Theoretical Works of

PERCY GOETSCHIUS

Applied counterpoint. As used in the invention, fugue, canon and other polyphonic forms. An exhaustive treatise on the structural and formal details of the polyphonic or contrapuntal forms of music.

Exercises in elementary counterpoint

Exercises in melody-writing. A systematic course of melodic composition, designed for the use of young music students, chiefly as a course of exercise collateral with the study of harmony.

Homophonic forms of musical composition. An exhaustive treatise on the structure and development of musical forms from the simple phrase to the song-form with "trio."

Larger forms of musical composition. An exhaustive explanation of the variations, rondos and sonata designs, for the general student of musical analysis, and for the special student of structural composition.

Material used in musical composition. A system of harmony originally designed for use in the English harmony classes of the Conservatory of Music at Stuttgart.

———

Write for a descriptive circular

G. SCHIRMER, INC., NEW YORK

THE
LARGER FORMS
OF
MUSICAL COMPOSITION

AN EXHAUSTIVE EXPLANATION OF THE VARIATIONS, RONDOS
AND SONATA DESIGNS, FOR THE GENERAL STUDENT
OF MUSICAL ANALYSIS, AND FOR THE SPECIAL
STUDENT OF STRUCTURAL COMPOSITION

BY

PERCY GOETSCHIUS

AUTHOR OF

*Exercises in Melody-Writing; The Theory and Practice of Tone-
Relations; The Material used in Musical Composition; The
Homophonic Forms of Musical Composition; Elemen-
tary Counterpoint; Applied Counterpoint;
Lessons in Music Form; etc.*

SIXTH ISSUE

NEW YORK
G. SCHIRMER, Inc.
1915

Printed in the U. S. A.

TO MY DEAR FRIEND

AND

FELLOW–STUDENT

EDGAR STILLMAN KELLEY

PREFACE.

"And the earth was without form and void; and darkness was upon the face of the deep."

— Genesis, I, 2.

"Order is heaven's first law."

— ALEXANDER POPE.

"Passion, whether great or not, must never be expressed in an exaggerated manner; and music — even in the most ardent moment — ought never to offend the ear, but should always remain music, whose object it is to give pleasure."

— MOZART.

"Inspiration without methods and means at its disposal will no more enable a man to write a symphony than to build a ship or a cathedral."
— C. HUBERT H. PARRY. "Evolution of the art of music."

"I have never believed it possible that any natural or improved ability can claim immunity from the companionship of the steady, plain, hardworking qualities, and hope to gain its end."
— DICKENS. "David Copperfield."

The present volume is a sequel to the *Homophonic Forms* and *Applied Counterpoint*, and is similarly designed for the use both of the student of analysis, and the student of practical composition.

It claims to be no more than a *guide* for the student through the successive stages in the evolution of the larger and largest forms of music structure. Therefore the *classic* point of view has been adopted and illustrated, not only because that would appear to provide the most reliable basis of technical habit, but also because the thorough knowledge of these older forms must precede the inevitable and desirable advance into the modern ones.

Without attempting any direct defence of conservatism, the author earnestly advises the young composer to *master* these classic forms by conscientious solution of each successive task given in the book. This will furnish him with a basis, both technical and conceptive, upon which he can most safely and most fully realize his personal artistic impressions and convictions. The classic designs are not lightly to be overthrown, for they are the cumulative product of a gradually dawning recognition of nature's musical laws, steadily progressing and crystalizing through the gathering and eliminating experiences of master-minds during many past centuries. It seems reasonable, therefore, to assume that true structural progress cannot be achieved by abandoning these, but rather by building upon them.

The student who desires to obtain a general view of this structural territory, or to proceed more quickly, *may limit himself to the paragraphs in larger type*, which are continuous and complete. The additional elucidations in smaller type, and the references, are so ample that they, also, may be partly omitted by those who prefer a shorter, though somewhat superficial, course. The analytic student will omit the given Exercises. The practical student must make faithful use of them.

It is narrow-minded to assume that these exercises, and the persistent application of "rules," will hamper genius. They need not be executed coldly and mechanically. Subjective, personal, enthusiasm may course just as hotly here as in the pursuit of any other occupation; and the student is nowhere invited to check this enthusiasm — only to control and guide it. Properly applied by the student, these exercises can thus only increase the power of his genius.

PERCY GOETSCHIUS.

New York City, *September*, 1915.

TABLE OF CONTENTS.

(The numbers in parenthesis refer to the paragraphs.)

DIVISION TWO.

THE RONDO-FORMS.

DIVISION THREE.

THE SONATA-ALLEGRO FORMS. 150

THE LARGER FORMS OF
MUSICAL COMPOSITION

INTRODUCTION.

1. The term "Larger Forms" refers specifically to those compositions which assume greater proportions, and therefore require greater breadth of design, and more concentration in the conception and arrangement of the structural factors. But length is not the distinctive trait; for a movement may be concise and fairly brief, and still comprise the characteristics of a Larger form.

2. The dimensions which Larger forms usually assume, and the increased necessity of sustaining interest by effective contrasts, lead naturally to the employment of all the resources of tone-combination, and, therefore, of both distinctive styles of composition — the homophonic and the polyphonic. For this reason, these Larger designs are sometimes called the "Mixed Forms."

3. The homophonic texture is that in which one single melodic line represents the chief contents, while all that goes with it is merely harmonic accompaniment. In the polyphonic texture, two or more, or all, of the lines are of equal melodic prominence and importance. Pure homophony is seen in the 25th (and others) of the Songs without Words of **Mendelssohn**; pure polyphony in the Fugues of **Bach's** well-tempered Clavichord. The numerous intermediate or mixed grades, between the two genuine styles — as in the Scherzo of **Beethoven's** 3rd pfte. Sonata — are called "polyphonic," but not "polyphony."

4. The larger forms may be classed in four distinctive Divisions:

    I. The Variation-forms;
    II. The Rondo-forms;
    III. The Sonata-allegro forms; and
    IV. Compound forms.

DIVISION I.

THE VARIATION-FORMS.

COMPARATIVE TABLE OF DIVISION I.

BASSO OSTINATO			VARIATION-FORMS		
Ground-motive.	Ground-bass, or Basso ostinato proper.	Passacaglia.	Chaconne.	Small Variation-form.	Large Variation-form.

THEMATIC BASIS

Motive of one or two measures, chiefly in bass.	*Phrase* of two or four measures, chiefly in bass.	*Period* (or repeated Phrase) of 8 measures, of which the burden is usually the *bass*-line.	usually the *chords* (incidentally the melody or the bass).	Double-period or 2-Part *Song-form*, 16 measures. *Melody* (chords, or bass, or formal design).	Usually 2- or 3-Part *Song-form*, 16 to 32 measures. *Melody* (chords, etc.)

DISTINCTIVE TRAITS

None.	None.	Minor mode. Triple measure ($\frac{3}{4}$, $\frac{3}{8}$ or $\frac{6}{8}$, $\frac{3}{2}$).	Minor or major mode. ($\frac{3}{4}$).	None.	None.

TREATMENT

Homophonic; changing melodic, rhythmic and harmonic forms in upper (added) parts.	Homophonic; changing forms, phrase-group design.	Preponderantly *polyphonic;* thematic accompaniment of *bass-theme.*	Preponderantly *homophonic;* varying patterns of (chiefly) harmonic figuration, with approximate retention of *Melody.* Partly continuous, partly separated, variations.	Chiefly homophonic, occasionally polyphonic; the variations completely separated, as a rule. Form of Theme retained, with unessential extensions.	Form of Theme treated with greater freedom, and transformed by Insertions and extensions. Elaboration, as well as Variation.

Structure continuous, with ordinary (transient) cadence interruptions.

CHAPTER I.

THE GROUND-MOTIVE.

5. The Ground-Motive is a brief melodic figure, usually one measure in length (sometimes less or more), placed, as a rule, in the bass part, and repeated there an optional number of times. These repetitions are generally exact, but may be modified. And the motive is occasionally transferred to another part. See Ex. 1, bass.

6. Its usual retention in one and the same part, however, distinguishes the Ground-motive from the motive of the Invention-forms, in which it is constantly *imitated* in changing parts. The term Ground-motive is adopted in this book, not alone because of its location in the bass (the "ground" part), but more particularly with reference to its object and character as *fundamental* motive, — even when placed in some upper part.

7. A sentence contrived with a Ground-motive is not a Variation-form in the recognized sense of the term; but it has a very similar technical basis, and should be regarded as an embryonic condition of the same process of thematic development which leads directly into the genuine Variation-form. It is more likely to occur during a certain section of a larger design (as in Ex. 1), than to form the basis of an entire composition (as in Ex. 6, No. 1).

8. At each repetition or recurrence of the Ground-motive the upper parts (or those others not holding the motive) are so changed as to constitute new melodic, harmonic, rhythmic, or contrapuntal associations with it. See Ex. 1, upper staff.

This indicates the relation of the Ground-motive to the Variation-form, which is defined as "a series of ingeniously modified (or variated) repetitions of an adopted Theme." Here, the thematic germ is simply smaller, being only a motive or figure.

9. It is customary, and wise, not to alter the harmonization at *every* successive recurrence of the Ground-motive, but to use the same, or nearly the same, form for two successive announcements (see Ex. 1, measures 1–2; 3–4; Ex. 4, measures 3–5). Also, to construct related (if not strictly similar) two-measure, or four-measure groups, in order to obtain the structural effect of phrase- and period-formations (see Ex. 1, measures 1–2; 5–6; Ex. 4, measures 4–5, 8–9). Also, to revert, later on, to preceding groups, so as to confirm the latter, and to intimate still larger designs (double-period, or even Song-forms). See Ex. 1, measures 2–4, 9–11; Ex. 6, No. 2, measures 11, 12, etc., like measures 1,

2, etc. Such confirmations or duplications constitute the only legitimate means of obtaining effective and intelligible *form*. Compare par. 12*c*, *d*.

10. For the sake of greater freedom and effectiveness, three licences are recognized as valid and permissible; but they are not to be applied until, in later recurrences of the motive, the necessity of avoiding monotony becomes evident:

1. Unessential (that is, slight, unimportant) melodic or rhythmic alterations of the motive itself. These may consist in the insertion of embellishing tones (passing and neighboring notes); dots; rests; shifting the position of the motive in the measure; an occasional modification by accidentals.

2. Transferring the Ground-motive to some other part,— as a rule, not until it has appeared several times in the bass (or whatever its own part may be).

3. Substitution of sequence for repetition, whereby the motive appears upon other scale-steps, or in different keys.

These points are all illustrated in the following example, from the Finale of **Brahms'** 1st Symphony:

Ex. 1.

*1) Ground-motive of four diatonic tones; one measure in length, but beginning at the *second* beat.   Observe that a Ground-motive may occupy any position in the measure.

*2) The melodic formation of the second measure is similar to that of the first; also meas. 4 confirms meas. 3 (as sequence); that is, the measures are "cast in pairs."

*3) The motive, in bass, is shifted up an octave.

*4) Measures 5-6 confirm measures 1-2, like a Consequent phrase in the period-form.

*5) The bass descends to its former register.   This measure and the next two agree with measures 2-4.

*6) The motive in bass is shifted up a 5th; that is, it is reproduced in sequence, instead of repetition.

*7) The melodic form is inflected by the accidental *e*-flat.

*8) The motive is transferred to the uppermost part, and, at the same time, it is rhythmically shifted—back one half-beat.

*9) The motive appears, in the same syncopated form, in "tenor."

11. Upon the recurrence of this passage, later in the movement of the Symphony, it assumes the following, more vital and interesting shape:

BRAHMS.

etc.

*1) The Ground-motive appears first in the soprano, then in bass; and this regular alternation of bass with the upper part continues to the end of the sentence.

12. *a.* The "variation" of the accompaniment to the successive recurrences of the adopted motive induces the composer to exercise unlimited ingenuity, and the result may be unique and effective.

b. The treatment of the added parts may be either homophonic or polyphonic, more commonly the former. But, in any case, the student must remember that no music is certain of its appeal without definite, and sustained, *melodic design;* and he should therefore direct his effort first to the conception of a good counter-melody.

c. It is also equally important to adopt and develop, beforehand, some perfectly definite plan for the entire sentence or composition, in order to avoid an absurd jumble of patterns, which would destroy the unity and effectiveness of the structural design as a whole. This is clearly illustrated in some of the following examples: Ex. 6, No. 1, of **Arensky,** is a Song-form with Trio; Ex. 6, No. 2, of **Brahms,** is a group of phrases approximating the 5-Part form (two returns to the first phrase); Ex. 7, No. 1, of **Bizet,** is a Song with Trio, the Ground-motive running through the Principal Song and its *da capo,* but abandoned during the Trio up to the retransition, where it re-enters; Ex. 7, No. 3, of **Lachner,** is a regular Three-Part Song-form.

d. The device most naturally employed for this purpose is (as hinted in par. 9) that of *duplication.* The term "duplication" is employed here, and throughout the book, to indicate the principle of repetition, reproduction, or recurrence, in the broadest sense, and may involve almost any degree of variation that could reasonably be included in a re-statement of any member or section of the form. Duplication means, then, the repetition (more or less exact, but possibly *greatly modified*), or the recurrence, of a measure, a phrase-member, a phrase, or an entire period.

For illustration: In Ex. 6, No. 1, measures 3–5 form an Antecedent phrase, duplicated, in the following three measures, as Consequent phrase (in contrary motion);
in the same example, at note *3), there is a recurrence or duplication of this 6-measure
Period; and at note *5), a return to the beginning and recurrence of the first 12
measures (in different rhythmic form).   In Ex. 7, No. 1, four successive announcements of the Ground-motive become the basis of a continuous 4-measure melody, as
Antecedent phrase, immediately duplicated as Consequent phrase.   Somewhat similar
is Ex. 7, No. 3, in which the duplication or repetition results in a 16-measure Double-
period of very definite and striking melodic form (as Part I), — followed by Part II,
of equally clear design, and, later, by Part III as recurrence of Part I.

Further illustrations:

*1) From the Finale of **Brahms'** 2nd Symphony.

*2) This Ground-motive is also one measure long, beginning at the unaccented second beat. It remains in bass throughout.

*3) Here the motive is shifted to the next higher step, and changed to the minor form.

*4) Again shifted up one step, and also *expanded* (by partial augmentation) to cover two measures.

*5) The sentence ends with this announcement of the first half of the motive only, in regular augmented form.

*6) The structural grouping, in sets of four similar measures, is apparent here.

*1) From the *Allegretto grazioso* of **Brahms'** 2nd Symphony. The Ground-motive may be interpreted to represent any location in the measure, but it was probably conceived as beginning with the third beat. The repetitions are not altered at all.

A somewhat similar passage occurs in the first movement of **Beethoven's** 7th Symphony, measures 50 to 29 from the end. The Ground-motive, derived from the beginning of the Principal Theme, is two measures long, and appears eleven times in succession in bass, without change (Ex. 5, No. 1). And also near the end of the first movement of **Beethoven's** 9th Symphony (Ex. 5, No. 2):

See further:

etc. 4 meas.

etc.
8 meas.

etc.
16 meas.

A. ARENSKY, op. 5.

Cadence

No. 2.

5-measure phrase

Gr.-mot.

5-meas. phrase

*7)

as at the beginning　　etc. 7 meas.

8va

*9)

*8)

8va

Similar to measures 2–5

BRAHMS, op. 116–2.

motive

etc.

*10)

No. 3.   From Parsifal.

R. Wagner.

*1) The Ground-motive includes *six* quarter-notes in *five*-quarter measure; at each recurrence it is therefore shifted forward one beat, with unique result.

*2) The melody here is the contrary motion of that at the beginning.

*3) Here the Ground-motive regains its original location in the measure, and the preceding phrase is repeated (and extended to 10 measures), while the motive appears in broken-octave form.

*4) This passage, with transposition to the dominant key, answers, in the form, to a "Trio," or Subordinate Song-form, with *da capo* 14 measures later. The Ground-motive retains its original letters, however, but the third note becomes *g*-sharp.

*5) The *da capo*, or return to the beginning, in more elaborate rhythmic form.

*6) The Ground-motive (after four measures) is shifted down a fourth.

*7) Here (again after four measures) it resumes its original location; but the recurrence of the first phrase does not appear until two measures later, — in consequence of the 5-measure phrases.

*8) Shifted upward a fourth.

*9) This measure, and the following three measures, constitute an Interlude, or sort of retransition.

*10) The Ground-motive is transferred to the inner part, and back, twice. The cadence follows. This entire extract forms the "Trio" of an Intermezzo, op. 116, No. 2.

*11) The Ground-motive here, and later, is abbreviated by omission of the final tone, or tones.

*12) Transferred, in abbreviated form, to an upper part.

See further:

Rheinberger, Organ Pieces, op. 156; No. 7, "In memoriam." Ground-motive of two measures: Reiterated in bass, exclusively, 42 times; frequently shifted to other scale-steps; no interludes; extended at the end by a brief codetta.

Rheinberger, Organ Pieces, op. 167; No. 12 (Finale); motive of one measure This is practically one tone only, as broken octave; it is frequently shifted to other steps, and often interrupted by interludes.

Tschaikowsky, 4th Symphony, first movement, measure 134 (*Ben sost. il tempo precedente*); through 22 measures, See also, the same Symphony, "Trio" of second movement (*più mosso*); motive melodically modified.

Arthur Shepherd, Pfte. Sonata, op. 4, second movement. Motive of two measures: Throughout the movement, but frequently interrupted, and modified.

Moszkowski, "Boabdil," No. 3, (Moorish Fantasia). Motive of two measures

First in bass (14 presentations), then in soprano *in contrary motion* (16 times), and again in bass; then in other, enlarged, forms, chiefly in the upper part, and finally again in bass.

Wagner, "Tristan und Isolde," Act. I, Scene V, *Da stand er herrlich, hehr und heil;* 2 measures, bass, four presentations.

Ottokar Nováček," Basso ostinato" in *f*-sharp minor. Motive of one measure:

It runs through the entire, fairly lengthy, composition, with occasional alteration of *d* to *d*-sharp — and a few other changes; also transferred briefly to the uppermost part. An interlude is inserted, near the end.

Nováček, "Basso ostinato" in *e*-minor. Motive of two measures:

An interesting illustration of consistent formal design.

Jean Sibelius, Pastorale from "Pelleas und Melisande" (op. 46, No. 5). The

Ground-motive, of six beats:

is announced in bass, and remains, throughout, in the same register; but other, lower, basstones are frequently added, which give to the motive the effect of an inner part. A melodic change occurs, at the end of the motive, in three of the presentations.

13. When the motive is announced — and retained — in some upper part, it is not a *Ground*-motive in the stricter sense of the word; but the principle, and the treatment, are exactly the same:

No. 1. "Le Carillon."

Ex. 7.

No. 2.
Moderato

Motive   *3)

AKIMENKO, op. 39.

etc.

No. 3.   " Trio "
Part I

*4)   Gr.-Mot.

Part II   FRANZ LACHNER, op. 113.

*1) From **Bizet's** orchestral suite, "L'Arlésienne," 4th movement. The motive, one measure long, is presented constantly in the inner part.

*2) The closing, re-transitional, measures of the "Trio."

*3) The motive of one measure appears as inner part, but is practically a bass, with the first tone held as organ-point. It runs through the entire composition (44 measures) without change.

*4) Similar: the motive is really in tenor, but the bass is chiefly an organ-point. See also: **Debussy,** Song with pfte., "Les cloches." The motive of one measure

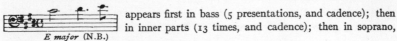 appears first in bass (5 presentations, and cadence); then in inner parts (13 times, and cadence); then in soprano, in the following three rhythmically modified forms, to the end:

 and final cadence.

This is a very beautiful and instructive example, worthy of close study.

Bizet, Suite "L'Arlésienne," first movement (*Prelude*), the passage with four-flat signature. The motive, two measures long: is presented constantly in the soprano (10 times), with one chromatic change (in the 9th presentation).

Maurice Ravel, Sonatine in *f*-sharp minor, last movement, measures 60–94.
NOTE. — Such examples as the following of **Chopin:**

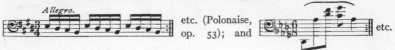

etc. (Polonaise, op. 53); and   etc.

(Berceuse, op. 57); — and **Tschaikowsky,** op. 11 (Andante), — cannot be classed among the Ground-motives, because they are not the *thematic* source and basis of the sentence, but merely *figural* motives, of distinctly accompanying character, whose uniformity, though characteristic and effective, is rather accidental than intentional.

EXERCISE I.

Write a number of sentences (brief, but complete), with Ground-motive. Use different kinds of measure, and various rhythmic forms, for each; also, motives of different length, and varied location in the measure, — but not beyond *two measures* in extent. Note, particularly, par. 12c.

CHAPTER II.

THE GROUND-BASS, OR BASSO OSTINATO.

14. The Ground-bass, or, as it is more universally called, the *basso ostinato* (persistent bass), differs from the Ground-motive only in *length*. In some of the above examples the term "basso ostinato" might apply quite as well as Ground-motive, and is actually employed by **Arensky** (Ex. 6, No. 1), **Nováček,** and others, for brief motives. The basso ostinato is, however, usually a complete four-measure phrase-melody, with cadence either on the tonic or the dominant. Sometimes, as stated, it is only two measures long; very rarely, a phrase of eight measures. See the Comparative Table, at the head of this Division.

15. When the *basso ostinato* is used as constructive basis, it leads, because of its length, to broader and more definite structural results than can be obtained with the Ground-motive. Therefore, it lends itself readily to development into a complete movement, with clearly defined form.

16. In its treatment it corresponds, in every essential detail, to that of the Ground-motive. As the name implies, it is supposed to appear in bass, and to be repeated there, throughout; and in older examples this is always the case.

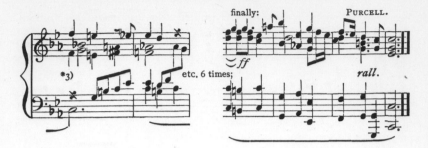

*1) From the opera "Dido and Aeneas" of **Purcell** (Novello edition), No. 2. The Ground-bass is a complete four-measure phrase, with strong tonic cadence.

*2) Here, about in the middle of the "Song," the motive is transferred to the dominant key, where it appears twice.

*3) Note the effective treatment (evasion) of the cadence here, to prevent monotony; also examine the other (earlier) cadences, which are "bridged over" without rhythmic interruption.

See also, in the same work: No. 6 (eight-measure phrase), No. 12, No. 24, No. 38 (four-measure phrases).

17. The added material, in the upper part, should be devised with the utmost ingenuity, in varying forms or patterns, for each successive recurrence of the Ground-bass. It may be, and usually is, homophonic; and, as usual, the melody of the upper part claims chief attention. But it may also be more or less imitatory, or even strictly polyphonic, — in which case it is likely to be assigned to the Passacaglia group, and to assume a correspondingly definite conventional character (par. 25).

18. The basic phrase may be a genuine *basso ostinato*, appearing only in the *bass* voice. But it may also be transferred, at times, to some other part; it may be shifted, as sequence, to other scale-steps, with or without change of key; and it may be unessentially modified, melodically or rhythmically. Comp. par. 10.

19. Here, again, the style or "pattern" of the added parts may be retained, with little change, for two (or even more) successive announcements of the Ground-bass. (Comp. par. 9.)

And the design of the sentence as a whole may (and should) represent the purpose and effect of such complete structural formations as the Three-Part Song-form and the like. (Comp. par. 12c, and par. 15.)

Or, in the absence of such definite structural traits, the whole may constitute a Group of phrases, with more or less evidence of some plan of continuous development, leading, through progressive stages of constantly increasing melodic, harmonic and (particularly) rhythmic interest and power, to a climax at, or near, the end.

20. The most effective result is likely to be achieved by interrupting the series of thematic announcements after a time — best near the middle of the entire movement — and interposing a section in distinctly contrasting style, as Interlude or "Trio." This should, of course, be followed by a resumption of the *basso ostinato*, either exactly as before, or, better, in new and more brilliant forms.

21. But, with this exception, no cessation of the repetitions of the *basso* is considered legitimate; and the successive variations are, naturally, not to be isolated by heavy cadence impressions, but should be as *continuous* as is compatible with effective structural presentation.

The monotony of the regularly recurring cadence of the bass theme may be avoided by skilful evasion of the cadence — ingenious harmonic and rhythmic treatment of the given cadence-tones. See Ex. 8, note *3).

Further:

BRAHMS.

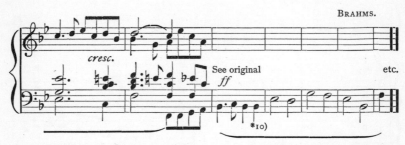

*1) The Finale of **Brahms'** Variations, op. 56, on a Theme of **Haydn.** — *2) Here the Ground-bass assumes its permanent rhythmic form.   It is a *five-measure* phrase, and this irregularity of form proves effective in removing the monotony of the cadences, which, though not evaded, always occur a measure later than expected. — *3) During these six repetitions of the bass, the rhythm of the added upper parts undergoes changes: at first a few ♩-triplets appear; then steady, emphatic quarter-beats; then eighth-notes; then sixteenths in the accompanying inner parts, against syncopated half-notes above; then 16th-note triplets; and then 8th-note triplets, carried over into the version at note *4). — *4) The theme begins to rise in register; at *5) it is in the tenor; at *6) the minor mode begins to assert itself; at *7) the theme is in soprano, and fully in minor; at *8) it is still higher.   Note the rhythms. *9) The thematic melody returns to the bass.   *10) Here the theme is dissolved into a coda, with bearing on the Theme of the Variations.

No. 4.   RHEINBERGER.

No. 5.   LADISLAS ALOÏZ.

*1) The "Crucifixus" from **Bach's** B minor Mass. The original should be thoroughly studied. The Theme is four measures long, with dominant cadence. It is presented 13 times, constantly in bass, and with but two modifications, in the last two announcements, — the final one is significant, as it cadences in *G* major.

*2) Here the four-part mixed chorus enters, and continues throughout, with most masterly and effective imitations (polyphonic).

*3) From "Judas Maccabæus," Nos. 38 and 39. The theme, four measures long, with dominant cadence, is retained in bass; but with frequent interludes, and shifted a 3rd higher during a later section.

*4) From "Serenade," op. 16, for orchestra (3rd movement). The *basso* appears only during the principal sections, is often shifted sequentially, and subjected to significant rhythmic alterations.

*5) From "Monologe," op. 162, for organ; No. 12. Motive, two measures long, in bass throughout, without modification.

*6) **Ladislas Aloïz,** Var. for two pianos, op. 28. Ground-bass, four measures long, as Introduction to the final Fugue.

22. The thematic melody may, as stated in par. 18, appear at times in an upper part; but it may also assume its legitimate place there, remaining in one or another of the upper parts, excepting when transferred occasionally to the bass. In this case it is, properly speaking, a *melodia ostinata* (the name adopted by **Rheinberger** in his op. 174, No. 11. See Ex. 11, No. 1).

No. 1. " Melodia ostinata "

Ex. 11.

No. 2. *Presto*

*1) The melody of this 8-measure Period is the Theme of the composition (op. 174, No. 11). It appears first in the upper part; then in the inner (tenor), and then in the bass; and this order of alternate upper, inner and lower part, is adhered to strictly, and without modification of the thematic melody, throughout.

*2) From **Beethoven's** 9th Symphony, the "Trio" of the Scherzo-movement. The thematic phrase of four measures is presented first in the Soprano, as *melodia ostinata*. It runs through the entire "Trio," with a few interruptions, and with no other changes than a modulation to the dominant, and systematic shifting of register.

*3) The motive is transferred to an inner part, and its contrapuntal associate appears above.

*4) Here the motive is abbreviated. See the original.

See also: **Beethoven,** pfte. Sonata, op. 28; "Trio" of the Scherzo. The motive is a *Soprano ostinato;* a four-measure phrase, whose repetitions run through the whole "Trio," with alternate change of *cadence,* in *b* minor and *D* major.

Rheinberger, op. 167, No. 10; *Soprano ostinato* throughout (see Ex. 15, No. 3).

EXERCISE 2.

A number of examples of the *basso ostinato,* and *melodia ostinata.* Employ various types of measure, and of rhythm. Limit the theme to four ordinary measures, or two large measures. The following given *basso* may be used for experimentation:

GOETSCHIUS.

CHAPTER III.

THE PASSACAGLIA.

23. The *Passacaglia* (French *Passacaille*) was originally a dance (probably of Spanish origin), always in the minor mode, and always in triple measure (usually $\frac{3}{4}$ — more rarely $\frac{3}{8}$ or $\frac{3}{2}$). It was commonly eight measures in length; sometimes, as period-form, with a light semi-cadence in the middle.

The practical availability of so brief a sentence for a complete and lengthy dance was secured by the simple device of numerous *repetitions*. These were at first probably nearly or quite literal; but it became the custom to modify or variate the repetitions more or less freely, though never elaborately — the "variations" consisting chiefly of simple harmonic figuration or arpeggiation (and slight melodic embellishment) of the original chords, in different rhythms. The *melody*, or tune proper, of the dance was treated with comparative indifference, or disregarded altogether; the basis of the sentence was its chords, and this lent paramount importance to the *bass-part*, which was retained almost unchanged, thus creating the impression of a *basso ostinato* throughout the many repetitions of the dance-sentence. See par. 25.

See **Bach,** Clavichord compositions (Peters Edition, No. 1959) No. 6, on page 40. The "Dance" (Passacaille) is an 8-measure Period of two parallel phrases upon the same bass. This Period is repeated 18 times with "variations," chiefly of a rhythmic nature. Between Variations 6–7, 9–10, and at the end, there is a *da capo*, or return to the original form of the thematic Period.

Very similar is the "Passacaglio" of **Frescobaldi,** cited in Ex. 15 (No. 9).

24. The idealized Passacaglia, in its *modern artistic form* (most common in organ literature), bears only a general resemblance to the original dance, though it has retained the name. That is, it is invariably $\frac{3}{4}$ (or $\frac{3}{8}$) measure; is in minor; and consists in a series of repetitions of the bass theme.

There is an inexplicable confusion of titles in a " Passacaille " of **Handel** (Suite No. 7 for the clavichord), which is in $\frac{4}{4}$ measure.

25. From the *basso ostinato*, to which class of composition it distinctly belongs, the modern Passacaglia differs only in certain characteristic traits: The bass theme is usually longer; sometimes more elaborate; the treatment is *preponderantly contrapuntal;* and the form as a whole may pursue a more definite design.   (It will be noted that a *basso ostinato* may be in any species of measure, in either mode, and of any rhythmic character.   The Passacaglia, on the other hand, has its fixed conditions, — par. 24.)   See the Comparative Table at the head of this Division.

26. The theme, in bass, is most frequently eight measures in length; sometimes more, rarely less.   It is generally of simple, almost austere melodic and rhythmic character; though occasionally more ornate and striking themes are chosen.   Compare the theme of **Bach**, in Ex. 14, with those given in Ex. 15; and with the following of **Max Reger**:

MAX REGER, op. 96.

27. The theme is usually announced first *alone* (as in the fugue), *in the bass,* where it best manifests its significance as actual thematic basis, — as principal tone-line, to which others are to be added by the polyphonic process.   It is then repeated, in that voice, under the same general conditions as those which govern the Ground-motive and Ground-bass; namely:

a) It may be rhythmically modified; see Ex. 14, notes *6) and *11).

b) It may be unessentially embellished, with neighboring notes or passing notes, especially when these are introduced in conformity with the imitatory "motive" adopted in the added (upper) parts; see Ex. 14, notes *6) and *14).

c) It may be transferred to another, higher, part; see Ex. 14, note *12).   Much more rarely, it may appear as sequence, on other steps, or in another key; see Ex. 15, note *2).   The simple change of mode is always permissible; compare Ex. 9, notes *6) and *7).

28. The treatment of the accompaniment in the upper (added) parts is preponderantly *polyphonic,* that is, contrapuntal or imitatory; but not necessarily wholly so, as purely harmonic patterns may occur from time to time.   It is, however, the *polyphonic* character of the Passacaglia that distinguishes it from the Chaconne, and Variation-forms in general.

29. Therefore, a "Motive" is chosen for each successive manipulation of the bass-theme, and is imitated and developed as in the Invention, or chorale-figuration. Here, again, the same (or a similar) motive may be used for two successive variations. Comp. par. 9; and see Ex. 14, notes *8), *9) and *19). And, as shown in the Ground-motive, and in the *basso ostinato*, a systematic increase in rhythmic animation is likely to occur; and other devices of progressive development may be so applied as to achieve an effective structural design in the entire series, with a view to providing the necessary contrasts and climaxes.

30. Interludes may appear, at proper intervals, between the variations; especially when caused by a natural expansion of the cadence-chord. It is especially effective and appropriate to insert a modulating interlude — perhaps extended by a dominant organ-point — immediately before the final announcement of the bass-theme, or at some other inviting point near the end.

31. An extension at the end, in the nature of a Codetta or Coda, is possible and desirable.

The following organ Passacaglia of **Bach,** one of the most masterly models of this form, illustrates the more important of the above details:

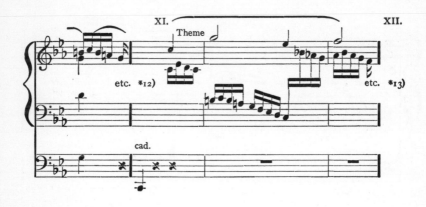

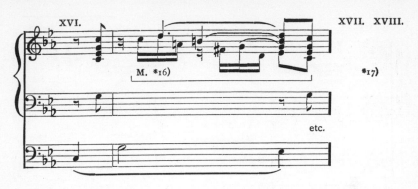

*1) Note the melodic structure of the Theme; the relation of the half-notes, at the beginning of each measure, to each other and to the key (the dominant note *g* with its lower and upper neighbors during the first phrase, and then the intervals of the tonic chord, in descending succession); and the manner in which nearly every one of these accented half-notes is preceded by its lower diatonic neighbor.

*2) The term "Var." is used here for convenience; it does not appear in the original. Var. I is homophonic, the motive in soprano being melodic only, not imitatory.

*3) Var. II is a duplication of Var. I, with new phrase-melody, built upon the same motive.

*4) Var. III is polyphonic, based upon the imitations of the adopted motive (in 8th-notes, as marked). It will be noticed that the motive, in this and all succeeding variations, begins during the cadence — before the Theme sets in, in bass.

*5) The rhythm is accelerated to 8ths and 16ths.

*6) Motive of 3 tones, harmonic form. The Theme, in bass, *is modified both melodically and rhythmically*, in order to participate in the imitation of the motive. Compare note *14).

*7) The rhythm again accelerated, to running 16ths.

*8) Var. VII is, in a sense, a duplication of VI, employing the same diatonic motive, but in contrary motion, and extended to two beats.

*9) Var. VIII is another duplication of VI (or VII), with the same diatonic motive extended to three, and more, beats.

*10) Similar to note *6), which see.

*11) A flowing motive of 3 beats, not imitated in alternate parts, but retained throughout in soprano. The rhythm of the Theme in bass is again rhythmically modified by shortening each half-note to a quarter.

*12) The Theme is transferred to the soprano. This Var. is a duplication of X, inasmuch as the line of 16th-notes is reproduced literally, in a lower part. The pedal-bass is discontinued, to emphasize the shifting of the Theme.

*13) The Theme is again in soprano, in Var. XII, accompanied polyphonically with a "jagged" motive of 3 or more beats in the lower parts.

*14) The Theme is in the alto, and modified melodically and rhythmically, as in Variations V and IX, in conformity with the adopted motive.

*15) Variations XIV and XV are both pure harmonic figuration; the presentation of the Theme, in the tenor (the pedal is silent), is unique: See the original.

*16) The "jagged" motive, in 16th-notes, is a direct allusion to the last five measures of the bass Theme, of which it is practically a diminution. The treatment is harmonic, — the measures are duplicates, without "imitation."

*17) Var. XVII accelerates the rhythm to 16th-triplets. Var. XVIII returns to the rhythm of Var. IV; the Theme in bass is modified by reducing each quarter-note to an 8th, with preceding 8th-rest.

*18) Note the singular "boring" effect of the motive (— two beats in length, suggesting $\frac{2}{4}$ measure).

*19) Var. XX is a duplication of XIX, with the motive doubled in 3rds.

*20) This variation concludes the Passacaglia proper. As Finale, a triple-fugue is added.

See, further, the following:

*1) Op. 132, Finale (Organ Sonata). The Theme, an 8-measure Period with tonic cadence, is stated first in bass alone. It appears chiefly in bass, but is transferred at times to an upper part, and occasionally slightly embellished. The treatment is polyphonic, and there is a progressive rhythmic design.

*2) Passacaglia, op. 156, No. 11. Theme, an 8-measure Period with dominant cadence. It is stated in bass, but immediately accompanied. The Theme appears constantly in bass, and is *transferred at each presentation to other steps*, chiefly in ascending sequences in the 3rd. The treatment is preponderantly harmonic, but occasional imitations and contrapuntal passages occur.

*3) Passacaglia, op. 167, No. 10. The Theme, an 8-measure Period with dominant cadence, is stated first in soprano alone, and is then retained in soprano throughout, as *melodia ostinata*. The treatment is polyphonic.

*4) Op. 85, No. 2. The Theme, 4 (large) measures with dominant cadence, appears first in bass alone; it is presented three times in *c* minor, then twice in *g* minor (with modified cadence at each change of key); then once in soprano in *c* minor, once in bass in *f* minor; then in *c* minor, in soprano, bass, soprano, tenor, and bass; again in soprano (*g* minor), bass (*c* minor, *g* minor, and *c* minor). This is followed by a Fugue, as Finale, whose Subject counterpoints the *basso ostinato*, which finally joins it, in the coda.

*5) Passacaglia upon the name B–A–C–H, op. 39. The Theme appears chiefly in bass. It occurs a few times in *B*-flat *major;* is considerably modified, both melodically and rhythmically — principally the latter. The treatment is almost entirely homophonic, preponderantly chromatic, and extremely brilliant.

*6) Passacaglia and Fugue, op. 10. An introduction, based upon the Theme in expanded form, leads into the Passacaglia. The Fugue ("Double") serves as Finale. A very effective and beautiful example, worthy of careful scrutiny.

*7) The Theme, an 8-measure phrase, modulates early into the dominant key (*f*-sharp minor) and cadences there. The treatment is largely polyphonic and involves many skilful melodic and rhythmic modifications of the Theme.

*8) A *basso ostinato*, but not "Passacaglia" of the conventional type, inasmuch as the Theme is in *major* (comp. par. 24; and par. 14).

*9) **Frescobaldi** calls it a "Passacaglio." This, though thoroughly scholastic and artistic in technical treatment, belongs more properly to the traditional type of the Passacaglia as *Dance*, — similar to the example of **Bach**, cited in par. 23. The Theme is an 8-measure Period, or, more properly, a repeated 4-measure Phrase; it is in *major;* the four-measure section is repeated 45 times (Nos. 14 to 32 in *g*-minor) in variated forms, with constant and direct reference to the *harmonic* basis — and to the melody. In this respect it bears closer relation to the Chaconne-forms (par. 34), especially as it is in major, and exhibits no *basso ostinato*. In many outward traits it is strikingly similar to the Chaconne of **Bach** for Solo Violin, cited in Ex. 19.

EXERCISE 3.

A number of examples of the Passacaglia, chiefly for the organ, but also for the pianoforte, or any ensemble of instruments with which the student is familiar. The themes cited in Ex. 15 (especially Nos. 1, 4, or 8) may be utilized; or — better — the student may invent and manipulate his own themes.

CHAPTER IV.

THE CHACONNE.

32. The *Chaconne* (Italian *Ciaccona*) was also originally a popular dance; it is very similar to the Passacaglia, and is often confounded with the latter.   It was always in $\frac{3}{4}$ (that is, triple) measure, usually eight measures in length; was either in major or in minor, and was many times repeated, with the same simple rhythmic and melodic modifications as those employed in the repetitions of the Passacaglia.

33. The artistic or idealized Chaconne, likewise, often closely resembles the modern Passacaglia, and has not escaped being confounded with, or even regarded as identical and interchangeable with, the latter.

But it appears possible to define (or, at least, to establish for the student's convenience) the characteristic traits of the Chaconne, as recognized and adopted in the majority of existing examples. See the Comparative Table at the head of this Division.

34. These distinctive traits are as follows:

a. The "theme" of the Chaconne is not a *basso ostinato*, but consists primarily in the *chord-successions* upon which the thematic sentence (usually eight measures, rarely only four) is erected.   Out of these chords emerges a Melody, the air or tune of the dance, in the uppermost part, which in many cases is so definite and lyric as to appear to be the real thematic thread.   And this may, to some extent, be the case, — the chords then representing the natural harmonization of that melody.

This view is borne out in the title to some of **Handel's** "Lessons for the harpsichord," namely: "Chaconne, *with Variations*" (Ex. 16).   In these, the "Air" seems to be the principal thematic thread, although it is the *chords* alone, ultimately, which control the conduct of the variations.   Further, in thus shifting the *melody* into greater prominence, the Chaconne approaches the nature of the conventional "Variation-forms," and is, indeed, to be regarded as the first or incipient grade of this class of compositions.   So, for example, the *c*-minor "Variations" of **Beethoven** (Ex. 18) are not called by him "Chaconne" at all, although they are a genuine type of that class.

It is, however, positively distinctive of the Chaconne that the *chord-succession* is retained as basis, with a few natural or interesting modifications and modulations, even when the original melody disappears, or assumes quite a different form.

Precisely as shown in par. 23, this retention of the chords leads as a matter of course to the more or less exact retention of the original bass-part, thus lending support to the impression of a *basso ostinato*. But the difference in the operation of this idea, and the actual distinction between a "retained bass" and a genuine "Ground-bass" (as thematic fundament), is quite as essential as it is obvious: In the Passacaglia the *basso ostinato* is the source and basis of the whole structure; whereas in the Chaconne the recurring bass is merely a consequence, by no means limited, of the retained *chord-successions* out of which the structure is really evolved. Comp. par. 25.

b. The treatment of the Chaconne is not polyphonic, as is that of the Passacaglia, but *preponderantly homophonic, or harmonic.* The successive modified repetitions (or variations) are but little more than figurations of the chords, in ingenious forms of broken and embellished harmony. Compare par. 28.

This distinction in the methods of treatment is the natural consequence of the location of the chief thematic thread: In the Passacaglia it is in the *bass*, as single tone-line, to which other lines are added, in contrapuntal texture: In the Chaconne it is in the *soprano*, as lyric product of the chords, which induce harmonic manipulation. The Passacaglia is built chiefly from the bottom upward; the Chaconne, from the melody downward.

c. The Passacaglia is not classed among the conventional variation-forms; but the Chaconne, as already noted, may justly be looked upon as the first or lowest grade of the Variation-form, inasmuch as it presents several features (absent in the Passacaglia) that are peculiar to this class of composition.

35. The manner in which the chords of the theme are broken, or figurated, constitutes what might be called the "pattern" of the variation, carried along in consistent recurrence through the entire series of chords, with sufficient modification, here and there, to avoid monotony.

Here, again, the same pattern, with change of register, is frequently used for two, or even three, successive variations; thus exemplifying the principle of *duplication*, defined in par. 12c as a vital element in the creation, and distinct presentation, of a structural design. Comp. pars. 9, 19.

Ex. 16.

*1) From **Handel's** "Lessons" for the Clavichord (or Harpsichord). The Theme (the Chaconne proper) is an 8-measure Period, with perfect cadence. The soprano-melody is the chief element; and, with its chord accompaniment, is traced more or less accurately through each variation. In the original version there are 62 variations.

*2) The bass corresponds exactly to that of the Theme, — but simply because the *chord-successions* are the same.

*3) The cadence-measure is so bridged over as to connect the variations without interruption (see par. 36).

*4) Var. III is a duplication of Var. II; that is, very nearly the same pattern is used for each. The same is true of Variations 9 and 10, — and many other pairs.

*5) This variation, like almost all which follow, consists clearly in nothing more than a *figuration* of the chords of the Theme. The pattern is defined simply by the manner in which the first chord is broken, melodically and rhythmically.

*6) A Canon in the octave, after one beat. See the original. See also the other Chaconne in **Handel's** "Lessons," — also in *G* major, and apparently a modified version of the above Theme.

See further:

*1) A *six*-measure Phrase, major mode. The Variations (five in *A*, four in *E*, two in *B*, and seven in *A*) all consist in purely harmonic figuration of the chords. Both melody and bass are retained nearly literally, throughout.

*2) Another curious confusion of styles, like that of the "Passacaglia" of **Handel** cited in par. 24 (in $\frac{4}{4}$ measure). This is called a "Chaconne," despite the fact that it is in $\frac{4}{4}$ measure. The Theme is a *four*-measure phrase, major mode. There are 25 Variations, all in *G* major, derived from the chords by simple harmonic figuration. The bass is retained almost literally; the melody has more modifications.

36. The variations of the Chaconne are often connected with each other (that is, are continuous), especially during such groups of two or three variations as are based upon the same pattern. But it is indicative of the relation of the Chaconne to the Variation-form proper, that an occasional complete break, or full stop, occurs, severing that variation from the following one. Such interruptions are not found in the Passacaglia, which is always strictly continuous. Comp. par. 21.

37. Partly in consequence of this incipient independence of certain separate variations, some liberty is permitted in the treatment of the tonality. Thus it is quite common, in the Chaconne, to alter the *mode* (from minor to major, or vice versa) during certain single variations, or groups of variations; see Ex. 18, note *12). This, however, is the only device employed; no change of *key-note*, or change of measure, is made, in the variations of the Chaconne; nor are alterations of the form, by extension of the Theme, considered legitimate. In a word, the connection between the Theme and its several variations is here still very close. The latter are referred directly to the Theme, of which they are usually closely related duplications, in all essential respects.

See further:

*1) The famous "*c* minor Variations" of **Beethoven** for pianoforte. It is evident that the *chords* form the Theme, and that the upper melody, beautiful and significant as it is, is an external auxiliary, not recognizably present in more than a half-dozen of the 32 variations. Note the bass-melody, also.

*2) The "pattern" appears alternately in ascending and descending form (contrary motion). The bass-part, throughout, conforms to that of the Theme.

*3) Note the change in the chord-form; in the Theme it is the dominant-7th of *f* minor (major), here the diminished-7th. Comp. note *6).

*4) The first variation has no rhythmic break at its cadence, but runs on into the next. The same is true of the second variation, and of several others.

*5) The same "pattern" is used for the second variation (par. 35), but transferred to the "other hand" (lower register). In variation No. 3, also, the same pattern is employed, but in both hands. In other words, Variations 2 and 3 are *duplications* of Var. 1.

*6) Another change of chord. Comp. note *3).

*7) This group of three continuous variations, with the same pattern, is here brought to a full stop, and severed from the next.

*8) Here there is an intimation of the thematic *melody* in the inner part. The bass-part corresponds to its progressions in the Theme.

*9) These three 8th-notes are derived from the three notes in the seventh measure of the Theme. See the original, and observe the manner in which Var. 5 ends.

*10) The pattern in the "left hand" is the same as that of Var. 7.

*11) The 32nd-notes in the pattern are borrowed from the melody of the Theme itself (end of the second measure). Var. 11 is the mate to Var. 10, with the two parts (hands) inverted.

*12) Here the mode changes, from minor to major. The melody of the Theme is plainly indicated, but in smoother rhythmic form.

*13) A complete change of the bass-part, and, consequently, a new chord-series, begins here. See the original. The bass has an ascending chromatic movement, instead of descending, as in the Theme.

*14) Variations 13 and 14 are both derived from Var. 12, as "duplications" of the latter. The melody, in shifted registers, is retained literally.

*15) Variations 15 and 16 (mated) are still in major.

*16) Var. 17 returns to minor. It is an "Invention with independent bass," and has its Motive, derived from the thematic melody.

*17) In Var. 20 the original bass appears as uppermost part. Var. 21 is its mate, or duplication, with inverted registers. Var. 22 is a Canon in the octave.

*18) Here a striking simplification of the Theme appears, in subdued rhythm.

*19) Var. 31 is an exact re-statement of the original melody, (as conventional *da capo*), with harmonic figuration in 32nd-notes. Var. 32 is its mate, or duplication, considerably embellished. This becomes the Finale of the composition, and consists, first, of the complete Var. (32); then an extension, as interlude (10 measures); then another variation, with evaded cadence and extension; and then a Coda of 18 measures, comprising three smaller sections. See par. 38, and par. 55.

38. The last presentation or variation of the Chaconne is usually extended by the addition of a Codetta or Coda, derived either directly from the pattern of the variation, or from the Theme itself, or from related material.

The distinction between codetta and coda is as follows: The codetta is a *single* section, — a phrase of four, or two, measures, duplicated (repeated, usually with some modification), and sometimes extended at the cadence. The coda, on the other hand, is a group of codettas, — contains, therefore, *more than one section*, of decreasing length, as a rule. See par. 55*b*. Examine carefully the last variation of **Beethoven** (Ex. 18), in the original; and also the coda of **Brahms** (Ex. 20).

Further illustrations:

*1) The Chaconne for Solo-Violin, from the 4th Sonata, **J. S. Bach.** The Theme is an 8-measure sentence, as *repeated phrase* (not Period), of the conventional type, $\frac{3}{4}$ measure, and in minor. Its actual thematic contents are the *chords*, of which the upper and lower lines (melody and bass) are rather the index than the cause.

*2) Note that the cadence is everywhere bridged over by maintaining the rhythmic movement, and beginning immediately the pattern of the following variation. Provision was made for this at the outset, by beginning with two "preliminary beats" (before the real first measure). In Var. 1, both the melody and bass of the Theme are closely followed.

*3) Var. 2 is a duplication of Var. 1, with chromatic bass.

*4) In Var. 3, the second phrase is a melodically embellished duplication of the first, — instead of a nearly exact repetition, as in the preceding presentations. In several instances this change of pattern *after four measures* is so radical that the Theme appears to be reduced to one of its two (similar) phrases; thus, Variations 15, 22, 29, 31, 32 and 33, are only four measures long. See the original.

*5) Variations 17 to 26 are in the major mode. Var. 27, and to the end, again in minor.

*6) The end of the series consists in a recurrence of the Theme as at the beginning (the customary "*da capo*"), the last 4 measures somewhat modified, and led to a strong tonic cadence. There is no codetta. Examine the original, and note the variety of "patterns," particularly with reference to their influence upon the *rhythmic* design as a whole.

Two ingenious and instructive transcriptions, or amplifications, of this Chaconne of Bach are: an arrangement by **Joachim Raff** for full orchestra; and an arrangement for the pianoforte by **F. Busoni.**

See further:

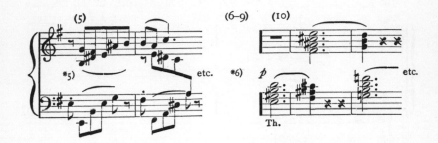

*1) The final movement of **Brahms'** 4th Symphony. The composer has given no name to this movement; it has been called, by different writers, both Passacaglia and Chaconne, most frequently the former. It appears to possess all the distinctive traits of the *Chaconne*-form, however. The Theme is an 8-measure phrase, the burden of which is the *melody* of the soprano, — and the chords which go with it. The bass-part has no thematic importance, excepting when it takes charge of this thematic melody (which it frequently, but by no means constantly, does). There is a noteworthy absence of the dominant harmony, in the first 6 measures; when it appears, in the 7th measure, it is in a rare altered form (with lowered second scale-step).

*2) The "variations" are not numbered or indicated in any way, in the original. They are marked here merely for convenience. In "Var. 1" the thematic melody is still in soprano, but an octave lower than before. The chords are retained exactly as in the Theme, but sharply enunciated on the second beat only.

*3) The thematic melody descends again one octave, to the tenor. Var. 2 is the only one of the whole series which has a polyphonic character; the motive of three diatonic tones, and its imitations, are unmistakable.

*4) Note, particularly, the treatment of the *cadence* measures (see the original). The tonic cadence-tone is always present, but always divested of its monotony. Comp. *12).

In Var. 3, the thematic melody reappears in the soprano; in Var. 4 it is, for the first time, placed in the bass.

*5) Var. 5 is a duplication of Var. 4.

*6) Variations 6 to 9 gradually increase the rhythmic pulse, through dotted 8ths, and 16ths, to 16th-triplets. Var. 10 subsides abruptly to a quiet rhythm of whole measures.

*7) In Var. 12, the measure changes to double its original length, the quarter-notes remaining equal, thus presenting the Theme in genuine "augmentation." The melody, in soprano, is dissolved into a *cantilena*.

*8) With Var. 13, the mode is altered from minor to major. The Theme still appears in augmentation.

*9) The thematic melody is delicately "pointed" out (for four measures) by the accent on the highest tone near the end of the measures.

*10) Var. 15 is a duplication of 14 (— thematic melody in bass).

*11) Here the conventional "*da capo*" takes place: the original mode and measure are resumed.

*12) Note the unusual manner in which the tonic cadence-note (*e*) is harmonized.

*13) Variations 24, 25, and 26 are equivalent to the significant "return to the beginning," which constitutes so vital a condition of clear and logical musical structure: Var. 24 is a nearly exact counterpart of Var. 1, — Var. 25 is similarly like Var. 2, — Var. 26 closely resembles Var. 3.

*14) Variations 27, 28 and 29 are of unusual melodic and harmonic grace. Var. 30 is extended or expanded four measures, at its end, in impressive preparation for the Coda.

*15) The Coda is, as usual, *sectional* in form (pars. 38 and 55*b*). The first section is based upon the first half of the thematic melody. At *16) the original *a*-sharp is changed to *b*-flat, and greatly emphasized, — see the original.

*17) Sections II, III and IV are each 8 measures in length (the extent of the Theme); each consists in the duplication of a 4-measure phrase; and each is based on a "diminution" of the thematic melody.

*18) This is followed by a Vth Section, similar to the IVth; and a final, VIth Section, of 9 measures, as reiteration of the cadence-chords.

See further:

Chopin, Berceuse, op. 57. This would scarcely be called a typical Chaconne, but it is nevertheless an example of the Chaconne-form. After two introductory measures (announcing the uniform alternation of tonic and dominant harmonies which oscillate uninterruptedly through the piece — to the Coda), the "Theme," a four-measure melody, is thus stated:

This 4-measure phrase recurs twelve times; in some cases the melody may be distinctly traced, but in the most of the presentations it is the *chords* (the "rocking" tonic-dominant) which provide the delightfully ornamental lines of the upper structure. After "Var." 12, a Coda of 16 measures is added; it consists of two Sections: the first Section introduces, for the first time, the subdominant chord and key; the second Section is the traditional "*da capo*," or direct reference to the original presentation of the thematic melody, — extended.

Brahms, op. 118, No. 5 (Romanze for pfte.); the middle Part (2-sharp signature). By no means a typical Chaconne, but a member of the same structural family: A 4-measure phrase, with five repetitions or variations, based strictly upon the *chords* of the thematic phrase, followed by a codetta (as retransition to the Principal Part of the composition).

Brahms, op. 119, No. 2 (Intermezzo for pfte.): Similar, but less genuine. This unique design is approximately a Group of phrases, with "Trio" in strict Three-Part Song-form. But it closely resembles the Chaconne-form, inasmuch as nearly every phrase in the group has the same thematic contents.

The thematic melody occurs in the first two measures, and is immediately duplicated and extended. These two thematic measures recur at measures 9, 11, 13 (transposed to *a* minor), 15 (sequence), 18 (transposed to *f* minor), 20 (in *e* minor, as at the beginning), 29; and again, in measure 36, expanded to four measures, as principal phrase of the "Trio," in *major;* thus:

Joachim Raff, Chaconne in *a* minor for the pfte. for four hands, op. 150. The Theme is announced after an Introduction. It is in *a* minor, $\frac{3}{4}$ measure, and *twelve* measures long. There are first 9 "variations" (not so called in the original) in *a* minor — the 9th one extended two measures at its end; then two in *C* major, 5 in *a* minor (some extended), 2 in *A* major, one each in *C* major and *e* minor; finally 3 in *a* minor; then a "*da capo*" statement, and a Coda, ending in major.

Erich W. Korngold, the final movement of Sonata, No. 1, for the pianoforte:

*1) The *Theme* (only) bears these initials, and is therefore plainly not original with Korngold, but its elaboration forms the last movement of his Sonata. It is not called "Chaconne," but obviously belongs to that tribe. The Theme is *seven* measures in length. Note the soprano, — all tones from the *d* minor chord. The principal basis is the chord-succession, though the *bass-line* is everywhere more or less evident; it is retained, as bass, during the first 5 or 6 statements; then presented, with varied modifications, in other parts. There are, in all, 13 variations in minor, 6 in major; the last 2 or 3 are in minor.

THE CHACONNE-THEME.

39. It is not easy to define the qualities of a good (original) working Theme. The predominant attribute should, however, be simplicity. A natural, unaffected chord-succession, with an attractive melodic upper line, will yield better results than a showy or dramatically impressive one can; a Theme that is elaborate in itself will admit of but little further elaboration; the art of variation is to develop unexpected effects not directly patent in the Theme. This is possible, with the exercise of sufficient *ingenuity*, and with the understanding that very great liberties may (and must) be taken with the Theme, on condition that these do not wholly destroy its *essential* elements.

At the same time, a Theme, while simple as a whole, must contain *one or more striking traits* which impart a distinct physiognomy to it, and establish a convincing point of contact between it and its variations. In this respect, note the irregular rhythm in measure 6 of Ex. 18 (**Beethoven**), and the chromatic bass; and the dissonant Second-dominant chord (II^7) on the first accent in Ex. 19 (**Bach**); the raised 4th scale-step in the 5th measure of **Ex. 20 (Brahms)**; and the striking harmonization of a very simple melody, in Ex. 24.

This latter trait — peculiar, irregular, abnormal harmonies — it is wise to shun, in the Theme, for nothing grows so quickly and inevitably wearisome as the regular recurrence of any abnormal feature.

Above all things, *monotony* (in the Theme, or in the rhythmic, melodic and harmonic treatment of its variations) must be rigidly guarded against.

EXERCISE 4.

A number of examples of the Chaconne-form; major or minor; almost, if not quite, exclusively in $\frac{3}{4}$ measure; with (chiefly) 8-measure Themes.

CHAPTER V.

THE SMALL (OR SIMPLE) VARIATION-FORM.

40. The distinction between the three grades of the Variation-form (chapters 4, 5 and 6), as shown in the Comparative Table at the head of this Division, is due primarily to the length of the *Theme*. In the Chaconne, it is usually an 8-measure sentence, or One-Part form. In the Small Variation, usually 16 measures, either as double-period, or Two-Part form; or, possibly, Incipient Three-Part form. In the Large Variation, usually 20 to 24 measures, as Three-Part form, sometimes Incomplete.

Other distinctions, concerning melody and formal structure, will be pointed out later.

41. This difference in the extent of the thematic sentence has an obvious, and significant, bearing upon the nature of the task, and, consequently, upon the attitude of the student. As the Theme becomes longer, the disposition increases to lay greater stress upon the melody or air; to separate the variations; and to direct more attention to the structural conditions (the "form"), — of each variation, and of the entire series.

42. The Theme of the Small variation-form, as stated in par. 40, is usually 16 measures in length, as double-period,* Two-Part Song-form,† possibly incipient Three-Part form.‡ The double-period is employed in **Beethoven's** "Righini Variations" (24, in *D* major); the Two-Part form in **Mendelssohn's** "Variations sérieuses" (*d* minor, op. 54); the Incipient Three-Part form in the 1st movement of **Mozart's** pfte. Sonata in A major (Schirmer ed., No. 9). Other dimensions are occasionally found, as, for example, a small Two-Part form (8 measures¶) in the Theme of **Brahms'** "Handel Variations" (*B*-flat major, op. 24). But 16 measures is the normal length.

The essential traits are similar to those given in the definition of the Chaconne Theme (par. 39, which review). But the Theme of the variation-form proper usually has a more pronounced *lyric* quality; its burden is the *melody*, or *air*, to which the chords are added as harmonic accompaniment. And although the earlier distinctive custom of writing variations upon some popular song, opera aria, or other favorite composition, has given way to that of preparing original Themes, the latter are generally far more melodious than harmonic in character.

43. *a.* In the Small form, with its 16-measure Theme, the variations, being longer than those of the Chaconne, are more independent of each other, and more likely to constitute separate sentences, each complete in itself.

b. The variations are, as a rule, no longer connected with each other. Each one receives its full perfect cadence, and is thus brought to a complete close.

Nevertheless, in some instances a few of the traits of the Chaconne still adhere to the Small variation-form: At times, the same "pattern," or a related one, is used for two (not more) successive variations; Ex. 25, notes *3), *4), *8). And occasionally a variation may be connected with the following one, — only by "bridging" the cadence, rhythmically; **Mendelssohn,** op. 54 (Ex. 25), Var. 1–2, 2–3, 3–4, 6–7, 9–10, 11–12, 16–17.

c. The variations may become somewhat more independent of their Theme, — not closely related duplicates, as in the Chaconne, but

---

* See the author's *Homophonic Forms,* chap. VIII.
† *Homophonic Forms,* chap. IX.
‡ *Homophonic Forms,* par. 84.
¶ *Homophonic Forms,* par. 76.

actual *variations*, more ingeniously differentiated from the Theme and from each other. They may be said rather to *allude*, than to refer, to their Theme; hence, greater liberty is exercised in the choice of "pattern," and in defining the character of each individual variation.

44. In this smaller grade of the Variation-form proper, the separate variations, as "modified repetitions of the Theme," should exhibit their relation to, and derivation from their Theme with convincing clearness; otherwise, in the absence of such recognizable proof of its thematic origin, the variation is, more accurately stated, an "improvisation" upon the Theme, and manifests only a remote or indirect relation to the latter.

45. For this reason, it is necessary to define the essential elements of the Theme, and to determine the principal points of contact to be maintained between it and its variations. Of these there are four, readily definable and recognizable:

    1. The *melody* of the Theme;

    2. The *chord-successions* (or harmonic body) of the Theme;

    3. The *bass* of the Theme; and

    4. The general *form*, or structural outline of the Theme.

46. *a*. In any case, the first step is to invent a motive or *Pattern* for the variation. See par. 35.

This is generally a brief figure, of one beat (rare), one-half measure, a whole measure, or two measures (rarely longer), which appears at the beginning of the variation, *and is then conducted through the variation, guided by the melodic and harmonic movements of the Theme, and in more or less close keeping with the adopted basis of contact* (par. 45).

Note the array of patterns in Exs. 18, 19, 20 and 25; and observe that it is the general melodic and, especially, rhythmic construction of the pattern that defines the style and effect of the variation.

The pattern is often derived from some feature of the Theme itself. See Ex. 18, note *9) and note *11). Also Ex. 25, note *2).

Theme. MENDELSSOHN, op. 54.
Andante   Var. 1. *Andante*
Ex. 25.   (See Ex. 30)   etc. *1)

*1) Only a portion of the Theme is given, sufficient to define the conception of the patterns. The pattern of Var. 1 might be defined as a "running inner part, with staccato bass, beneath the original melody." It is adhered to throughout.

*2) The "motive" of the pattern, in the lower staff, is derived from the last member of the Theme (measures 15 and 16 — which see), to the *bassnotes* of which it exactly corresponds.

*3) Var. 4 is the mate to Var. 3; it utilizes the same "motive" of four tones, but in contrary motion.

*4) Var. 9 is the mate to Var. 8.

*5) A fughetta; see par. 54*d*.

*6) The thematic melody in tenor, nearly literal, throughout.

*7) Change of mode; melody in tenor.

*8) Var. 17 is the mate to Var. 16; it is followed by a long Coda of four Sections (see par. 55*b*). In every one of these "patterns" the presence of the *first two* melody tones of the Theme (*a* and *g*-sharp) is clearly recognized.

b. It is by no means necessary to adhere strictly to the adopted pattern throughout, although this is generally done. The effort to defeat monotony, and the natural exhibition of ingenuity and freedom, will lead to occasional slight — or even great — alterations of the pattern; these, however, seldom affect the rhythm. This freedom of treatment is frequently conspicuous in the variations of **Beethoven,** in which, instead of continuous reiterations of the same pattern, often a number of motives (always closely assimilated, particularly in respect of rhythm) appear, in the successive phrases, periods, or Parts of the same variation.

47. Of the four essential thematic elements enumerated in par. 45, the most important and indicative is the Melody. The more or less constant adherence to the air or melody is by far the most natural and common method of establishing contact between Theme and Variation. And this is the reason why the Theme of a small variation-form should present a more distinctly *lyric* appearance (should have a more prominent melody-line) than that of the Chaconne.

48. (First glance at par. 58.) When the *melody-line* is thus adopted as the basis of the variation, it may be traced quite, or nearly, literally:

a. In the same (upper) part.

Mendelssohn, op. 54, Var. 1 — literally; Var. 2 — nearly literally. Such nearly exact retention of the melody of the Theme is very apt to occur in the *first* variation, which naturally represents a direct re-statement and confirmation of the Theme, before its more elaborate variation is undertaken. The succeeding variations then diverge more and more widely from the thematic melody — for a time — until it seems effective to return and state the melody again in its original form (as quasi *da capo*, from time to time). In this respect, the above variations of **Mendelssohn** (op. 54) are typical.

b. Or the melody may be placed in an inner or lower part — again, either quite, or nearly, literally; perhaps with different harmonization, and always with new and ingenious patterns.

Mendelssohn, op. 54, Var. 13 (very nearly literal, in tenor); Var. 14 (nearly literal, in tenor, during the first Part; then more obscured); see Ex. 25, notes *6) and *7).

Beethoven, "Russian" variations (12, in *A* major), Var. 4 (melody in tenor, nearly exact, during first and third Part). Op. 26, *A*-flat major pfte. Sonata; Var. 2 (in bass — later in inner part — nearly exact).

Schumann, Symphonic Études (op. 13), Var. 2 — melody in bass, later in inner part. **Brahms,** op. 9, Var. 1, — melody in bass.

c. Or the successive members of the melody may appear in alternate parts.

This is seen in the variation just cited — **Beethoven,** op. 26, Var. 2; and in the following:

*1) The original melody tones are here indicated by – – –, which, of course, do not appear in **Mendelssohn's** version; the o denotes the absence of an original note.

See also **Mendelssohn,** op. 82, Var. 3. **Brahms,** "Handel Variations," op. 24, Var. 10; Var. 18 (alternate left and right hand).

d. The melody may be elaborately ornamented, or dissolved into a florid cantilena or "aria" (similar to the process sometimes applied to a chorale melody: See the author's *Applied Counterpoint,* par. 107).

Beethoven, op. 35 (15 variations in *E*-flat major), Var. 15. Also his op. 120 ("Diabelli" variations), Var. 31; and op. 34 (6 variations in *F* major), Var. 1, and the *adagio molto* in the Coda; also 13 variations in *A* major (Dittersdorf), Var. 12.

e. In variations for the organ, especially in so-called Chorale-variations, the thematic melody is likely to be retained as more or less strict *cantus firmus,* with polyphonic treatment of the accompanying parts.

Bach, organ compositions, Vol. 5 (Peters edition), Second Division (page 60); four sets of Chorale-variations. The word "partite" is used instead of "variations" in Nos. 1 and 2. No. 4 is a series of canonic variations. The Chorale–theme appears, as *cantus firmus,* in various parts — most frequently in soprano; usually retained literally, sometimes modified here and there, or dissolved by ornamentation into a florid aria.

f. The successive tones of the melody are often presented in detached or fragmentary order. This is especially apt to be the case when the chord-basis is prominent (par. 49), or when the pattern is of a figural character. See also par. 51. For illustration:

g. In case the melody of the Theme is chosen as chief line of contact, it goes without saying that the original chord-harmonization, and the bass, may be partly or wholly changed. Comp. pars. 49 and 50. For example:

*1) The Theme (and its melody) are in E-flat major. In this variation, *the melody remains in its original place*, but it is harmonized in *c* minor.

*2) The bass continues in broken octaves.

*3) This note (*e*-flat in the Theme) is the only one changed to accommodate the new key.

*4) Very similar: The melody of the Theme is in B-flat major; in this variation it is in *g* minor — pointed by the short grace-note in each beat. *See the original* ("Handel" variations, op. 24).

*5) The notes of the thematic melody retain their position on the staff, but both the key and the harmony are greatly changed.

*6) Here the original line is changed, and then abandoned.

*7) The melody corresponds note for note to the original, excepting the two inserted tones marked o. The chord-analysis shows the radical change in harmony.

49. When the *chords* are adopted as the principal basis of the variation, with more or less exact adherence to the harmonic and modulatory movements of the Theme, much liberty may be taken with the original melody-line. It may be vaguely represented by its salient fragments, or it may disappear altogether. This style of variation reverts, in a sense, to the character of the Chaconne-form.

Beethoven, op. 35 (Ex. 28, No. 1), Var. 2, 3, 4, 11, 12, 13.

Beethoven, 8 Variations in F major (Süssmayer), Var. 1, 4.

Beethoven, 10 Variations in B-flat major (Salieri); Variations 1 to 7 all bear but little trace of the original melody. In Var. 5, a wholly new melody appears, as product of the original chords.

50. When the original *bass-line* of the Theme is adopted, the original melody, and the chord-successions, may be more or less completely transformed. (This style constitutes an allusion to the *basso ostinato*.)

In the E-flat major Variations of **Beethoven,** op. 35 (subsequently utilized in the Finale of his Third Symphony), very marked prominence is given to the bass-part. It is used, in four literal presentations, for the Introduction to the entire work, somewhat after the manner of a *basso ostinato*, but shifted successively, each time an octave higher; in the first presentation it is alone, in all the characteristic and unlovely rigor of a genuine bass-line; in the second presentation one melodious part is added; then two, then three; — and upon its fifth presentation the actual melodic Theme of the work is erected upon it, followed by 15 variations, and a Finale. *See the original.* In many of these variations, the bass-line (especially the first four, and the last four — and often more — measures) is persistently present. In Variations 4, 6, 7, 8, 10, 11, 12 and 15 it is less conspicuous, its place being represented by the chords in general; in Var. 14 it is especially significant, being used as uppermost part during the first 8 measures. The Finale, with which the set concludes, consists of four Sections (see par. 55c): The first is a fairly strict Fugue, whose subject is derived from the first 4 or 5 measures of the thematic *bass;* Section two is a sort of *da capo*, or statement of the Theme in very nearly its original form, with modified repetition of the second Part; Section three is another complete (and extended) variation, with the melody in bass; Section four (last 9½ measures) is a codetta, based upon reiterations of the first two measures of the melody.

Very similar, in every essential respect, is op. 5 of **Schumann** (called "Impromptus," instead of variations, for pfte.), which see.

A very unique application of the bass-line, as bearer of the variation, is shown in op. 9 of **Brahms** ("Schumann" variations), Var. 2:

*1) There is a curious transformation of the meter, through which four original measures are expressed in *one* measure; — consequently, this whole variation is only six measures long (but then repeated). The bass-line is retained almost literally, throughout, while the original melody and harmony are but vaguely intimated, here and there.

51. N. B. In none of these cases is *strict, continuous, adherence to the adopted basis necessary*. Thus, one of the three principal guides (melody, chords, or bass-line) may be pursued for a time, and then abandoned for another, so that the variation may exhibit, in different phrases, different points of contact.

The only requisite is, that the connection between the variations and their Theme be plausibly recognizable, in a general way at least; certain single points of contact, sufficiently frequent and numerous, should be established; especially those points where the Theme exhibits somewhat characteristic or striking features. In a word, the hearer should obtain a glimpse, here and there at least, of the melody or the original harmony, and of the fairly prominent traits of the Theme. Compare par. 48*f*.

52. When the greatest freedom is desired, the variation cuts loose from the usual guides (melody, chords, or bass) and demonstrates its relation to the Theme only by general structural coincidence. This is the case when *the form, or the general structural outline* of the Theme is adopted as basis, — see par. 45, condition 4. The Theme is, so to speak, reduced to its skeleton, and this is re-clothed with, at times, wholly new melodic and harmonic material. For example:

*1) The structural outline of the Theme may be defined as follows:

A member (one measure), reproduced (by sequence); a third member (two measures), beginning as reproduction (sequence) of the preceding, and leading to a semicadence in the 4th measure. Then a member corresponding to the first one (as repetition), reproduced (by sequence); a third member leading to a perfect cadence in the 8th measure.

*2) The structural outline of the Variation is defined as follows:

A member (one measure), reproduced (by repetition); a third member (two measures) beginning as reproduction (repetition) of the preceding, and leading to a semicadence in the 4th measure. Then a member corresponding to the first one (as sequence), reproduced (by repetition); a third member leading to a perfect cadence in the 8th measure.

Upon careful comparison, the student will perceive that the two *structural outlines* are identical. But "repetition" is substituted for "sequence" in three places, and "sequence" for "repetition" in one place, — thus arriving at a wholly new result, from precisely the same scheme of *reproduced* members. The cadences occupy the same points, but the second (perfect) one is merely in a different key. The "glimpses" of the thematic melody are revealed at the letters A and B.

Analyze the remaining half of this Var. (**Mendelssohn,** op. 54); and also the following Var. (No. 9). It will be observed that Var. 9 is *twenty* measures long, — increased from the original number (sixteen) *by repeating the last phrase.* See par. 53.

The "structural outline" of a Theme is defined by its length (number of measures), its form, the number and harmonic character of its cadences, the presence of repetitions or sequences, and of characteristic traits of melodic progression. All these traits may be preserved in the variation, but so differently interpreted as to form a wholly new picture. For instance, by an unimportant alteration of an important trait — retaining the *location* of the cadences, but changing their harmony or key; substituting "sequence" for "repetition," and vice versa; substituting "ascending" for "descending" sequence; and so forth.

53. The rule for the variation-form, during the classic period, was that the form of the Theme should undergo no change; that is, that each variation should contain the same number of measures as the Theme (excepting the final one, to which a Codetta or Coda might — or should — be added).

This rule is not considered binding, in the more modern era.   But it is characteristic of the *Smaller* variation-forms that no *essential* alterations of the design of the Theme are permissible.   The *unessential*, and therefore permissible, extensions, are those which result from the simple *repetition* of a phrase, or of a phrase-member, — naturally with modification; or from the process known as Expansion (prolonging a single prominent melody-tone or chord; see *Homophonic Forms*, par. 29c).

Mendelssohn, op. 54 (Ex. 30); Variations 1 to 8 are all 16 measures long, like the Theme; Var. 9, as already pointed out, is 20 measures long, because of the repetition (an octave higher) of the fourth 4-measure phrase; Var. 13, similarly, has a repetition (an octave lower) of the fourth phrase; Var. 10 is extended, at the end, to 18 measures.

In Beethoven, op. 34 (*F* major) there is an Expansion, as "cadenza," in the 5th measure from the end.

Beethoven, 8 variations in *F* major ("Süssmayer"); the Theme (with its repetitions) contains 24 measures; Var. 7 contains 28 — measures 19–20 of the Theme being extended, by reiteration, to 6 measures.

Beethoven, 24 variations in *D* major ("Righini"); in Var. 23 each of the two 8-measure Periods is repeated, with elaborate modifications.

More vital transformations of the thematic design, peculiar to the Larger variation-form, are shown in par. 63.

54. Besides these specific details, there are certain alterations of a general character which may affect some of the variations as a whole. These are:

a. The change of *mode*, — referred to in par. 37, and encountered already in the Chaconne (Ex. 18, Variations 12 to 16).

See Ex. 25, Var. 14.

Beethoven, op. 120 ("Diabelli"); the Theme is in *C* major; Variations 9, 29, 30, 31 are in *c* minor.

b. The change of *key*.

This more significant alteration is usually limited, in the Smaller form, to *next-related* keys, or to the so-called Mediant keys, which, though remote, exhibit peculiarly vital ties of relationship.

See Ex. 28, No. 1; Var. 6 is in the relative minor key. Ex. 28, No. 2; **Var.** 21 is in the relative minor key. Ex. 28, No. 3; Var. 5 is in the tonic-mediant key (*f*, tonic=mediant, third step of *D*-flat major).

Brahms, op. 9 ("Schumann" variations); the Theme, and variations 1 to 8, are in *f*-sharp minor; Var. 9 is in *b* minor (the subdominant); Var. 10 in *D* major (subdominant-relative); Var. 11 in *G* major (remote), ending in *f*-sharp minor; Var. 15 in *G*-flat major (= *F*-sharp, change of mode); Var. 16 in *F*-sharp major.

Tschaikowsky, op. 19, No. 6 (Ex. 31, No. 1); the Theme, and variations 1 to 4, are in *F* major; Var. 5 is in *D*-flat major (the tonic-mediant key); Var. 6, *F* major; Var. 7, in the Phrygian mode on *A* (ecclesiastic); Var. 8 in *d* minor (the relative key); Var. 9 in *B*-flat major (the subdominant); Var. 10 in *f* minor (the change of mode); Variations 11 and 12 again in *F* major.

In **Beethoven,** op. 34, a singular systematic change of key occurs, in descending thirds from variation to variation. The Theme is in *F* major; Var. 1 in *D* major (mediant = dominant); Var. 2 in *B*-flat major (tonic = mediant, with the preceding key); Var. 3 in *G* major (mediant = dominant); Var. 4 in *E*-flat major (tonic = mediant); Var. 5 in *c* minor (mediant = dominant); this keynote, *c*, is the dominant of the original key, *F;* being in the minor form, an Interlude follows (par. 54*g*), during which the triad changes to its major form and becomes the true dominant of *F;* Var. 6, and the Coda, are then again in *F* major. Such extreme changes of key are more likely to occur in the Larger form.

c. The change of *meter* (time-signature).

Tschaikowsky, op. 19, No. 6; the Theme, and variations 1 and 2, are in $\frac{3}{4}$ measure; Var. 3 is in $\frac{3}{8}$ measure; Var. 4 in $\frac{9}{16}$ measure (Ex. 31, No. 1); Var. 5 in $\frac{3}{4}$; Var. 6 in $\frac{9}{8}$; Var. 7 in $\frac{3}{2}$; Var. 8 in $\frac{3}{4}$; Var. 9 in $\frac{3}{8}$; Var. 10 in $\frac{4}{4}$; Var. 11 in $\frac{2}{4}$; Var. 12, and Coda, again in $\frac{3}{4}$ measure. It is unusual to change the measure in this manner in almost every variation. In **Mendelssohn,** op. 54, there is no change at all; in **Beethoven,** op. 35, there is but one change from $\frac{2}{4}$ measure — in Var. 15, to $\frac{6}{8}$ measure.

d. The adoption of some *conventional type* or style of composition for one or another of the variations. Thus, a variation may assume the character of a March, Minuet, Waltz, Mazurka, Gavotte, Aria (par. 48*d*), Invention, Fughetta, Canon, or any other type, — with corresponding change of time-signature (par. 54*c*).

Beethoven, op. 35; Var. 7 is a Canon in the octave (compare Ex. 16, note *6)). Also his op. 120 ("Diabelli" variations); Var. 1 is a March; Var. 19, canonic; also Var. 20; Var. 22 is patterned after Leporello's first aria in Mozart's "Don Giovanni"; Var. 24 is a Fughetta; Var. 30, an Invention; Var. 31, an Aria; Var. 32, a Fugue.

Brahms, op. 9 ("Schumann" variations); Var. 8 is a Canon in the octave; Var. 14 a Canon in the second; Var. 15 a Canon in the third; Var. 10 a "Quodlibet"; **Var.** 9 is patterned after a composition of **Schumann** (from his op. 99).

Tschaikowsky, op. 19, No. 6; Var. 9 is a Mazurka (Ex. 31, No. 1).

Arensky, Suite (Variations) for two pianos, op. 33: Thême, Dialogue, Valse, Marche triomphale, Menuet, Gavotte, Scherzo, Marche funèbre, Nocturne, Polonaise.

e. Transformations of the *rhythm.*

This extremely effective process is applied to the first melodic member of the Theme (at least, — sometimes carried on consistently through the entire Theme), and consists in *so shifting the tones in the measure* that the accented and unaccented points are exchanged, or otherwise modified.   For example:

*1) From **Tschaikowsky's** Trio in *a* minor, op. 50 (last movement).

To this class of rhythmic modifications belongs also the *augmentation* of the Theme, whereby one measure of the latter is so expanded as to cover two, or more, in the variation.

See Ex. 31, No. 2 (**Liadow,** Var. 7). Also **Glazounow,** op. 72, Var. 8 (double-augmentation) and others. Of similar nature is Ex. 20 (**Brahms**), Var. 12. The less common *diminution* is seen in Ex. 29.

f. The *double-variation.* In this rare species of the form, two strongly contrasted patterns are alternately applied, usually to the complete repetition of each phrase or Part.

Beethoven, 24 Variations in *D* major ("Righini" Theme); Var. 14.

Beethoven, Sonata, op. 109, third movement, Var. 2.

g. In rare cases, an *Interlude* is inserted, as transitional passage, between two variations. Comp. par. 65.

Beethoven, op. 34, between Variations 5 and 6.

55. The entire series of variations is almost invariably rounded off (as in all the larger designs) with an addition at the end, in the nature of a Coda. This final extension may assume three different dimensions; partly according to the extent of the Theme itself, or of the entire composition; and partly in keeping with the character of the last variation, and the general necessity of instituting good balance, and effecting an adequate ending. Thus:

a. The addition may be limited to a brief *Codetta*, of one section, with the customary repetition, or duplication, and extension, — attached to the last variation. (See the author's *Homophonic Forms*, par. 51.) A typical illustration of the "Codetta" is seen at the end of Ex. 34.

Beethoven, 6 Variations in *F* ("Schweizerlied"); the last two full measures. Also, 6 Variations in *G* (original Theme); last 14 measures (called "Coda" in the original, but belongs to the Codetta class, because it consists of *one* section only, — two measures, repeated 3 times, and further extended by 5 or 6 repetitions of the cadence-chords).

b. Or the addition may be a complete *Coda*. (*Homophonic Forms*, par. 98.)

The design of a Coda is invariably *sectional*. That is, it consists of a number of successive "Sections," the character and extent of which can be determined only by the composer's judgment and sense of proportion. The Coda is therefore an essentially indefinite and formless factor, which, for precisely this reason, forms an important contrasting element in the otherwise logical and systematic structure; and, in dismissing the constraint of definite structural arrangement, it affords the writer full freedom to exercise his imagination, and create an effective climax.

The term "Section" is here applied to any episode of *indefinite form*, — in distinction to the terms Phrase, Period, Part, etc., whose structural conditions are more or less accurately fixed. Its use in the analysis of the Fugue, Invention, Fantasia, and a few other forms, is encountered in the author's *Applied Counterpoint*.

The number of sections is optional.

The length of a section is optional. The final ones are apt to decrease in extent, and the very last one is practically identical with a Codetta.

The contents of each section are optional, though it is natural that each should refer more or less directly to the various members of the Theme, particularly to the *first* melodic member. A section may constitute an additional variation (perhaps extended — perhaps abbreviated), in which some new pattern is utilized. This may occur in several successive sections, as incomplete variations. It is not unusual to devote one section of the Coda to a re-statement of the Theme, or of its first phrases, as traditional *da capo*.

Schubert, Impromptu, op. 142, No. 3, *B*-flat.

See also, **Beethoven,** op. 34; op. 35; and the 33 variations in *c* minor. The Coda in each of these sets contains additional complete variations.

It is also possible to introduce new material (though not wholly irrelevant) in one or more of the sections.

The sections may be separated from each other by fairly complete cadences, or — as is more common — each may be carried over uninterruptedly into the following one. The beginning of a new section, in case of such unbroken transition, is shown by a positive change of rhythm, or of pattern.

A section is frequently duplicated, in sequence.

In a general sense, the Coda (and also the "Finale") is a free, fantasia-like, manipulation of salient *fragments* of the Theme, thus differing from the variations, in which the whole theme is present.

Ex. 32.

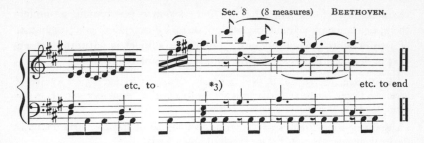

*1) A Russian dance. The Theme, 19 measures long, is Incipient Three-Part form.

*2) The Coda is attached to the 12th (last) variation. It will be observed that each of its seven Sections utilizes the first melodic member of the Theme. Section 1 is a three-voice Invention, in double-counterpoint.

*3) Section 8 is the final "Codetta": The two measures here shown, duplicated and extended.

See also: **Beethoven,** 24 Variations in *D* major ("Righini"). The Coda, which is attached to the last variation, begins with a section of 8 measures, consisting of a new (but related) melodic member; it is repeated and extended, and closes with a complete tonic cadence, of intentionally humorous character. Section two, based upon the first phrase of the Theme, is 8 measures long; then repeated and skilfully spun out (30 measures). Section three (*allegro*) grows out of the end of this, and is 16 measures long, with a strong dominant semicadence. Section four (*presto assai*) 48 measures long, to the end, is based upon the first period of the Theme, and humorously drawn out, in four successive augmentations.

Rubinstein, *c* minor pfte. Sonata, op. 20, second movement. The Coda, attached to the 4th Var. (which has an evaded cadence), consists of three brief sections, each of which reviews the pattern of foregoing variations; then a fourth section of 11 measures, to the end.

Liadow, op. 51 (Ex. 31, No. 2), has a Coda, attached to the last variation, consisting of a section based upon the first melodic member (8 measures, duplicated and spun out, 20 measures); and a second section, with slightly different treatment of the same member, 11 measures, to the end.

Mendelssohn, op. 54. The Coda follows the 17th Var.; its first section is based upon the last phrase of Var. 16 (24 measures, very brilliant); section two is a partial *da capo*, — the first Part of the Theme, extended (14 measures, with strong dominant semicadence); section three (*presto*), 21 measures long, is a partial variation; section four (12 measures) is a partial duplication of section three; section five, similar, is 8 measures long; section six, its duplication and extension, comprises 20 measures, to the end.

c. The "Finale" is wholly independent of the last variation, and therefore constitutes a separate movement, by itself. In design, it corresponds to the Coda, being sectional in form. But it is somewhat characteristic of a Finale, that its first section is polyphonic, assuming the appearance of a fugue-exposition, or of an extended, genuine fugue, of two or more *fugato* sections. For this a subject is naturally chosen that is derived directly from the initial phrase of the Theme.

Beethoven, op. 35 (Ex. 28, No. 1), Finale. The first section is quite a lengthy, ingenious Fugue, whose subject represents the *bass* of the Theme (see par. 50, in the notes to which, the whole Finale is described).

Brahms, op. 56 (orchestral variations on a Theme of **Haydn**). The Finale is the *basso ostinato* given in Ex. 9; dissolved into a Coda.

Or the entire Finale is a Concert-fugue, — sectional, of course.

Brahms, op. 24 ("Handel" variations), Finale.

Or some later section of the Finale may develop into a *fugato*.

E. Rudorff, Variations for orchestra, op. 24 (Ex. 31, No. 3), Finale. A masterly, extremely ingenious work. The Finale consists chiefly in a series of fragmentary variations, including a *fugato*.

Otherwise, or in addition to these polyphonic sections, the Finale is similar in character to the Coda, and is subject to the same conditions. The impression conveyed is, as stated, that of fragmentary manipulation, with a view to brilliancy and an effective climax.

The student should make a thorough study of as many of the following Variation-forms as he can procure, and of any others which he may encounter (— first glance at pars. 65 and 66):

Mozart, pfte. Sonata, No. 9 (Schirmer edition), first movement.

Mozart, pfte. Sonata, No. 15, last movement.

Beethoven, 12 Variations in *A* ("Russian"; Ex. 32).

Beethoven, 24 Variations in *D* ("Righini").

Beethoven, op. 35 (Ex. 28, No. 1). And other Variations of **Beethoven,** easily recognizable as Smaller form.

Beethoven, pfte. Sonata, op. 14, No. 2, *Andante.*

Beethoven, pfte. Sonata, op. 109, *Andante.*

Beethoven, pfte. Sonata, op. 57, *Andante.*

Beethoven, pfte. Sonata, op. 111, second movement (in some respects, Larger form).

Beethoven, Fantasia, op. 77, *Allegretto.*

Beethoven, Sonata for pfte. and violin, op. 12, No. 1, second movement.

Beethoven, Sonata for pfte. and violin, op. 30, No. 1, third movement.

Beethoven, Sonata for pfte. and violin, op. 96, last movement.

Beethoven, pfte. Trio, op. 1, No. 3, second movement.

Beethoven, pfte. Trio, op. 11, last movement.

Beethoven, String-quartet, op. 18, No. 3, second movement.

Schubert, Impromptu, op. 142, No. 3, *B*-flat.

Mendelssohn, Sonata for pfte. and 'cello, op. 17.

Mendelssohn, Variations for pianoforte, op. 54 (Ex. 30).

Brahms, pfte. Sonata, op. 1, *Andante.*

Brahms, pfte. Sonata, op. 2, *Andante.*

Brahms, pfte. Var., op. 24 ("Handel"; Ex. 28, No. 2).

Brahms, String-sextet, op. 18, *Andante.*

Brahms, String-sextet, op. 36, *Adagio.*

Brahms, String-quartet, No. 3, op. 67, last movement.

Brahms, pfte. Var., op. 21, No. 1.

Brahms, pfte. Var., op. 21, No. 2 (quasi Chaconne-form).

Schumann, Impromptus, op. 5.

Karl Nawratil, pfte. Var., op. 7.

Tschaikowsky, pfte. Var., op. 19, No. 6 (Ex. 31, No. 1).

Paderewski, Var. and Fugue, op. 11 (comprising some traits of the Larger form).

Paderewski, op. 16, No. 3 (ditto).

EXERCISE 5.

A number of examples of the Theme with variations in the Small or Simple form, with Codetta, Coda, or Finale. The student may select a Theme from any source (but see par. 40); or may invent original Themes. The following Theme is submitted for manipulation:

GOETSCHIUS.

CHAPTER VI.

THE LARGE (OR HIGHER) VARIATION-FORM.

56. The distinction between the Small and Large grades of the variation-form is defined primarily by the length of the Theme, which, in the higher grade, is usually the Three-Part Song-form (**Beethoven,** op. 34), — sometimes Incomplete (**Mendelssohn,** op. 82, and op. 83). Comp. par. 40, and see the Comparative Table at the head of this Division.

57. But the two grades are differentiated in a much more vital respect, and this concerns the whole artistic aspect and the consequent treatment, which is more creative than imitative, and more elaborate.

58. The mass of directions in the preceding chapter, which might be feared to hamper and stultify the student's original conception, were given in systematic detail because these constitute the *technical basis* of the problem of variation; and this must be mastered before it is wise to break loose from the lines of the Theme, and venture to develop it with freedom.

59. But in the higher grade, the student gives free rein to his imagination, and evolves more independent results from his Theme. In this grade, the variations are more properly *Elaborations* than mere modified duplications of the Theme.

Hence it is that, while a longer Theme is usually chosen, as affording a wider field of operation, it is nevertheless possible to develop an imposing work, decidedly "large" in spirit, from a comparatively brief Theme. Two conspicuous examples of this are the variations by **Glazounow**, op. 72, on a Russian melody of only seven measures (Ex. 35); and those by **Rachmaninow**, op. 22, on the *c* minor Prelude of **Chopin**, which is a period of 8 measures.

60. *a.* The leading purpose in the smaller grade is *technical* manipulation, — "variation," with fairly direct reference to the Theme.

In the larger grade the leading purpose is imaginative and *creative* manipulation, — "elaboration," with only general allusion to the Theme. The variation is not the prime object, but becomes the *means to an eminent artistic end.*

b. It must be understood, however, that not every variation assumes broader proportions; the first few variations are always more directly related to the Theme, and the impulse of freedom grows as the form advances. In this respect the variations of **Glazounow** (op. 72) are typical and highly effective.

61. Such a creative process cannot always be carried on, with the necessary freedom, within the exact limits of the Theme. The confines of the latter must be broken through, its lines broadened, its scope widened, to make room for the unrestricted exercise of imagination, and to provide increased opportunity for free development.

This manipulation and expansion of the structural design of the Theme may be conducted in two ways:

1. So as to secure *unessential* extensions of the Theme, by mere repetitions, or Expansions, which do not alter the form; and

2. So as to effect more or less complete *transformation* of the design.

62. *a.* The first class, unessential extensions, may be applied in both the smaller and larger grades of the variation-form. Their operation in the smaller grade is explained in par. 53, which review.

b. The second class, transformation of the design (always as enlargement), involves a number of independent additions to the original members of the Theme, which may all be classed under the head of *Insertions.*

63. There are three kinds of independent insertions, as follows:

a. The insertion of a Codetta, possible at any *important* (tonic) cadence in the course of the variation; and, of course, even more plausible at the end of the variation.

This is always feasible, because a Codetta is defined as "an extension at the cadence," — not *of* the cadence itself, but sufficiently independent of it to constitute a fairly distinct member of the design; and this may be applied to *any tonic cadence* in the course of the design, especially to any one which terminates a "Part" (or Period) of the form.   (See *Homophonic Forms*, par. 98*a* and, particularly, 98*c*).

For illustration:

LIADOW, op. 51.

*1) This variation is a transposed presentation of the Theme, from *A*-flat major to its relative minor.

*2) This Insertion of four measures is practically an Expansion of the cadence-chord (chord of *c* — first as tonic of *c* minor, and later, with *e*-natural, as dominant of *f* minor); but it is so distinct in style as to become an independent "Codetta."

*3) The second Period is exactly similar to the first Period, excepting that its Consequent phrase is shifted a 4th higher, precisely as in the Theme.

*4) Here the Insertion is a genuine 4-measure Codetta, with the customary duplication and extension. See the original.

b. The insertion of a Duplication; — either as complete sequence of a phrase (or other member of the form); or as reproduction (quasi repetition) of a phrase, with a different ending (cadence).

Such reproductions, contradicting the principle of mere "repetition," as they do, constitute actual alterations of the form, and therefore contribute to its enlargement. The "Sequence" is shown in Ex. 35, note *3).

The "Duplication" (with new cadence) occurs in Var. 11 of the same work (**Glazounow**) : The first Phrase, corresponding to the first half of the Theme (Ex. 35), is 8 measures long, because two of its measures represent one measure of the Theme; it begins in *F*-sharp major, and cadences on the dominant; the second Phrase is ostensibly a "repetition" of this — but proves to be a "duplication," as it cadences on the tonic of *A* major. (See par. 12*d.*)

c. The insertion of an entire Part. This is the most significant method, as it results in complete transformation of the design.

This is best illustrated by a diagram, — applied to the simple Period-form: Given a period, as follows, in *parallel* construction (the Consequent phrase beginning, at least, with the same melodic member as the Antecedent phrase):

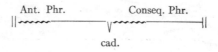

If the two phrases are drawn apart, thus:

far enough to admit of a genuine Insertion *as actual Departure,* or *Second Part,* the Consequent phrase becomes a Third *Part,* with its evidence of a "Return to the beginning" (being parallel with its Antecedent), and the simple Period-design has been transformed into a Three-Part Song-form. The Antecedent phrase can easily be extended to the dimension of an adequate First Part, by the means indicated in par. 63*b* (above). **Thus:**

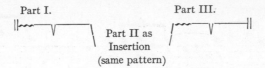

Part I.   Part III.

Part II as
Insertion
(same pattern)

Though a digression, or "departure," it is obvious that this inserted Second Part — in common with all Insertions — must consist of strictly related, homogeneous material. It will, at least, always utilize the same, or a very similar, pattern.

For illustration of *all three* of the above classes of Insertion:

*1) The construction of the Theme (Period-form) is parallel; that is, the Conse-
quent phrase begins like the Antecedent.

*2) At this point the second measure of the (Antecedent) phrase is omitted —
hence the abbreviation to *seven* measures. In every variation this wanting measure
is inserted; see note *7).

*3) The Insertion is a sequential duplication of the first phrase (par. 63*b*).

*4) This cadence, for emphasis, fills an extra, fifth, measure.

*5) The Insertion is equivalent to a complete Second Part (par. 63*c*), which, though a new member of the design, is developed out of the pattern of the First Part, and alludes (in the uppermost part) to the first member of the thematic melody.

*6) The "return to the beginning," corresponding here to the Consequent phrase of the Theme (comp. note *1).

*7) This is the inserted measure, referred to in note *2).

*8) The Codetta is built upon the prevailing pattern, and coincides with Part II.

This work of **Glazounow** will repay thorough analysis; the student should endeavor to verify the following traits: Var. 1 is practically a re-statement of the Theme, with full harmony, and "corrected" to 8 measures. Var. 2, similar (melody exact). Var. 3, similar, — extended at the end to 9 measures. Variations 4, 5 and 6 (each 8 measures) abandon the direct line of thematic melody, but refer closely to it. Var. 7 is the "transformed" design, shown in Ex. 35. Var. 8 is a curious double augmentation (four measures equal to one of the Theme); the melody is traceable as described in par. 48*f*; a Codetta, with duplication and extension, is added (last 14 measures). Var. 9 (*A* major) is in 3-Part Song-form: Part I is the 8 measures of the Theme, but with "false" cadence — in *F* major; Part II is an Insertion, based on the prevalent pattern; Part III is a partial recurrence of Part I, but transposed, and extended by a brief Codetta, and an Expansion. Var. 10 is also transformed into 3-Part Song-form: Part I is the 8-measure Theme, with correct cadence — a complete variation; Part II is an Insertion, based on the second member of the Ant. Phrase (presented four times in sequence); Part III is like Part I, but "Incomplete" — consisting of the Conseq. Phrase only; a Codetta is added. Var. 11 (*F*-sharp major) is also 3-Part Song-form; Part I (16 measures — two measures to one of the Theme) is, like Var. 9, the Theme with "false" cadence — in *A* major; Part II is based on the prevailing pattern; Part III like Part I, but "Incomplete," also stating the Conseq. Phrase only; a Codetta, with duplication and extension, is added. Var. 12 is a sort of Fantasia (sectional form), approximating a Group of (four) Parts; the whole variation is a unique combination of the first and second members of the Ant. Phrase (measures 1–2, 3–4) — the latter member everywhere in "Diminution"; a brief Codetta is added. Var. 13 is a Group of (three) Phrases: Phr. 1, the Antecedent; Phr. 2, a Sequence (representing the Consequent); Phr. 3, another Sequence, greatly extended; a Codetta is added, the duplication of which is the Conseq. Phrase complete. Var. 14 — an exquisite example of creative evolution — is also a 3-Part Song-form; Part I is the Theme complete, with the melody in the tenor, and a "Counter-melody" in the soprano; Part II, an Insertion, is the sequential development of this Counter-melody; Part III is a literal recurrence of Part I; three brief Codettas are added. The following number is a genuine Finale (named, erroneously, "Var. 15," — comp. par. 55*c*).

See also: **Liadow**, op. 51 (Ex. 34). In Var. 1 the form of the Theme is unchanged. In Var. 2 it is extended by unessential repetitions. Var. 3 is extended: by an Introduction of two measures (see par. 65–2); and by the Insertion of an additional 2-measure member (duplicated) at the end of Phr. 2 — and Phr. 4. In Var. 4, the form is enlarged by the insertion of a Codetta at the end of Phr. 2 —

and Phr. 4, and an additional brief Codetta at the end. In Var. 5 the form is unchanged. In Var. 6 (a partial Canon) the form is enlarged by extensions, and Codettas (as in Var. 4 and Var. 8). Var. 7 contains an inserted Codetta at the end of Phrase 2; this Codetta is duplicated and extended; the corresponding Codetta appears at the end of the 4th Phrase, duplicated, and extended; the extension is "dissolved" (see par. 78) into a "Transition" into the next variation (see par. 65–4). Var. 8 is illustrated in Ex. 34. Var. 9 is extended by the simple (exact) repetition of the second Period. Var. 10 is enlarged by an independent Introduction, and by extensions and Codettas; and to this Var. is added the Coda: Section 1, eight measures, is based on the first melodic member; it is duplicated and greatly extended; Section 2, similar, covers the last 11 measures.

64. In the higher form of the variation, where such transformations of the design are undertaken, it is almost obligatory to adopt, and adhere to, the *melody-line of the Theme* (in a certain sense as if it were a Fugue-subject), as this is the only line of contact which will demonstrate with sufficient clearness the relation of the (quasi distorted) variation to its Theme.

65. Besides the Insertions, described in par. 63, which enter into the very grain of the Theme, and develop it from within, there are other — extraneous — additions, which may be attached to certain variations, or to the whole series, namely:

1. An independent Introduction to the entire work.

Beethoven, op. 35.

2. A brief Introduction to any single variation.

Liadow, op. 51, Var. 3 and Var. 10.

3. An Interlude between two successive variations (par. 54g).

4. A Transition from one variation into the next.

Liadow, op. 51, Var. 7 into Var. 8.

5. And the usual Coda or Finale — which is almost indispensable. The directions for these are given in par. 55b and c.

66. Earnest thought should be directed to the series of variations *as a whole.* It is advisable to compose a number of variations (possibly a much larger number than will be needed), as the moods come, and then to select from this number (rejecting in cold blood the less effective or obviously superfluous ones) those that will constitute an effective dramatic succession, with a view to good contrasts, and to the proper number and degree of climaxes. As already stated (par. 60b), the first few variations are simpler than the later ones, and refer more directly to the Theme. The changes of key, rhythm, and *tempo*, constitute the chief means of obtaining variety and progressively accumulating interest.

Here, again, the student is advised to make a conscientious study of the following variation-forms, in all of which the traits of the Larger or Higher grade are present:

Haydn, pfte. variations in *f* minor (unusually long Theme, in the form of a "Song with Trio").

Beethoven, Sonata for pfte. and violin, op. 47 ("Kreutzer"), second movement. — Pfte. Sonata, op. 26, first movement. — Pfte. variations in *F* major, op. 34. — Pfte. var. in *C* major, op. 120 ("Diabelli").

Schubert, pfte. Sonata, No. 1, *Andante.*

Brahms, op. 9 ("Schumann"). This set has no Coda.

Brahms, orchestra variations, op. 56 ("Haydn"); see Ex. 9, which is the Finale.

Brahms, pfte. Trio in *C* major, op. 87, *Andante.*

Brahms, pfte. var., 4 hands, op. 23 ("Schumann").

Mendelssohn, pfte. var., op. 82, and op. 83.

Chopin, pfte. var., op. 12.

Chopin, Concert-variations, pfte. and orchestra, op. 2 ("Don Juan").

Schumann, pfte. Sonata, op. 14, third movement.

Schumann, pfte. var., op. 1 ("Abegg").

Schumann, Symphonic Études, pfte., op. 13. The remote reference to the Theme, in some of the numbers, induced Schumann to substitute the term Étude for Variation.

Schumann, Var. for two pianos, op. 46.

Mrs. H. H. A. Beach, "Balkan" variations, op. 60.

Dvořák, pfte. var., op. 36.

Arensky, Suite (Var.) for two pianos, op. 33.

César Franck, Symphonic var. for pfte. and orchestra in *f*-sharp minor, — a work of broad design and most masterly execution.

Karl Nawratil, pfte. var., op. 15.

Ed. Schütt, pfte. var., op. 62. — Also op. 29 (Var. and Fugato).

Grieg, Ballade for pfte., op. 24.

Liadow, op. 51 (Ex. 34).

Glazounow, op. 72 (Ex. 35).

Rachmaninow, op. 22 (Chopin-Prélude, *c* minor).

Paderewski, e-flat minor, op. 23 (Fugue-Finale).

Saint-Saëns, Var. for two pianos, op. 35 ("Beethoven").

D. G. Mason, Elegy in free var.-form, op. 2.

E. R. Kroeger, pfte. var., op. 54.

Rudorff, Var. for orchestra, op. 24 (Ex. 31, No. 3).

EXERCISE 6.

A. An example of the Larger variation-form, with Coda or Finale, upon a Theme in 3-Part Song-form, without *essential* change of form.

B. An example upon a Theme in 2-Part Song-form, with Insertions (Codettas, — and enlargement to 3-Part form) in some of the later variations; and with Coda or Finale.

C. Several examples upon a brief Theme (not less than Period, or Double-period, — preferably in parallel construction), with Insertions that effect complete transformation of the form into larger designs, in some of the later variations; and with Coda or Finale. See par. 65, *and par. 66.*

DIVISION TWO.

THE RONDO-FORMS.

INTRODUCTION.

67. The constructive Basis of the several forms of musical composition may be classified as follows:

a. That of the Phrase is the *melodic figure,* or member, borne out by the chord-successions.

b. That of all Homophonic Forms (Period, Double-period, Two- and Three-Part Song-forms, with or without "Trio") is the *Phrase.*

c. That of the Invention, and other smaller polyphonic forms, is the *Motive* (or Phrase-member).

d. That of the Fugue is the *Subject,* or complete melodic phrase.

e. That of the Canon is the continuous melodic *Leader.*

f. That of the Variation, and all other Larger forms (Rondo, Sonata), is the *Theme,* or complete musical sentence.

68. A "Theme," as shown in the variation-forms, is an *independent musical sentence*, distinctive in style and character, and usually complete in its structural design. Therefore its smallest dimension will naturally be a Period-form — eight ordinary measures — consisting of *two* Phrases which balance and complement each other, and therefore enclose definite and sufficient contents.

But it is more likely, especially in broader designs, to be *more than a single Period*, and is perhaps most commonly a full Song-form, of two or three Parts, — though rarely, if ever, longer than the latter, excepting when extended by unessential repetitions.

A Theme may be of any melodic, harmonic, or rhythmic character; but its message must be clearly expressed, and must be significant, — for only such are available for effective development.

Comp. par. 39; but note that the definitions there given refer to a Theme designed for *variation*. The Theme of a Rondo or Sonata should be more vitally individualized; not only for its own sake, as standard-bearer of the composition, but also in order to invite logical manipulation and development. See par. 72.

69. In all of the Larger Forms (beyond the Variation-form) there are at least *two Themes;* each one distinct in character, and well contrasted with the other, and frequently (though not always) complete in its design.

Of these, the one which first appears is called the *Principal Theme*, and the other, or others, *Subordinate*.

70. The structural principle underlying all **Rondo designs** is that of **Alternation**, — the alternation of a Principal Theme with one or more Subordinate Themes. The extent of the design depends upon the number of times that a digression from the Principal Theme occurs.

In the *First Rondo form* there is one digression (or, one Subordinate Theme), and, consequently, one return to, and recurrence of, the Principal Theme, — that is, *one* complete alternation of the two Themes.

In the *Second Rondo form* there are two digressions (or, two Subordinate Themes), and two returns.

In the *Third Rondo form* there are three digressions and (usually) three returns.

CHAPTER VII.

THE FIRST RONDO FORM.

71. The diagram of the First Rondo form is as follows:

PRINCIPAL THEME	Transition	SUBORDINATE THEME	Re-transition	PRINCIPAL THEME	CODA
Any Part-form.		Different key, usually (next)related. (Codetta).		As before, possibly modified.	

THE PRINCIPAL THEME.

72. The design of the first Theme, in the First Rondo form, is generally the 3-Part Song-form; in rare instances only One-Part form (Period, Double-period, or Phrase-group) — perhaps extended by complete or partial repetition; still more uncommon is the 2-Part form.

It should be a simple, *clear*, but characteristic statement, of preponderantly lyric (melodious) character; not fragmentary, but conceived as a sustained, tuneful melodic idea, and not too elaborately extended. Comp. par. 68.

The character of the Rondo Theme is optional; it may proceed from any mood, from the most sombre to the most gay, though the lyric is probably the most appropriate.

The student should not confound the traditional Rondo *style* (usually graceful and moderately animated) with the Rondo *form*. The latter designates a *structural design*, which may be applied to any style of music.

See **Beethoven,** pfte. Sonata, op. 2, No. 1, *Adagio* (the Principal Theme is Incipient 3-Part form, 16 measures).

Beethoven, pfte. Sonata, op. 31, No. 1, *Adagio* (Incomplete 3-Part form, 34 measures, Part I a parallel Double-period).

Beethoven, Sonata, op. 2, No. 3, *Adagio* (Period, extended, 11 measures).

Schubert, pfte. Sonata, No. 6, op. 147, *Andante* (Complete 3-Part form, 27 measures).

Brahms, Symphony No. 3, *Andante* (Group of four Phrases, quasi 3-Part form, 24 measures).

73. The Principal Theme, in the First Rondo form, usually ends with a *complete tonic cadence*, in its own key. See Ex. 36, note *1).

Other methods of treatment, including the process of "Dissolution," will be shown later — par. 77c.

One Theme being thus definitely terminated, conceptive action turns to the following Theme, and the question arises: How can a good connection be established between the two Themes? All that takes place at this point is comprised under the general head of "Transition," and may assume very many (equally normal and effective) forms, that admit of classification as below.

TRANSITION.

74. *a.* The definite cadence of the Prin. Th. (in case this method of termination is adopted) is sometimes followed by an immediate announcement of the Subordinate Theme — that is, without any transitional material, — with an abrupt change of key.

See Ex. 36, No. 1.

Also **Beethoven**, Sonata, op. 2, No. 2, *Largo*, measure 19 (20).

The illustrations of the structure of the Larger Forms which follow are limited chiefly to the pianoforte Sonatas and other works of **Beethoven**; partly because of their unquestioned authority, and partly because the student will find them convenient of access.

b. Such total absence of transitional material is, however, unusual, because incompatible with the desirable continuity and unity of the design. The least that is likely to intervene, between the Themes, is a transitional "bridging" of the cadence-measure, — possibly involving the necessary modulation. For illustration (Ex. 36, No. 2):

*1) In both cases, this is a complete tonic cadence, in the original key.
*2) Sonata, op. 7, second movement.   See the original.
See also, **Beethoven,** Sonata, op. 31, No. 1, *Adagio*, measure 34 (35).

c. In some rare instances there is still less evidence of transition; the Prin. Th. ending with an *elision* of its cadence, which represents at the same moment the beginning of the Subordinate Theme.

See **Beethoven,** Sonata, op. 2, No. 3, *Largo*.   The Prin. Th., an extended period, ends in measure 11; the Sub. Th. begins at the same point, with change of signature.   The fact that the cadence-chord, on the accent of the actual cadence-measure, is *at the same time* the beginning (first accent) of the next Theme, is proven by the abrupt and complete change of style, rhythm, tempo, key, and dynamics.
(Other, more elaborate, forms of transition are shown in par. 77.)

THE PROCESS OF TRANSITION.

75. The primary object of a transition is to approach the *key* in which the following Theme is to appear.   Its aim is, therefore, usually the *dominant* harmony of the coming key, since that is the legitimate and most convenient medium through which a tonic may be reached.

The process as a whole is generally divided into two, sometimes very distinct, successive stages or moves (or, as they might aptly be called, "acts"):

The first stage, or act, consists in *leading the harmonies to the desired position,* — as stated, usually to the prospective dominant; either the dominant triad, or dom.-7th chord, with root in bass; or the dominant note, in bass, without reference to the chords involved.

The second stage, or act, consists in *establishing this dominant, by dwelling upon (or near) it* for a few beats or measures, until the most appropriate or effective moment arrives for its resolution into the first melodic member of the new Theme.

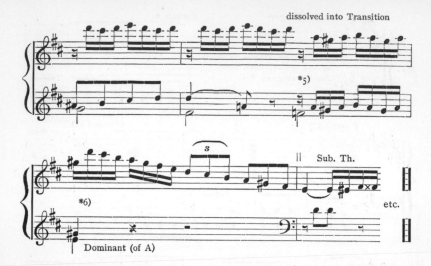

*1) This is not a First Rondo form, but that does not affect the illustration. As stated in par. 69, all these Larger Forms, without exception, contain two Themes (at least), which are presented one after the other; and this successive presentation takes place, in every instance, as first and chief object of the whole design. From this it follows that *all* the Larger Forms are practically identical (in general structure) up to the point where this double presentation is accomplished, — as may be seen by comparing the given diagrams. For this reason, illustrations of these initial processes may be chosen from any of the Larger designs, with a view to desirability only.

*2) At this point, with the insertion of the deflecting accidental (though no modulation takes place), the process of "dissolution" (see par. 78) begins to operate; and this also marks the actual beginning of the "first act" of transition.

*3) Here the modulatory movement culminates upon the chord of *f*-sharp, whose root — *f*-sharp, in bass — is the *dominant note* of the prospective key and Theme. And therewith the "second act" of transition begins, continuing solidly upon the dominant note (as organ-point) for five measures.

*4) Here the dominant is finally resolved (no longer as tonic chord of *F*-sharp major, but as dom.-seventh chord of B), into the first melodic member of the Subord. Theme.

*5) This is a very brief transitional passage; the "first act" begins (as dissolution of the form, by modulatory deflection) with this beat — *f*-natural in bass, and leads quickly to the prospective dominant.

*6) The "second act" runs only through this one measure, as bridging. See also, **Beethoven,** Sonata, op. 2, No. 2, *Largo,* measures (29, 30) 31.

Sometimes one or the other of the two transitional "acts" is not only thus brief (Ex. 37, No. 2), but is omitted altogether, for some obvious reason or other.

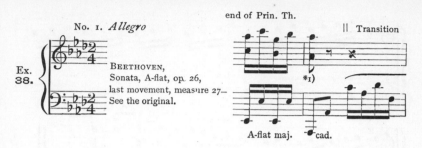

Ex. 38.

No. 1. *Allegro*

BEETHOVEN,
Sonata, A-flat, op. 26,
last movement, measure 27—
See the original.

end of Prin. Th.

‖ Transition

A-flat maj.   cad.

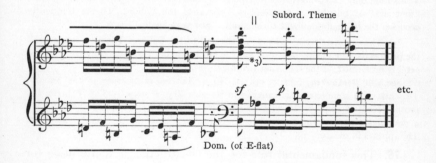

‖ Subord. Theme

etc.

Dom. (of E-flat)

No. 2. *Poco allegretto*

BEETHOVEN,
Sonata, op. 7, E-flat,
last movement, meas. 47—
See the original.

end of Sub. Th. *4)

ff

B-flat major

*1) Complete tonic cadence, at the end of the Prin. Theme, in the original key.

*2) The "first act" of actual transition (modulatory deflection) begins here, and leads to the prospective dominant, *b*-flat, in bass.

*3) The "second act" would enter here, but is omitted, because unnecessary, — the Sub. Theme itself beginning (and dwelling) upon the dominant harmony.

*4) This is the reversed order of Themes, and the process involved is called *Re-transition* (par. 86).   The principle, and the process, are exactly the same as in the Transition, only excepting that it is chiefly in this direction that the omission of the "first act" is possible, and necessary — because the Subord. Theme frequently occupies the original dominant throughout.   See next *note.

*5) The complete tonic cadence, at the end of the Subord. Theme.   Being itself the prospective dominant, the "first act" is not needed.   Therefore only the "second act" is performed, in the following two measures.

See also, **Beethoven**, Sonata, op. 31, No. 2, *Adagio;* in measure 38 the Subord. Th. ends with complete tonic cadence in its own key, *F* major.   This *F* being the prospective dominant (of the next Theme), no "first act" is required; the following 4 measures represent the "second act" — dwelling upon the dominant; the Prin. Th. appears in measure 43.

76. This fundamental rule for the construction of a transition (or re-transition) is, however, often modified.

a. The objective point of the transition may be some other tone than the prospective dominant; for example, the Second-dominant (2d scale-step); or any other tone or chord that will lead powerfully into the new Theme (the 6th scale-step, probably lowered, — the raised 4th scale-step, — the leading-tone).

See **Beethoven**, Sonata, op. 31, No. 1, *Adagio*, measures (34) 35 (36).   The *C* at the end of the Prin. Theme is prolonged (two measures), with change of mode, and becomes the Mediant (3rd scale-step) of the following key — *A*-flat major.
    Also:

*1) The "first act", induced by dissolution of an extended Transition-Phrase (par. 77*a*), has been going on for some time; at this point it makes a decisive move towards *a* minor, and soon reaches the tone *A* and the chord of *A* (major).

*₂) This *A* is the Second-dominant (dominant-of-the-dominant) of the prospective key — *G* major, — and is chosen as aim of the transition, because the Subord. Theme chances to begin on the *dominant* harmony of *G*.   The "second act" of transition extends only through the cadence-measure, as bridging, and is signalized by the *g*-natural, which gives the chord of *A* a dominant significance.

*₃) The root of this chord, *B*-flat (upon which the "second act" of retransition is based, for ten measures) is, as *A*-sharp, the leading-tone of the following key and Theme.

b. At times, the transition leads to the dominant of some other than the coming key, and is then followed by an unexpected "false" resolution (on the principle of Cadence-modulation):

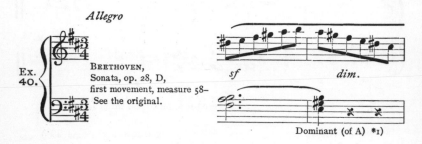

Ex. 40.   BEETHOVEN, Sonata, op. 28, D, first movement, measure 58– See the original.

sf   *dim.*

Dominant (of A) *₁)

End of Transition   Subord. Th.

p   *pp*   etc.

F-sharp minor   *₂)

*₁) This dominant note, *E*, is reached several measures before (in meas. 55) and is dwelt upon, as "second act" of transition, up to the Subord. Theme, which sets in, however, in an unexpected key.

*₂) The first phrase of the Subord. Theme *ends*, nevertheless, in the proper key, *A* major, thus ultimately vindicating the transitional tone *E*.

See also, **Beethoven,** Sonata, op. 10, No. 1, last movement, measure 16, — dominant of *c* minor, followed abruptly by the Subord. Theme in *E*-flat major (measure 17).

c. In rare instances, the transition leads to the *tonic itself* of the coming key and Theme; and this tonic is then usually retained for one single measure, which assumes the nature of an introductory anticipation of the accompaniment of the new Theme.   Thus:

*1) The legitimate aim of this transition, in view of the coming key (*E* major), would have been the tone and chord of *B*, its dominant. Instead of which, it drives straight at the coming tonic, and then enters it passively, without resolution.

See also, **Brahms,** Symphony, No. 3, *Andante* (Ex. 39, No. 1), measures 77–84; these are the "second act" of retransition, dwelling upon *C*, the *tonic* and key of the following Theme (which begins in meas. 85). A notable and masterly example of a most uncommon and hazardous process.

Beethoven, Sonata, op. 22, *Adagio*, measure 18 (end of transition on *B*-flat); meas. 19 (beginning of Subord. Theme in *B*-flat). **Beethoven,** Sonata, op. 49, No. 1, second movement; meas. 30–32. **Beethoven,** op. 49, No. 2, first movement; meas. 20–21.

This is, naturally, a somewhat misleading and dubious method of transition, as the tonic note has no urging force into "itself."

77. Reverting to par. 74, which review, there are still other forms of transitional material, as follows:

a. Quite frequently, the complete tonic cadence at the end of the Principal Theme is followed by a phrase of more or less independent character (new), which is designed to serve the transitional purpose. If this inserted member is a definite phrase, with cadence, it may be called the *Transition-Phrase*. The treatment consists, naturally and usually, in re-stating the Transition-phrase, as duplication; this duplication is then dissolved and led, as "first act" of transition, to the prospective dominant; the latter generally prolonged, as "second act", and resolved into the Subord. Theme.

For example:

Also, **Beethoven,** Sonata, op. 28, first movement. The Transition-phrase (new) appears in meas. 40–43; duplicated in sequence, meas. 44–47; these eight measures are repeated (modified); the "second act" covers meas. 56–62; Subord. Th. in meas. 63. (Shown in Ex. 40.)

Beethoven, Sonata, op. 13, last movement. The Transition-phrase (new) appears in meas. 18–21; followed by a sequence leading to the *tonic* (meas. 25) of the Subord. Theme, which follows immediately. Also Sonata, op. 22, last movement, — very similar (Transition-phrase, new, meas. 18–22).

Beethoven, Sonata, op. 31, No. 3, first movement. The Transition-phrase (new), measures 26–32, is followed by a curious prolongation of the transitional operation, consisting in the wholly unexpected insertion of a reminiscence of the Prin. Theme (in meas. 33–45) leading to the prospective dominant, and followed by the Subord. Theme (meas. 46). This insertion is the *second Section* of the entire transition. (See par. 55*b*, in reference to the "Section"; and note that sectional arrangement may occur in any portion of the form which is not subject to *definite* structural conditions: in the Coda, the "Development" [par. 150], the Re-transition, — most rarely in the Transition, as here.)

Beethoven, Sonata, op. 2, No. 2, last movement. The Transition-phrase covers meas. 17–20; it is duplicated, dissolved, and led to the *tonic* of the next Theme, — as shown in Ex. 41. **Beethoven,** Symphony, No. 2, *Larghetto*, meas. 33; the Prin. Th. is a full Two-Part form, with repetitions, otherwise this Transition-phrase would be "Part II".

Schubert, Sonata No. 6, op. 147, *Andante*. The Transition-phrase enters abruptly, with an *elision* of the cadence-measure of the Prin. Theme, in meas. 27. Its complete change of style verifies the elision, and also gives it the appearance of an almost foreign link; it proves, however, to be directly related, thematically, to the Subord. Theme, which begins in meas. 32.

b. Often the Transition-phrase, instead of being thus independent, or new, in its construction, is derived from material of the Prin. Theme itself. In this case it is "independent" only in its location, while thematically relevant, and consistent with its surroundings.

See **Beethoven,** Sonata, op. 14, No. 1, first movement; the Transition-phrase (meas. 13) is so similar to the Prin. Theme, that it sounds at first as if a duplication of the latter were intended. (Shown in Ex. 37, No. 1.) Also Sonata, op. 10, No. 3, first movement, very similar (meas. 17–22).

Beethoven, Son. op. 26, last movement; the Transition-phrase is derived from the thematic figure of the Prin. Theme (Ex. 38, No. 1).

Beethoven, Son. op. 27, No. 1, last movement; Transition-phrase from Prin. Theme, meas. 25–32; "second act", meas. 32–35; Subord. Theme, meas. 36.

Beethoven, Son. op. 31, No. 3, *Scherzo;* Transition-phrase derived so exactly from Part II of the Prin. Th., that here again the intention of duplicating the latter is intimated; meas. 29–32; "second act", meas. 33–34; Subord. Theme, meas. 35. (Shown in Ex. 55, note *2.)

Brahms, Symphony 3, *Andante;* the Transition-phrase is, at first, a re-statement of the first member of the Prin. Theme (meas. 24–25), and is, therefore, a direct deduction from the chief thematic proposition. It is duplicated, dissolved, and led to the Second-dominant of the next Theme, as shown in Ex. 39.

c. Or the transitional process may maintain still closer adherence to the Prin. Theme (than that of thematic derivation), *and proceed directly out of some phrase of the latter, by dissolution of the form.* The following illustrations will be better understood by first reading par. 78.

For example:

*1) This is unquestionably the Second Part of the Prin. Theme, and not to be confounded with a Transition-phrase, although it is finally utilized as transition, by extension and dissolution.

*2) The first sign of weakening of the principal key, for modulatory deflection, is exhibited in this *c*-sharp.

*3) This melodic figure runs through the entire transitional extension.

*4) Here the transitional modulation is consummated, leading, at note *5), to the dominant, *A*, of the coming key and Theme (*D* major).

*6) The "second act" of transition is performed upon the dominant note, *A*, maintained as organ-point unyieldingly in bass, for 7 measures.

See also, **Beethoven**, Sonata, op. 31, No. 2.   Part II of the Prin. Theme begins in measure 21 (with elision); it remains in its key, *d* minor, up to meas. 31, where it is deflected into *a* minor; therewith, the "first act" of transition begins, and extends to meas. 41, where it cadences on *E*, the dominant of the coming Theme; the "second act" is simply the bridging of this measure; the Subordinate Theme appears in meas. 42, upon the same dominant harmony (of *a* minor).   See also the last movement of the same Sonata, similar in every respect.

Beethoven, op. 10, No. 1, *Adagio*.   The Second Part of the Prin. Th. begins in measure 17, is dissolved in meas. 21, reaching the prospective dominant in meas. 22; the Subord. Th. follows in meas. 24, on the same dominant harmony.

Beethoven, op. 31, No. 2, *Adagio*.   Part II of the Prin. Th. begins in measure 18; is dissolved, in meas. 23, immediately into the prospective dominant (*C*), which is prolonged, as "second act", to meas. 30; the Subord. Th. appears in meas. 31, in *F*.

Beethoven, op. 10, No. 3, last movement; Part II dissolved.   See Ex. 37, No. 2.

Beethoven, op. 28, last movement.   The transitional process starts in measure 17, with a phrase in contrasting rhythm, which *may* be regarded as Part II of the Prin. Theme, but has somewhat more of the appearance of an independent Transition-phrase (par. 77a).   It is duplicated and dissolved in the usual manner; the "second act" covers measures 26–28; Subord. Th. in meas. 29.

Beethoven, op. 31, No. 1, first movement.   Part I of the Prin. Th. to measure 30; Part II to meas. 45; *Part III* begins in meas. 46; is dissolved in meas. 53, — the prospective dominant (*f*-sharp) appearing in meas. 54; the "second act" extends to meas. 65; Subord. Th. in meas. 66.

Beethoven, op. 7, first movement.   Part. I of the Prin. Th. to measure 17; Part II to meas. 24; the next measure (25) is an ostensible return to the beginning — therefore the index of Part III; it is, however, abruptly deflected (dissolved) by the *D*-flat, and extended, as "first act" of transition (with infusion of new material) to measure 35, where it subsides upon the prospective dominant; "second act", measures 35–40; Subord. Th. in meas. 41.

Beethoven, op. 22, first movement.   The Prin. Th. is a group of four phrases (measures 1, 5, 9, 12).   The fourth of these Phrases, like the first one, and therefore suggestive of the intention of duplication, is utilized as transition; dissolved in meas. 13, and led to the prospective dominant in meas. 16; "second act," meas. 16–21; Subord. Th. in meas. 22.

Brahms, Symphony, No. 1, *Andante*.   The Prin. Th. is a Group of six phrases (measures 1, 5, 10, 14, 18, 22), ending with complete tonic cadence in meas. 27.   A Transition-phrase follows, which (as in **Beethoven**, op. 28, last movement) may be regarded as Part II.   It is duplicated, dissolved, and led to the prospective dominant in meas. 34; "second act" to meas. 38; the Subord. Th. begins in meas. 39.

Broad comparison of the preceding paragraphs (and par. 82) will reveal the three possible locations of the transitional movement:

Par. 74b, and par. 77a, — independent transitional material *inserted between the two Themes*.   Frequent.

Par. 77c, — transition effected *during the later course of the Prin. Theme itself, involving dissolution.* Fairly frequent.

Par. 82, — transitional act performed *during the early course of the Subord. Theme.* Very rare.

DISSOLUTION OF THE FORM.

78. A phrase is said to be "dissolved" when, instead of closing with its *expected cadence,* upon its own tonic, it is deflected (by modulation), and conducted (perhaps with extensions) to some other key and chord, — most commonly to a *dominant,* and generally the dominant of the coming Theme.

The process of dissolution is applied invariably to the *final* phrase of some member of the form: To the Third Part of a Three-Part form (which would then be defined as a "Three-Part form with dissolved Third Part"); or to the Second Part of a Two-Part form (illustrated in Ex. 43); or to the Consequent phrase of a Period (single or double); or to the last phrase in a phrase-group form. Illustrations of all these species are given in par. 77.

79. Dissolution of the form occurs, naturally, only in connection with the process of *transition* (or re-transition — par. 86); and its real object consists solely in achieving the "first act" of a transitional movement.

For this reason, dissolution is also very commonly applied to a Transition-phrase (as shown in Ex. 38, No. 1), — or, more frequently still, to the *duplication* of such independent single phrases as the Transition-phrase, and the Codetta to a Theme.

Such phrases as these, which appear where the passage into another Theme is imminent, are often first stated in simple form, with their legitimate cadence, and then duplicated, with dissolution. The definition of this would be "phrase with *transitional* (or dissolved) duplication." One illustration will suffice:

Ex. 44.

BEETHOVEN, Sonata, op. 13, last movement, measure 50— See the original.

end of Codetta I

Codetta II *1)

cad.

*1) This is the second one of two Codettas, added to the Subordinate Theme. See par. 88. It is the material designed for the retransition (par. 86), and proves to be a "phrase with dissolved duplication," extended into the usual "second act" on the prospective dominant.

*2) The dissolution is induced by the modulatory deflection through this b-natural.

See also Ex. 41: The transition, the end of which is shown in the example, is a phrase with dissolved duplication.

80. In the First Rondo form, the Transition, as seen in the diagram, leads from the Principal Theme into

THE SUBORDINATE THEME.

81. It is a fundamental condition of the Subord. Theme, that it should appear in a *different key* from that of the Prin. Theme. And with but very few exceptions this is the case.

The exceptions to this rule are more common in the works of **Beethoven** than in those of any other writer. He not infrequently *begins* his Subord. Theme in the same key (often the opposite mode), and then leads it over into the "right" key (par. 82). See his String-quartet, op. 18, No. 6, *Adagio*, meas. 17; and String-quartet, op. 74, *Adagio*, meas. 25. The most unusual example occurs in his *Polonaise*, op. 89, a Second Rondo form, in which *both* Subord. Themes are in the same key as their Prin. Theme.

See also, **Beethoven,** Sonata, op. 2, No. 3, *Adagio;* the Subord. Th. is in the same key as the Prin. Theme, *E,* but in the opposite mode — *e minor.*

The most common and effective keys for the Subord. Theme are, the dominant key after a major Prin. Theme; or the relative major key after a minor Prin. Theme.

But any other related key — near or remote — may be chosen; and even a wholly unrelated key is possible, if justified by the nature of the Themes and the special structural purpose.

Beethoven, Sonata, op. 2, No. 1, first movement: Prin. Theme in *f* minor; Sub. Th. in *A*-flat major.

Same Sonata, *Adagio:* Prin. Th., *F* major; Subord. Theme, first in *d* minor, and then *C* major.

Same Sonata, last movement: Prin. Th., *f* minor; Sub. Th., *c* minor (dominant key, after a *minor* Prin. Th.).

Sonata, op. 2, No. 2, first movement: Prin. Th., *A* major; Sub. Th., *e minor* (instead of *E* major) — later major.

Sonata, op. 7, *Largo:* Prin. Th., *C* major; Sub. Th., *A*-flat major (tonic-mediant relation). Ex. 36, No. 2.

Sonata, op. 31, No. 1, first movement: Prin. Th., *G* major; Sub. Th., *B* major, later minor (relative of the dominant).

Sonata, op. 31, No. 3, *Scherzo:* Prin. Th., *A*-flat major; Sub. Th., *F* major, later *E*-flat major.

Sonata, op. 53, first movement: Prin. Th., *C* major; Sub. Th., *E* major (mediant-tonic relation).

It is least favorable to choose the *subdominant* key, as this is dull in effect.

82. In very rare cases, the Subord. Theme *begins,* immediately after the cadence of the Prin. Th. (without transition), *in the same key,*—

that of the Prin. Th.; and then gradually swings over into its proper key; thus, so to speak, including the transition within itself.

See **Beethoven,** Sonata, op. 7, last movement: The Prin. Theme, an Incipient 3-Part form, comes to a complete tonic ending in measure 16. The Subord. Theme *follows immediately*, in the same key (*E*-flat); its first phrase is deflected (meas. 19) into *c* minor, and then into *B*-flat major — the proper key (meas. 23). What emphasizes this curious irregularity (an instance of almost oppressively close logic), is the fact that this first phrase is *derived directly from the Second Part of the Prin. Theme* (meas. 8–9). Opinions may differ concerning this analysis; but it appears impossible to define the actual beginning of the Subord. Theme at any later point, so persistent is the continuity, — unless it be in meas. 25, where a somewhat striking rhythmic modification, and the proper key, asserts itself. Almost exactly the same conditions prevail in **Beethoven,** *Andante favori* in *F* major (measure 30).

83. Besides the change in key, there should also be a sufficiently marked change in style. For the Subord. Theme, while preserving close and evident organic relations with its Prin. Th., must nevertheless be *well contrasted* in general effect, — perhaps chiefly with regard to its rhythmic character. The two Themes should be well mated, but differentiated in appearance and in "mood".

This is, naturally, one of the most difficult problems of effective composition, and one whose solution cannot be indicated by rules. The student should make a careful study of the Themes thus associated in the Sonatas and other works of **Beethoven, Brahms,** and other modern masters; and, for the rest, exercise his own musical imagination and — above all things — his judgment.

If the Prin. Th. is lyric, the Subord. Theme may be dramatic; and *vice versa.* If one is serious, the other may be of a somewhat lighter character; and so forth. The most striking distinction between the Themes will usually rest upon their *rhythms,* — either the rhythmic nature of the thematic melody, or of the accompaniment, or both.

84. The old rule (in force during the early classic eras of strict thematic unity) that the Subord. Theme should be derived from the Prin. Theme, or at least be thematically related to it, is generally abandoned in modern music, because of the greater difficulty of creating the necessary contrast.

Its influence is still traceable here and there in **Beethoven** (op. 26, last movement — Ex. 45, No. 1; op. 2, No. 1, first movement — the melodic member of the Subord. Theme is the same as that of the Prin. Theme, in contrary motion; Symphony, No. 5, *c* minor, first movement; also Sonata, op. 7, last movement — cited in par. 82; and, very pointedly, in op. 14, No. 1, last movement, where the Subord. Theme, beginning abruptly, without transition, in measure 14, is derived directly from the consequent phrase of the Prin. Theme, from which it differs chiefly in key). Also in **Brahms;**

and again, with some evidence of a reactionary spirit, in recent works: **Glazounow,** pfte. Sonata, op. 75, *e* minor, first movement — Ex. 45, No. 2; **Vincent d'Indy,** String-quartet, op. 45, *E* major, first movement.

It is evident, however, that when the Subord. Theme is thus derived from, or thematically related to, the Prin. Theme, it must nevertheless assume a sufficiently independent aspect; must present the usual contrast in *style*. It may adopt thematic material from its Prin. Theme, but it must work it over into a *new thematic condition*, assuring its characteristic independence. This, as intimated, may best be brought about by some essential alteration of the rhythmic conditions. For example:

*1) The thematic figure of the Prin. Theme, in contrary motion, and transferred to the lower part, as accompaniment, is the basis of the Subord. Theme; but the distinctive line of the latter is, nevertheless, the sharp staccato figure in the upper part, which creates a marked contrast in style with the foregoing.

*2) The melody of the Subord. Th. is patterned exactly after that of the Prin. Theme. The necessary contrast is amply provided by the complete change of "mood" (*dolce*), and the change of rhythm, both in the melody and in the lower part (triplets).

*3) The wholly new melody of the Subord. Theme is *a counterpoint to that of the Prin. Theme,* which appears, below, as shown by the – – –. The change of mood is very marked.

85. The form of the Subord. Theme is optional, but it is somewhat likely to be a shorter, more concise, design than that of the Prin. Theme. It is therefore frequently no more than a One-Part form (Period, Phrase-group, or Double-period). And, as will be shown, a Codetta is often added (par. 88).

At least *one* of the two Themes should be more than One-Part form, or the whole rondo will represent a total of but three *Parts*, and therefore will create the impression of 3-Part form only.

N.B.—Every composition in which there is a "return to the beginning" (after an actual departure) is an example of the *tripartite* design. But there are many such tripartite forms, which differ from each other in size or extent, and, though fundamentally similar, become independent of each other through their several degrees of dimension, of scope, and of purpose. Not that *dimension alone* differentiates musical designs; for there are quite genuine First Rondo forms that are very short, while others are unusually long. But dimension, in connection with frequency of cadence and changes of thematic contents, does contribute in some degree to the definition of the form, since all these elements *together* are involved in the presentation of the adopted purpose.

Compare **Schumann**, Sonata, op. *22*, *Andantino*. This is only a 3-Part Song-form; but the 2nd Part (meas. 22–38) is of so different a style, in its later course, as to assume the importance and effect of a Theme. And **Chopin**, Nocturne, No. 4, op. 15-1; also 3-Part form only, but decidedly suggestive of First Rondo form, because of the radically independent style of its 2nd Part. **Beethoven**, Violin Sonata, op. 96, *Adagio*. The Prin. Th. is an extended Period, only. What follows is practically a Second Part, — one phrase, with extended duplication; and a rather long retransition which illustrates the effective swaying back and forth around the prospective dominant; then the Prin. Th. and Coda. The design is, probably, only 3-Part Song-form, but with decided "Rondo" effect.

Mendelssohn, op. 16, No. 3; the Prin. Th. is a period, with introductory phrase; it is dissolved into a brief transition, followed by a Subord. Th. in phrase-group form, with a Codetta, from which a fairly lengthy retransition leads to the Prin. Theme, extended to phrase-group form and followed by a brief Coda. It is only 3-Part Song-form, but has the breadth of the Rondo.

Schubert, Sonata, No. 5, op. 143, *Andante;* — a very concise First Rondo form, in which the Subord. Theme (meas. 21–30) is but little more than an Interlude between the Prin. Theme (in 2-Part form) and its *da capo* (partly transposed). But it is sufficiently characteristic to represent a "digression."

Beethoven, Sonata, op. 79, *Andante;* — a genuine, though small, First Rondo form. The Prin. Th. is in diminutive 2-Part form; the Subord. Th. a 4-meas. Period, extended to 7 measures, with a Codetta, duplicated and dissolved (as shown in Ex. 48).

The Re-transition.

86. The term Re-transition is applied by the author to the passage *back* into the previous Prin. Theme, in distinction to the Transition into a *new* Theme. The process is practically the same in both cases, though a difference in treatment may assert itself, in consequence of the difference in location and aim. The Retransition is often longer and more elaborate than the Transition, and not infrequently separates into two or more sections. Illustrations have already been given, in Ex. 38, No. 2; Ex. 39, No. 2; and Ex. 44; which see.

87. The Retransition, like the Transition, may be initiated in a number of ways:

a. The Subord. Theme may close with a complete tonic cadence (that is, *without* dissolution of the form), usually in its own key, — more rarely in some other key, though quite as completely. In this case, the Retransition will have its independent beginning, and will include its "two acts" within itself.

Assai allegro   end of Sub. Th.   Retransition-phrase

Ex. 46.   Beethoven, Sonata, op. 14, No. 2, last movement. See the original.

*1)   *2)   cad.

duplication

extension ("first act")   "second act"   Prin. Theme

etc.

Dominant (of G)   G major

*1) A complete tonic cadence in the key of the Subord. Theme, *C* major.

*2) The Retransition-phrase is *derived* from the chief member of the Prin. Theme. Avoid the blunder of jumping at the conclusion that this *is* the Prin. Theme, because it chances to resemble it. It is not in the right key, nor is it the *entire* Theme. See par. 123.

See also: **Beethoven**, Sonata, op. 7, last movement, — the second ending after the last double-bar (with repetition marks).

Beethoven, Rondo, op. 51, No. 1, C major. The Subord. Th. (a *Second* Subord. — par. 104) is in *c* minor; it ends with complete tonic cadence in that key, therefore already on the original tonic. For that reason, the retransition is long, including three sections, in order to get away from, and return to, the key of C. The first Section is a one-voice passage (meas. 72–75); Sec. 2 is derived from the Prin. Th., in a remote key, leading to the prospective dominant (meas. 76–83); Sec. 3 is the "second act" of retransition (meas. 83–91).

Sonata, op. 10, No. 3, last movement. The Subord. Theme (a *Second* Subordinate), is in *B*-flat major; it makes its cadence, however, on the tonic of *E-flat* major, in meas. 41; the retransition starts immediately, and contains three brief sections: Section 1 (meas. 41–45), new, but so closely related that it might be regarded as the final phrase of the Subord. Theme; Sec. 2 (meas. 46–49) derived from the Prin. Theme — in a remote key, but dissolved and led to the prospective dominant (chord of *A*, in *D* major); this is the "first act" of actual retransition; Sec. 3 (meas. 50–55) is the "second act," and is a quaint demonstration of the principle of dwelling upon, or near, the dominant; Prin. Theme in meas. 56. — Sonata, op. 22, last movement. Subord. Th. (Second) in *f* minor; complete tonic cadence in *b*-flat minor (meas. 103); followed by the two distinct acts of retransition.

b. If, as is likely, the Subord. Theme is in the dominant key, its complete tonic cadence will itself be the prospective dominant, and, consequently, no "first act" of transition will be necessary, — only the "second act."

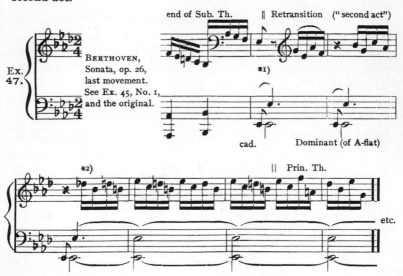

*1) Complete tonic cadence in the key of the Subord. Theme (*E*-flat). This chord is already the prospective dominant, wherefore no "first act" of transition appears. In such cases, the "second act" prolongs and establishes the dominant, as usual, but its function is centred upon the *addition of the minor 7th*, which transforms the chord (as tonic of the former key) into an actual dominant (dom.-*7th* chord) of the coming key.

*2) This *d*-flat is the 7th in question, and records the decisive operation of the retransitional act.

See Ex. 38, No. 2.   The transforming dominant-7th (*A*-flat) first appears with the first note of the Prin. Theme.

See also, **Beethoven,** Sonata, op. 28, last movement; the retransition begins in meas. 43 (as "second act" only); in meas. 47, the dominant-7th (*g*-natural) is introduced, securing the identity of the bass tone *A* as dominant, — no longer tonic.

Similar, Sonata, op. 10, No. 3, last movement, measures 23–24.

Also, Sonata, op. 2, No. 1, *Adagio,* measure 31 only.

88. As stated above, it is quite common to add a Codetta, or even more than one, to the Subordinate Theme.   This may consist of any thematic material, wholly new, or more or less directly related to or derived from the foregoing.   But it is perhaps most common and effective to borrow it from motives of the Prin. Theme (as in **Beethoven,** op. 2, No. 1, *Adagio,* meas. 27–29).

The Codetta is generally a comparatively brief phrase, of two or four measures, and is, as a very general rule, duplicated.   (If there are two Codettas, the first one is likely to be longer, four or eight measures, duplicated as usual.)

The duplication may have the complete tonic cadence, and be followed by the independent retransition.   But it is more natural (if necessary — see par. 87*b*) to dissolve this duplication, thus transforming it into the "first act" of retransition.   See Ex. 44, — applied to the *second* Codetta.

If the Subord. Theme, and therefore its Codetta, is in the dominant key, then, as shown in par. 87*b*, the retransition will be limited to its "second act" alone.

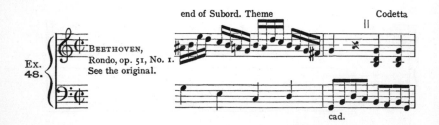

*1) This *F*-natural initiates the actual transitional movement, by changing the tonic, *G*, into a dominant (of *C*).

See also: **Beethoven,** Sonata, op. 2, No. 1, *Adagio*, meas. 27–31; the retransition is merely bridging, in meas. 31, with insertion of the dominant-7th, *B*-flat.

89. When, on the other hand, the Subord. Theme does not close with a complete tonic cadence (be it in its own, or some other, key), it is because the principle of "dissolution" has been active. This method is less clear, because definite cadences are of great assistance to the hearer, who profits by distinct structural outlines, — but it may be quite as effective, and is, of course, more artistic, as it establishes more complete continuity. (Compare par. 197, No. 1.) The final phrase of the Subord. Theme, in this case, is dissolved, and this dissolution (or modulatory deflection) constitutes, as usual, the "first act" of retransition, leading to the prospective dominant (or whatever may be chosen as leading factor), whose prolongation covers the "second act."

See Ex. 39, No. 2; and the following:

*1) The Subord. Th. is a Group of (3) phrases, the third — and last — one of which (patterned after the first one) is dissolved, as shown, and thus led to a cadence upon *G,* the dominant of the coming Theme.

*2) The retransition is unusually elaborate, and separates into three sufficiently distinct sections. This would not appear to have been necessary; but the creative imagination of the tone-master dictated it; and it serves to illustrate and confirm the countless ways in which a fundamental principle may be carried out. Section 1 sways around the dominant, *G,* and then slips away from it — to return, *soon.*

*3) Section 2 is an *allusion* (only) to the principal melodic member, in a remote key, and fragmentary. This insertion, very characteristic of **Beethoven,** must not be hastily called the "Principal Theme." Section 3 returns to the dominant, and prolongs it, quite steadily, up to the announcement of the Prin. Theme. See par. 123.

A similar long retransition, — similar also in its sectional arrangement, occurs in **Beethoven,** Rondo, op. 51, No. 1, cited in the notes to Ex. 46.

Also, **Beethoven,** Sonata, op. 13, last movement: The Subord. Theme (Second) is in 3-Part Song-form, of which the Third Part is dissolved (in meas. 104), leading to the prospective dominant (G) in meas. 107; from there to meas. 120 this dominant is persistently maintained, as "second act" of retransition.

Sonata, op. 2, No. 2, *Largo;* the Subord. Theme is a Group of (3) phrases, the last one of which (meas. 27) is dissolved, and led to the prospective dominant in meas. 31; the Prin. Th. appears in the following measure, — the retransition being unusually brief.

90. The "second act" of transition and retransition — the maintaining or establishing of the dominant — is often somewhat characteristic in style; but it should not be so striking in contents as to invite the impression of a *Theme.* Usually it is but little more than the harmonic figuration of the chord or chords in question, so simple as not to disturb the effect of merely dwelling upon, or circling about, the dominant (or whatever the leading factor may be).

The retransition, especially, is quite likely to contain more or less direct allusions to the initial melodic member of the coming (Principal) Theme, — naturally *not* in the same key.

See Ex. 46; Ex. 47; and all the retransitions in **Beethoven,** Sonata, op. 22, last movement.

Also Ex. 49, section 2 of the retransition.

In retransitions, it is wise to avoid any *conspicuous* presentations of the *tonic* harmony of the coming key. The latter may be touched, in passing, if the transitional movement sways back and forth around the dominant; especially when the opposite mode of the tonic chord is used; or when the latter appears as 6–4 chord. But the "tonic" element should not be so prominent as to anticipate and weaken the effect of the *da capo* (recurrence of the Prin. Theme).

THE RECURRENCE OF THE PRINCIPAL THEME.

91. In the First Rondo form, the recurrence of the Principal Theme (or the "da capo," as it is often called) may be an *exact* reproduction of its first presentation — a literal copy.

Mozart, Sonata, No. 14 (Schirmer edition), *Adagio.*

Beethoven, Sonata, op. 2, No. 3, *Adagio.*

But this is rare. It is far more likely to be somewhat embellished, or even considerably variated and elaborated.

Beethoven, Sonata, op. 2, No. 2, *Largo;* Sonata, op. 2, No. 1, *Adagio;* Sonata, op. 7, *Largo.* **Brahms,** Symphony, No. 1, *Andante sostenuto.*

92. *a.* The Prin. Th., upon its recurrence, may, and often does, close with a complete tonic cadence in its own key, in which case the Coda (or, if brief, the Codetta) which follows will be "independent."

> **Beethoven,** Sonata, op. 2, No. 1, *Adagio,* measure 47.

b. But, perhaps quite as commonly, the final phrase of the Prin. Th. is dissolved, or its cadence evaded, so as to lead over without interruption into the Coda. In this case, the dissolved portion of the Prin. Th. becomes the first section of the Coda.

> **Beethoven,** Sonata, op. 2, No. 3, *Adagio,* measure 30 from the end; an evasion of the expected cadence. Sonata, op. 7, *Largo,* meas. 17 from the end; an elision of the cadence. **Beethoven,** Violin Sonata, op. 12, No. 2, *Andante,* meas. 30 from the end; the form is dissolved by expanding the *dominant* chord, at the cadence. **Schubert,** Sonata, No. 6, *Andante,* meas. 16 from the end; the Third Part of the Prin. Th. is dissolved, as first section of the Coda. **Mendelssohn,** "Midsummer Night's Dream," *Notturno,* meas. 40 from the end; a beautiful example of dissolution, or merging in the Coda; for this purpose, the Prin. Th. (as *da capo*) is reduced to its First Part, the last two measures of which are spun out, extended by the introduction of a phrase from the Subord. Theme and further allusions to the first phrase of the Prin. Theme — all closely coherent, and developed into a group-form of singular charm and effectiveness, as first section of the Coda. A second section follows (last 18 measures).

THE CODA.

93. The Coda here has the same design and treatment as in the variation form and elsewhere. That is, it is invariably *sectional* in form; the number of sections, the extent, and the contents of each, are wholly optional, and subject only to the obvious necessity of good proportion; of interesting and effective structure, especially in regard to contrasts; and of sufficiently close relation to the motives and moods that have gone before. Review, carefully, par. 55*a,* and, particularly, *b.*

One or another of the sections is fairly certain to allude directly to material of the Prin. Theme; and in some Codas there is a disposition to revert to the Subord. Theme. Occasionally, a section, if not too lengthy, may present wholly new (though strictly affiliated) material.

> **Beethoven,** Sonata, op. 2, No. 1, *Adagio.* The Coda (last 14 measures) contains two sections: Section 1 (5 measures) is derived from the second phrase of the Subord. Theme; Section 2 (to the end), from the Codetta of the Subord. Theme.
>
> Sonata, op. 2, No. 2, *Largo.* The Coda (last 30 measures) contains four sections: Section 1 (8 measures) is derived from the Second Part of the Prin. Theme, — a phrase, duplicated; Section 2 (10 measures) is derived, after an evaded cadence, with elision, from the Prin. Theme; Section 3 (8 measures), is a fairly accurate re-

statement of the first phrase of the Prin. Theme, and a new Consequent phrase; Section 4 (to the end), a Codetta, with the customary repetition and extension.

Sonata, op. 2, No. 3, *Adagio.*   The Coda (last 30 measures) contains four sections: Section 1 (two measures) is derived, after an evaded cadence, and elision, from the Prin. Theme;   Section 2 (12 measures), from both Parts of the Subord. Theme; Section 3 (11 measures) is a nearly complete re-statement of the Prin. Theme; Section 4 (to the end), a Codetta, alluding to the Prin. Theme.

Sonata, op. 7, *Largo.*   The Coda contains four sections (last 17 measures): Section 1 (5 measures) is derived, after an elision, from the Subord. Theme; Section 2 (6 measures), from the second measure of the Prin. Theme;   Section 3 (2 measures), is entirely new, but related; Section 4 (to the end), a re-statement of the first phrase of the Prin. Th., with characteristic chromatic harmonization.

Sonata, op. 31, No. 1, *Adagio.*   The Coda (last 21 measures) contains two sections: Section 1 (10 measures — a 5-measure phrase, duplicated) follows the complete tonic cadence, and is closely related to traits of the Prin. Theme; Section 2 (to the end) is a Codetta, based upon the first two measures of the Prin. Theme, with unusually persistent reiterations and extensions.

Brahms, Symphony, No. 1, *Andante sostenuto.*   The Coda (last 28 measures) contains two sections: Section 1 (14 measures) follows an elision of the cadence, and is an extended statement of the fifth phrase of the Prin. Theme;   Section 2 (to the end) is new, but closely related, — a 6-measure phrase, duplicated.

94. In rare cases, the Coda has but one section — as Codetta:

Beethoven, Sonata, op. 79, *Andante,* last 5 measures.

Or, still more rarely, the Coda is entirely omitted, — as will be seen, in later forms.

Relation of the First Rondo Form to the Song–form with Trio.

95. The observant student will have perceived that the First Rondo form has the same *fundamental* design as the Song-form with (one) Trio, or the "Minuet-form," — the Trio being the equivalent of the Subordinate Theme.

In fact, the First Rondo form bears about the same relation to the Minuet, as does the scholastic Chaconne or Passacaglia to the primitive dances of those names (par. 24); and may be defined as an artistic or refined version of the dances that are cast in the mould of the Song-form with Trio.   The chief distinction is, that while the Song with Trio (in keeping with its inferior rank) displays simple Part-forms, clearly separated by frequent and decisive cadences, the First Rondo form is one continuous whole.

96. The gradual progressive idealization of the Song-form with Trio passes, naturally, through many intermediate grades; some more closely approaching the one or other extreme, and some which defy exact qualification.

The traits which contribute to the widening distinction between the typical Song-form with Trio (**Beethoven,** Sonata, op. 2, No. 1, *Menuetto*) and the genuine First Rondo form (the same Sonata, *Adagio*), may be classified as follows:

1. The insertion (in the Song with Trio) of a retransitional passage, from the Trio into the *"da capo."*

Beethoven, Sonata, op. 7, third movement, last two measures of the *Minore* (or Trio).

2. The addition of a Coda, to the Song with Trio.

Beethoven, Sonata, op. 14, No. 1, second movement; the end of the *Maggiore* (or Trio) is dissolved into a retransition, and a Coda follows the *da capo.*
Sonata, op. 2, No. 3, *Scherzo*, the same, in both particulars.

3. The modification or variation of the *da capo*, which, consequently, is written out, instead of being merely indicated by the letters D. C., or their equivalent.

Beethoven, Sonata, op. 10, No. 2, second movement. A retransition follows the Trio (indicated only by the change of signature), and leads into the *da capo*, which is a recurrence of the Prin. Song, modified by syncopation.
Sonata, op. 27, No. 1, *Molto allegro*, similar. Also, Sonata, op. 28, *Andante.*

4. The character of the digression ("Trio"), and also its key. The Song-form (dance) and its Trio are separate sentences, whose association is apparently accidental and external; the Subord. Th. of the rondo, on the other hand, should blend intimately with its Prin. Theme, as an outwardly contrasting aspect of the same mood. Further, the key of the Trio is often the same as that of its principal dance, sometimes with change of mode. But in the genuine Rondo, the Subord. Th. is always in a different key; or if (as in **Beethoven,** op. 2, No. 3, *Adagio*) the Subord. Th. *begins* in the same key, or its opposite mode, it soon passes over into, and asserts, its proper key.

Beethoven, Sonata, op. 28, *Andante* — a vexing hybrid, which eludes strict classification. It is clearly Song-form with Trio up to the *da capo*, and then quite as clearly First Rondo form to the end, with its variated *da capo*, and its significant Coda. It suggests a possible and not unnatural change of **Beethoven's** attitude during the composition, — as if his interest in his Themes increased, and induced him to refine the structure more and more as he proceeded.

Chopin, Mazurka, No. 26 — probably Rondo form, though a "dance"-species.

Chopin, Nocturne, op. 9, No. 1 — probably Rondo form, though its cadences are all very definite. Also Nocturne, op. 9, No. 3 — probably Song with Trio. Also Nocturne, op. 27, No. 1 — probably Rondo form.

Beethoven, Violin Sonata, op. 30, No. 3, *Tempo di menuetto;* probably Song with Trio (both in same key and mode); the Trio and *da capo* are repeated, with abbreviation, and Coda.

Beethoven, String-quartet, op. 18, No. 2, *Adagio* (decidedly Song with Trio in effect).

Brahms, Symphony, No. 3, third movement.

The student is urged to make thorough and thoughtful analysis of all the following examples of the First Rondo form, as nothing is more illuminating than to follow, observantly, the workings of a mastermind. Some of them have been repeatedly cited, above, for the illustration of some details; but they should now be scrutinized *as a whole:*

Beethoven, Sonata, op. 2, No. 1, *Adagio.* — Sonata, op. 2, No. 2, *Largo.* — Op. 2, No. 3, *Adagio.* — Op. 7, *Largo.* — Op. 31, No. 1, *Adagio* (very broad). — Op. 79, *Andante* (very concise).

Beethoven, Bagatelles, op. 33, No. 1; irregular; the Subord. Th. is in the same key (opposite mode), and brief. — Op. 33, No. 3; irregular; "Subord. Th." only an Interlude. — Op. 33, No. 5; like No. 1. — Op. 33, No. 6; brief Subord. Theme, derived from the Prin. Theme.

Beethoven, Violin Sonatas: Op. 12, No. 2, *Andante.* — Op. 12, No. 3, *Adagio.* — Op. 30, No. 2, *Adagio.* — Op. 96, *Adagio* (very concise — probably only 3-Part Song-form).

Beethoven, String-quartet, op. 18, No. 6, *Adagio;* the Subord. Theme *begins* in the same key, opposite mode. — Beethoven, Trio, op. 11, *Adagio;* (Coda, a frank reminiscence of the Subord. Theme).

Schubert, pfte. Sonata, No. 6, op. 147, *Andante.* — Sonata, No. 9, *A, Andantino;* the Subord. Theme is represented by an episode of fantastic character, in sectional form. — Sonata, No. 10, *B-flat, Andante;* broad. — Sonata, No. 5, op. 143, *Andante;* concise; *da capo* partly transposed. — Impromptu, op. 90, No. 3; very broad, many repetitions; Subord. Th., Two-Part form. (The preceding Impromptu, op. 90, No. 2, is a First Rondo form, suggestive of the Song with Trio.)

Schumann, Symphony, No. 1, *B-flat, Larghetto;* Prin. Th., Three-Part form, Part III transposed; *da capo* abbreviated to Part I.

Mendelssohn, *Notturno* from "Midsummer Night's Dream." — Pfte. Concerto in *g* minor, *Andante.* — Op. 43, *Andante* ("Serenade"). — Violoncello Sonata, op. 45, *Andante* (very elaborate Coda, *suggestive,* only, of a second digression). — Pfte. Trio, op. 49, *Andante* (Subord. Theme begins in same key, opposite mode). — Pfte. Trio, op. 66, *Andante* (similar).

Chopin, Nocturne, op. 32, No. 2 (possibly Song with Trio). — Nocturne, op. 48, No. 1 (probably Song with Trio; Subord. Theme in same key, opposite mode). — Nocturne, op. 48, No. 2, similar. — Nocturne, op. 55, No. 1. — Nocturne, op. 55, No. 2; the design irregular in *dimensions*, but rendered recognizable by the cadences; Prin. Theme, 3-Part period, to meas. 12; Subord. Theme. Two-Part Song-form, 22 measures long; retransition, one measure; *da capo* abbreviated to four measures; long Coda, four sections, the first and second derived from the Subord. Theme. — Nocturnes, op. 62, No. 1; op. 62, No. 2; op. 72, No. 1 (No. 19). — Pfte. Sonata, op. 4, *Larghetto;* Subord. Th. begins in same key. — Sonata, *b* minor, op. 58, *Largo.* — Barcarolle, op. 60; very broad; Section 1 of the Coda an almost literal recurrence of Part Two of the Subord. Theme.

Brahms, Intermezzo, op. 118, No. 2 (possibly Song with Trio). — Ballade, op. 118, No. 3 (similar). — Intermezzo, op. 116, No. 6 (similar). — Intermezzo, op. 10, No. 3 (similar). — Serenade, op. 16, *Adagio non troppo.* — Pfte. quartet, No. 1, op. 25, *Andante* (elaborate "sectional" transition and retransition). — Horn-trio, op. 40, *Adagio mesto* (concise). — String-quartet, op. 51, No. 1, *Romanze* (Subord. Theme begins in the opposite mode of the principal key). — String-quartet, op. 51, No. 2, *Andante moderato* (Parts I and II of the *da capo* transposed). — Pfte. quartet, No. 3, op. 60, *Andante.* — String-quartet, op. 3, op. 67, *Andante* (in the *da capo*, the Prin. Theme is partly transposed). — Symphony, No. 1, op. 68, *Andante* (Part I of the Prin. Theme extended, in the *da capo*). — Pfte. Concerto, op. 83, *Andante* (elaborate retransition, four sections, one entirely new). — Symphony, No. 3, op. 90, *Andante.* — Violoncello Sonata, No. 2, op. 99, *Adagio.* — Violin Sonata, No. 1, op. 78, *Adagio.* — Violin Sonata, No. 3, op. 108, *poco presto;* broad, but regular; Prin. Theme, 2-Part form, duplicated; no transition; Subord. Theme, 2-Part form, duplicated; retransition, 22 measures; Coda, three sections.

Maurice Ravel, Sonatine in *f*-sharp minor, second movement. Prin. Theme, 3-Part form (Part III transposed and abbreviated — meas. 23–26); Subord. Th., measure 27, begins in same key; Part II extended, as retransition.

Glazounow, Sonata, No. 1, op. 74, second movement (Part II of the Prin. Th. reconstructed in the *da capo*).

EXERCISE 7.

It is of the utmost importance that the student should fully master the *First Rondo form,* because this design presents the fundamental conditions of all the larger forms, namely: The conception of different (related, but contrasting) Themes; their effective connection, through a suitable transition, and retransition; and the Coda. Until the ready solution of these problems becomes almost automatic, the composer cannot cope with the still larger designs, with any hope of success. Therefore, persistent and exhaustive practice in this Exercise is earnestly recommended. See, first, par. 197, 1 to 6.

A. Construct a First Rondo form in major; Prin. Theme, a 3-Part Song-form, possibly Incomplete, or Incipient grade, preferably in slow *tempo;* brief transition, as "bridging"; Subord. Theme in the Dominant key, 2-Part Song-form, with complete tonic cadence; retransition, "second act" only; recurrence of Prin. Theme (*da capo*) nearly literal; independent Coda, brief (quasi Codetta).

N.B. — For this exercise, any instrument, or ensemble, may be chosen. But the student is advised to limit himself to the pianoforte, or pfte. and violin (or 'cello), and to avoid any elaborate ensemble whose difficulties will divert his attention from the *structural* conditions he is aiming to master.

B. Rondo in minor; Prin. Theme, a 2-Part Song-form, complete tonic cadence; transition-phrase, dissolved and led to prospective dominant; Subord. Theme, Double-period, complete tonic cadence; retransition, both acts; *da capo* somewhat modified; Coda, one or two sections.

C. Rondo in major; Prin. Theme, a 2-Part Song-form, the last phrase dissolved, as "first act" of transition, followed by brief "second act"; Subord. Theme, a Phrase-group, the last phrase dissolved, followed by a longer "second act"; *da capo* elaborated; Coda, two or more sections.

D. Rondo in minor; Prin. Theme, optional form, complete tonic cadence; Subord. Theme beginning in same key and modulating soon to the proper key; Codetta, duplicated and dissolved, as retransition; *da capo* elaborated, the last phrase dissolved, as first section of the Coda.

E. Rondo, all details of structure optional. — And many more examples, similarly optional.

CHAPTER VIII.

THE SECOND RONDO FORM.

97. See par. 70. The diagram of the Second Rondo form is as follows:

Prin. Th.	Transition	*I. Sub. Th.*	Codetta	Retransition	*Prin. Th.*	Transition	*II. Sub. Th.*	Retransition	*Prin. Th.*	Coda
Any Part-form.		Related key.			as before, possibly abbreviated.		usually a more remote key.		as at first, or modified, or merged in the Coda.	

THE PRINCIPAL THEME.

98. In the Second Rondo form, the Prin. Theme may be either Two- or Three-Part form; perhaps more effectively the former, because of the greater length of the composition, and the consequent desirability of more concise thematic members.

THE FIRST TRANSITION.

99. *a.* As before, the Prin. Theme may close with its complete tonic cadence, in which case the transition will be "independent." Review par. 73, and par. 74*a* and *b*. It then generally assumes the nature of a Transition-phrase, dissolved, or duplicated and dissolved, leading to the prospective dominant (or whatever the basis of the "second act" may be). Review par. 77*a*, and *b*.

b. Or the final phrase of the Prin. Theme may be dissolved, as "first act" of transition. Review par. 77*c*.

c. Or, much more rarely, the Subord. Theme may follow the tonic cadence of the Prin. Theme immediately, in the *same key*, and include its transition into the proper key, within itself. Review par. 82.

THE FIRST SUBORDINATE THEME.

100. In a structural design which is to contain *two* Subord. Themes, it is evident that each of the two should not only form an effective contrast to their Prin. Theme, but that they should also differ strikingly *from each other*.

The proper attitude will be gained by conceiving the First Subord. Theme as a comparatively moderate or narrow digression, and the Second Subord. Theme as a more positive, wider and longer digression from the Prin. Theme.

Therefore, the First Subord. Theme is usually placed in a nearly related key (the dominant from major, or the relative from minor), and is likely to be concise in form, — generally only one Part (period or phrase-group). But, as usual, a Codetta may be added (par. 88).

Beethoven, Rondo in *C*, op. 51, No. 1: Prin. Theme (*C*), an Incipient 3-Part form; the I. Subord. Theme (*G*), a period, slightly extended, with a 2-measure Codetta. — Sonata, op. 10, No. 3, last movement: Prin. Theme (*D*), a 2-Part form, dissolved; the I. Subord. Theme (*A*), a regular period, dissolved, but not extended. Sonata, op. 14, No. 2, last movement: Prin. Theme (*G*), an Incomplete 3-Part form; I. Subord. Th. (*e* minor — *a* minor), a group of four phrases.

On the other hand: **Mozart,** *a*-minor Rondo: Prin. Th. (*a* minor), a complete 3-Part form; I. Subord. Theme (*F* major), a complete 3-Part form, with Codetta to both the First Part and the Third Part.

THE FIRST RETRANSITION.

101. This follows exactly the same course as in the First Rondo form, excepting that it is not likely to be lengthy. Review par. 86, 87*a* and *b*, 89.

THE FIRST RECURRENCE (OR DA CAPO) OF THE PRIN. THEME.

102. The first *da capo* may be a complete re-statement of the Prin. Theme; but it is very common, in favor of concise form, to *abbreviate it to its first Part*, or its equivalent.

Beethoven, Rondo in *C*, op. 51, No. 1: Prin. Theme, 3-Part form; first *da capo*, its first Part only (8 measures). — Sonata, op. 10, No. 3, last movement: Prin. Theme, 2-Part form; the first *da capo*, its first Part only, with evaded cadence. — On the other hand: Beethoven, Sonata, op. 14, No. 2, last movement; the first *da capo* is a complete and literal re-statement of the Prin. Theme.

THE SECOND TRANSITION.

103. The passage from the Prin. Theme into the Second Subord. Theme is frequently omitted altogether, — the latter beginning abruptly, in its own key.

Or a brief transitional "bridging" intervenes, within the cadence-measure.

And, of course, an independent transition is possible; or one that is induced by dissolution, from the end of the first *da capo*.

Beethoven, Rondo in *C*, op. 51, No. 1: no second transition. — Sonata, op. 10, No. 3, last movement: The *da capo* closes in meas. 33 with an evasion of the expected cadence; two measures of transitional material follow, based on the coming *tonic* (not on the usual dominant); II. Subord. Theme in meas. 35. — Sonata, op. 14, No. 2, last movement: The *da capo* ends in meas. 64 with complete tonic cadence; a Transition-phrase follows, derived directly from Part Two of the Prin. Theme — duplicated and extended to meas. 72.

THE SECOND SUBORDINATE THEME.

104. For the second of the two digressions, or Subord. Themes, it is common (though by no means imperative) to choose both a more remote key, and a larger form; and also to institute a more complete and striking change in style.   The signature frequently changes here.

Beethoven, Rondo in *C*, op. 51, No. 1: II. Subordinate Theme, in *c* minor and *E*-flat major, complete 3-Part form. — Sonata, op. 14, No. 2, last movement: Prin. Theme in *G;* I. Subord. Theme in *e* and *a* minor; II. Subord. Theme in *C* (the *sub-dominant* key, — a fairly common choice), complete 3-Part form, with repetitions and extensions. — Sonata, op. 10, No. 3, last movement: Prin. Th. in *D;* II. Subord. Theme, in *B*-flat and *E*-flat, an extended phrase, only.

THE SECOND RETRANSITION.

105. As the Second Subordinate Theme is usually a more striking digression, both in key and in length, it follows that the second retransition may require to be more extended and elaborate than the first.

It may be independent, — following the complete cadence of the Subord. Theme; in which case it will comprise both of the transitional "acts," and may even be sectional in form.

Or it may emerge, by dissolution, out of the final phrase of the Subord. Theme.

Beethoven, Rondo, op. 51, No. 1 (the second retransition of which is analyzed in detail in the notes to Ex. 46). — Sonata, op. 10, No. 3, last movement, — also analyzed in the notes to Ex. 46. — Sonata, op. 14, No. 2, last movement (shown in Ex. 46, which see). — Sonata, op. 49, No. 2, last movement: Prin. Th. in *G* major; Second Subord. Theme in *C* major (the subdominant — at the change in signature); it is a concise double-period, the fourth phrase of which is dissolved, becoming the "first act," and followed by three measures of "second act."

The Second Recurrence (or da capo) of the Prin. Theme.

106. The final *da capo*, in the Second Rondo form, is generally a complete re-statement of the Prin. Theme, but may, of course, be abbreviated; and is not infrequently dissolved and merged in the Coda. Review paragraphs 91 and 92.

Beethoven, Rondo, op. 51, No. 1: the final statement of the Prin. Theme (measure 92) is complete up to the *first measure* of its Third Part (measure 105); this first measure is halted, and followed by swift modulations into *c* minor and *D*-flat major, to measure 109; these five measures constitute, therefore, the first Section of the Coda. — Sonata, op. 10, No. 3, last movement: In this Rondo, the Principal Theme undergoes a curious transformation at each recurrence; at first (as seen) it is a Two-Part form, dissolved; as first *da capo* it is abbreviated to its First Part, with evaded cadence; upon its final recurrence it is *enlarged to a complete Three-Part form*, by an effective extension of the former Second Part; it has a complete tonic cadence (in meas. 22 from the end), — followed by an independent Coda. — Sonata, op. 14, No. 2, last movement: the final *da capo* is a complete, and literal, re-statement of the Prin. Theme.

The Coda.

107. This is subject to precisely the same conditions as in the First Rondo form. Review, thoroughly, par. 93.

Beethoven, Rondo, op. 51, No. 1: The first Section of the Coda (as already seen) emerges from the dissolution of the Third Part of the Prin. Theme; Section 2 (suggestive of the first two measures of the II. Subord. Theme) is six measures long; Section 3 (new), five measures; Section 4 (from the Prin. Theme), eleven measures; Section 5 (from the Prin. Theme), four measures, to the end. — Sonata, op. 10, No. 3, last movement: The final *da capo* closes, with a complete tonic cadence, in measure 22 from the end; the first Section of the Coda (derived from the Prin. Theme) is seven measures long — to the ⌒ *; Section 2 (Prin. Theme), two measures; Section 3 (new, but derived *rhythmically* from the first measure of the Prin. Theme), five measures; Section 4 (combination of Prin. Theme and I. Subord. Theme), seven * measures, to the end. — Sonata, op. 14, No. 2, last movement: The final *da capo* closes, with complete tonic cadence, in meas. 160; the first Section of the Coda (derived directly from the Second Part of the Prin. Theme) is 14 measures long; Section 2 (from the Prin. Theme), fifteen measures; Section 3 (new, but related), twenty-four measures; Section 4, a nearly exact duplication of Section 3; Section 5 (from the Prin. Theme), seventeen measures, to the end.

Relation of the Second Rondo form to the Song–form with Two Trios.

108. This relation is the same as that of the First Rondo form to the Song-form with One Trio, though less apparent and much less frequent. Review par. 95, and 96.

Schubert, Sonata, No. 7, op. 164, *Allegretto quasi Andantino.* (The first *da capo* is transposed, from E major to F major. Glance at par. 167.)

Beethoven, Sonata, op. 27, No. 1, first movement, — probably Rondo; I. Subord. Theme in same key.

---

109. The Second Rondo form, like the First, is sometimes very concise, the Themes being limited to a One-Part form. In this case, the design approaches the Five-Part Song-form (see *Homophonic Forms,* par. 106e), but falls within the domain of these Larger forms, in character, when the Parts are so distinctly individualized as to create the impression of legitimate *Themes.* Review par. 68, and par. 85, small type.

Beethoven, Sonata, op. 13, *Adagio:* apparently a Five-Part Song-form, since each "Theme" is in small (One-Part) form; the Prin. Theme, a repeated period, 16 measures; I. Subord. Theme, a 7-measure phrase, eked out with a Codetta (duplicated and dissolved, as retransition); Prin. Theme, one statement of the period; II. Subord. Theme an 8-measure period, followed by a retransition, which may be regarded as a Second Part, dissolved; Prin. Theme as at first, followed by a Codetta, duplicated and extended, to the end.

* N.B. — Since there is no elision in the cadence-measure — 22 from the end — the student must beware *of counting this measure twice.* The "first measure" of the Coda is, therefore, *measure 21* from the end. This same, somewhat confusing, condition prevails in many places, and demands strict discrimination on the student's part. The tones which thus often fill out the cadence-measure constitute that species of "bridging" known as *preliminary tones* of the actual phrase — not its "first measure." See *Homophonic Forms,* par. 2a, small type ; and Ex. 66, with its context.

Beethoven, Violin Sonata, op. 30, No. 1, *Adagio;* broader than the preceding example, and obviously Rondo form — possibly *First* Rondo, with Prin. Theme as 3-Part form (abbreviated to One-Part in the *da capo*), and a fairly long Coda.

Mozart, Sonata, *c* minor (Schirmer ed., No. 18), *Adagio.*

The following list of examples of the Second Rondo form should also be most diligently studied:

*1) The Prin. Theme (meas. 1–23) is a Two-Part form, with Codetta, and complete tonic cadence.

*2) There is no transition — only this "bridging."

*3) The I. Subord. Theme begins in the same key (opposite mode); it is a Two-Part form (meas. 24–34; 35–48), with a cadence-extension, quasi Codetta, leading to the prospective dominant; the "second act" of retransition (meas. 52–61) is given in the above example.

*4) The Prin. Theme recurs in exactly the same "form" as before, but considerably ornamented, as shown.

*5) Again, no transition. The II. Subord. Theme (meas. 85–100) is a period, duplicated.

*6) It makes its full cadence, exceptionally, on the *original tonic*.

*7) For this reason, the second retransition must perform the task of leaving, and returning to, this tonic. It begins, as seen, with a direct allusion to the Prin. Theme (in minor), and persists in an ingenious presentation of the initial figure (*c–d–c–b*) throughout the "first act," until it reaches the dominant, as shown in the example, one measure before the reappearance of the Prin. Theme.

*8) The second recurrence of the Prin. Theme, like the first, is unchanged in form, but again modified in treatment; its cadence is evaded by substituting (or retaining) the dominant chord — thus merging in the first section of the Coda.

*9) The Coda (meas. 137–167) contains four brief sections, dealing with the I. Subord. Theme, the Codetta of the Prin. Theme, the first motive of the Prin. Theme, and an extended cadence.   See further:

Beethoven, Rondo, op. 51, No. 1 (cited above, but to be analyzed here as a whole). — Sonata, op. 10, No. 3, last movement (ditto). — Sonata, op. 14, No. 2, last movement. — Sonata, op. 49, No. 2, last movement. — Sonata, op. 79, last movement (concise, small Themes). — Sonata, op. 53, last movement (very broad, unusually long Coda). — Polonaise, op. 89 (all three Themes in the key of C — major and minor). — *Andante favori* in F major (the I. Subord. Theme begins in the principal key, with material from the Prin. Theme). — Trio, op. 1, No. 1, *Adagio*. — Trio, op. 9, No. 2, *Andante quasi Allegretto.* — String-quartet, op. 74, *Adagio* (Ex. 50).

Mozart, Rondo in a minor (large Themes). — *Don Giovanni,* No. 24 (*Elvira,* "Mi tradì quell'alma ingrata").

Carl Maria v. Weber, Sonata, No. 1, op. 24, last movement (*Perpetuum mobile*).

Schubert, pfte. Sonata, No. 2, op. 53, last movement (II. Subord. Theme a Song-form with Trio). — Fantasia, op. 78, last movement.

Josef Suk, pfte. Suita, op. 21, last movement.

Brahms, pfte. Sonata, op. 1, last movement. — Sonata, op. 5, last movement (elaborate Coda). — Symphony, No. 1, *Poco Allegretto.* — Violin Sonata, No. 1, op. 78, last movement.

EXERCISE 8.

A number of Second Rondo forms; different *tempi* and character, *Adagio, Larghetto, Andante, Allegretto cantabile, Allegro maestoso, Allegro con brio,* etc. See par. 197, 1 to 7.

N.B. — Any instrument, or ensemble, may be employed; but see Exercise 7, A.

CHAPTER IX.

THE THIRD RONDO FORM.

110. See par. 70.　The diagram of the Third Rondo form is as follows:

First Division			Middle Division	Recapitulation		
Prin. Th.	*I. Sub. Th.*	*Prin. Th.*	*II. Sub. Th.*	*Prin. Th.*	*I. Sub. Th.*	*Prin. Th.*
Any Part-form	Related key	Possibly abbreviated	Broader form, probably a remote key	As before	As before, but **transposed** (to principal key)	(and) *Coda*
Trans.	*Retrans.*		*Retrans.*	*Trans.* (par. 121*b*)		

111. The thoughtful consideration of this diagram reveals several significant traits which distinguish it from the preceding Rondo forms. First of all, it is another example (and the largest) of the "tripartite" form, and represents the most extreme evolution (in extent) of the structural principle of "Statement–Departure– and Return," which underlies every grade of the Three-Part form. Review par. 85, N.B.

The progressive stages of this evolution are thus distinguished:

1. The *Three-Part Period* (of which each "Part" is a phrase, only, — the third a confirmation of the first);

2. The *Three-Part Song-form* (of which each Part is, usually, a Period, or more, — the third like the first);

3. The *Song-form with Trio* (each division an entire Song-form); and its refined counterpart

4. The *First Rondo form* (each division an individual Theme, the third a recurrence of the first);

5. The *Third Rondo form* (the first division a complete First Rondo form, the middle division an emphatic Departure, and the Recapitulation a confirmation of the first division).

Other manifestations of this sovereign principle of musical structure will be encountered later (par. 143).

112. The Third division of this form is called the Recapitulation, because it is a *collective* re-statement, — of several individual factors.

This act, and therefore the name, occurs here for the first time in the process of formal evolution, but is a distinctive and indispensable trait of all the succeeding Larger forms.

113. Probably the most significant technical feature of a Recapitulation is *the transposed recurrence of the First Subordinate Theme* (as a rule, shifted to the principal key).

The consequence of this is, that while there are three digressions from the Prin. Theme, they are not all *different* departures: The third digression — the Subord. Theme in the Recapitulation — corresponds to the first digression, or First Subord. Theme.   But this recurrence transcends in importance the common, unaltered *da capo* of the Minuet and allied dance-forms, and also averts monotony, by appearing in a *different key*.

That the principal key should usually be chosen, in confirmation of the ruling tonic centre, is obviously logical.

114. This transposition of the I. Subord. Theme naturally, and almost inevitably, exerts an important influence upon the treatment of the transition and retransition, as will be shown.

THE FIRST DIVISION.

115. In view of the length of the Third Rondo form, it would be unwise (under ordinary conditions) to choose large designs for the Themes.   At the same time, it is not uncommon to mould the Prin. Theme in the Three-Part Song-form, — though usually concise (Incomplete, or Incipient grade).   The I. Subord. Theme is rarely more than a One-Part form, though a Codetta is frequently added.   And, as a rule, the first *da capo* (recurrence of the Prin. Theme) is abbreviated to one, only, of its Parts.

On the other hand, the Themes should not *both* be so brief as to reduce the whole first division to a mere Three-*Part* form (par. 85).

The end of the first division is often marked with a double bar.   This is not by any means a necessary element in the Third Rondo form, but appears, as a technical expedient, *only when the signature is changed for the key of the middle division.*   For all the Rondo forms are distinguished by their almost unbroken continuity from beginning to end.   Nevertheless, it is effective, and customary, to mark the close of the first division quite emphatically, by a strong cadence, and by an abrupt announcement of the II. Subord. Theme (without transition).

See **Beethoven,** Sonata, op. 2, No. 2, last movement:

Principal Theme, A major, 3-Part form, Incipient grade (to measure 16);

Transition-phrase (to measure 20), duplicated, dissolved, and led to the prospective *tonic* (measure 26);

I. Subord. Theme, E major, period-form, Consequent phrase extended and dissolved, as retransition (measures 27–39); "second act" to meas. 40;

Prin. Theme (measures 41 to 56), as before, slightly modified. It ends with a complete tonic cadence, and is followed immediately (that is, without transition) by the II. Subord. Theme, in *a* minor and *C* major. A double-bar appears at this point, in consequence, *only,* of the change of signature.

In **Beethoven,** Sonata, op. 7, last movement, the recurrence of the Prin. Theme (*E*-flat major) is abbreviated, — only its first and second Parts are stated (to measure 62); two measures of chromatic transition follow, leading to the prospective *tonic;* the II. Subord. Theme begins, with double-bar (on account only of the intended repetition), in measure 65, in *c* minor.

In **Beethoven,** Sonata, op. 2, No. 3, last movement, no double-bar appears between the first and middle divisions; but the alteration of style is very marked in the II. Subordinate Theme, which is reached by a brief chromatic transition (measures 101–102).

116. The transition and the retransition are made precisely as shown in the First Rondo form.

An excellent example, just cited, is the **Beethoven** Sonata, op. 2, No. 3, last movement: *Principal Theme, C* major, 3-Part form; Part III is dissolved (in meas. 22) and led to the prospective dominant (meas. 29); the *I. Subord. Theme, G* major, is a period (measures 30–39), duplicated and extended, closing on its tonic, *G,* in meas. 55; a two-measure Codetta is added, and three times repeated; the "second act" of retransition extends from meas. 64 to 69, where the *Prin. Theme* reënters. The latter is abbreviated to its first Part (meas. 69–76) which is, however, duplicated, greatly extended, and led to a complete tonic cadence upon *A* — the *mediant* of the coming Theme (meas. 77–101). As stated above, two chromatic measures lead to the II. Subord. Theme.

THE MIDDLE DIVISION.

117. The second division of the Third Rondo form consists solely of the II. Subordinate Theme, with its retransition back to the Prin. Theme. Both the Theme and the retransition are therefore likely to assume greater dimensions, and a more striking appearance, than the foregoing factors. Hence the frequent change of signature, and a marked contrast in style, especially in *rhythmic* character, and in "mood."

See **Beethoven,** Sonata, op. 2, No. 3, last movement (just cited): The *II. Subordinate Theme,* in *F* major (meas. 103), is a fairly broad 3-Part form with repetition of Parts II and III; the latter is dissolved (in meas. 147), "spun out," and led to the prospective dominant (measure 164), therewith closing the "first act" of retransition; the "second act" extends to meas. 181 — where the Recapitulation begins.

Beethoven, Sonata, op. 28, last movement: The II. Subord. Theme (meas. 68) is a 2-Part form; the Second Part (meas. 79), imitatory, is extended, and led to the prospective dominant (meas. 101); the "second act" of retransition extends to meas. 113; the Recapitulation begins in the following measure. There is, in this example, no transition into the II. Subord. Theme, no change of signature, and, consequently, no double-bar. The keys are *D* major and *G* major.

118. It is evident that the design, up to this point, agrees exactly with that of the Second Rondo form. But the student will appreciate that this similarity is, nevertheless, more external than vital. A composer should, surely, always be fully conscious of his larger purpose; and this consciousness should inform him whether he has in mind to employ the Second form or the Third. For this choice, despite complete external likeness in *design*, must determine many finer details of conception.

THE RECAPITULATION.

119. The salient feature of the Recapitulation is, that all the Themes are (as a rule) *in the same key* — the original key. The consequent danger of monotony must be averted by judicious treatment of the transition and retransition, and also by interesting variation in the presentation of the Themes themselves.

120. The Prin. Theme, at the beginning of the Recapitulation, is usually presented in its complete form, as at first (that is, not abbreviated), though it is often variated and ornamented, sometimes considerably.

Beethoven, op. 2, No. 2, last movement: The Recapitulation begins at the third double-bar, where the signature is again changed to three sharps; it extends through 16 measures; compare carefully with the first 16 measures of the movement.

Beethoven, op. 7, last movement: The Recapitulation begins in the seventh measure from the last double-bar with two endings; compare with the first 16 measures of the movement, and note the ornamentation in triplets.

Beethoven, op. 22, last movement: The Recap. begins in meas. 112; compare with the first 18 measures of the movement; note the transferring of the melody to the inner register, and other (rhythmic) changes.

In **Beethoven,** op. 26, last movement, the Prin. Th. is re-stated, in the Recapitulation, *exactly* as at first (meas. 13 from the last double-bar with two endings).

121. From the fact that the recurrence of the I. Subord. Theme, at this point, takes place in the *same key* (par. 119), it is evident that the transition here must pursue a course widely different from that of the ordinary transition, as exhibited in the First division.

a. One way — the most simple, though inartistic, and therefore rare method — is to take advantage of the similarity of key, and *omit the transition* altogether.

This happens in **Beethoven,** Rondo, op. 51, No. 2 (*G* major): The Recap. begins at the "Tempo I," where the signature is changed from four sharps back to one sharp; the Prin. Theme extends through the following 24 measures, closing with a complete tonic cadence, and followed *immediately* by the I. Subord. Theme (in *G*).

b. But the opposite course is generally adopted: Instead of shortening, or omitting, this transition, it is made longer than before, so as to admit of *getting away from the principal key, and returning to it.* This is indicated by the arrows in the diagram (par. 110), which compare.

This more extended course of the transition almost invariably includes a more or less emphatic modulation in the *subdominant* direction, — for several reasons, chief among which is, probably, the fact that the I. Subord. Theme, in the First division, is usually placed *above* the Prin. Theme (in the dominant key, at least from major), and therefore reappears, in the Recapitulation, in a key which is the subdominant of its first location.

This is disclosed by comparing the succession of keys in, say, **Beethoven,** op. 28, last movement:

Prin. Th.	I. Sub. Theme	Pr. Th.	II. Subord. Th.	Prin. Th.	I. Sub. Th.	Pr. Th. & Coda
D maj.	*A* maj. *1)	*D*	*G* maj. etc.	*D*	*D* maj. *1)	*D*

*1) The I. Subord. Theme appears first in *A*, then in *D*, — consequently it is finally transposed to the *subdominant* of its first key.

The subdominant infusion is clearly shown in the Sonata just cited (op. 28, last movement): The Recap. (*D* major) begins in meas. 114; the transition, in meas. 130, is exactly as before (meas. 17); in meas. 135 it modulates downward into the subdominant keys, *G* major and *e* minor; the prospective dominant (*A*), and the "second act" of transition, runs through measures 138–144; the I. Subord. Th. enters in meas. 145. The transition is three measures longer than at first, in consequence of this modulatory excursion (compare with measures 17–28, 29).

Beethoven, op. 26, last movement: The transition (in the Recap.) begins in meas. 42 from the end, exactly as in meas. 28 (from the beginning); comparison with measures 28–32 shows that here it is considerably longer, including two subdominant modulations, into *b*-flat minor (*i.e.*, from four flats into five). In **Beethoven,** Violin Sonata, op. 12, No. 3, last movement, the Prin. Th. *itself* is partly transposed to the subdominant key (at the beginning of the Recapitulation).

c. As usual, the process of dissolution may be applied to the final phrase in the recurrence of the Prin. Theme (or a part of it), leading smoothly into the I. Subord. Theme.   This method of transition, also, usually exhibits the subdominant tendency.

*1) The Prin. Theme is a period, with repeated Consequent phrase, and a two-measure Codetta, the duplication of which is here shown.

*2) A full tonic cadence, followed (in the first division) by a 4-measure transition, leading to the I. Subord. Theme in E-flat major (see the original).

*3) This is the duplication of the Consequent phrase, extended and dissolved as shown.

*4) Here the subdominant infusion (into *four* flats) asserts itself.

*5) The I. Subord. Theme appears in *C* major — see par. 122.

d. In **Beethoven,** Sonata, op. 2, No. 2, last movement, the transition is exactly as before, excepting an unimportant abbreviation of two measures (not affecting its cadence, upon E).

This first transition is given in Ex. 41, and, as there pointed out, it leads to the prospective *tonic* (E) — instead of the usual dominant. But this same note, E, *is the dominant* of the key in which the I. Subord. Theme is to stand in the Recapitulation (the principal key, A major), — therefore it serves the transitional purpose here, without change, even better than before. See measures 24–25 from the change of signature (to three sharps).

e. The connection of Themes is somewhat peculiar in **Beethoven,** Sonata, op. 7, last movement:

The peculiarity is cited in par. 82, which review; namely, the I. Subord. Theme begins (in measure 17) in the same key, *E*-flat major, and makes the transition to *B*-flat major within itself — during its first half-dozen measures. In the Recapitulation, precisely the same conditions prevail: The I. Subord. Theme *begins,* as before, in E-flat major; it modulates soon into the subdominant (f minor), and thence makes its way back again to its proper key, E-flat major, — again containing its transition within itself.   See measures 23–31, etc., from the last double-bar with two endings.

122. The First Subordinate Theme, in the Recapitulation, is transposed, almost always, to the principal key, as intimated in the diagram.

a. The chief exception occurs in Rondos in minor, where a *change of mode* is not uncommon.   Thus, in the last movement of the Beethoven sonata, op. 13:

Prin. Th.	*I. Sub. Th.*	*Prin. Th.*	*II. Subord. Th.*	*Prin. Th.*	*I. Sub. Th.*	*Pr. Th. & Coda*
c minor	E-flat maj. *1)	c min.	A-flat maj.	c minor	C major *1)	c minor

*1) The I. Subord. Theme appears at first, as is usual, in the relative *major* key. In the Recapitulation it would be expected to stand in the principal key, *c minor;* but this would involve an alteration of the mode which might be embarrassing, and might impair the Theme.   Hence the natural inclination to change the mode of the *Rondo,* rather than the mode of the Theme.   The change is illustrated in Ex. 51, note *5), which see.

The return to the original mode (minor) may be made at any point, during the later course of the Subord. Theme, or in the retransition.   In some cases, a similar change of mode (from minor to major) occurs in the Coda, leading to a final cadence *in major.*   **Beethoven,** Sonata, op. 10, No. 1, last movement.

b. The deliberate choice of some other, unexpected, key is seen in **Beethoven,** Sonata, op. 14, No. 1, last movement:

The I. Subord. Theme, derived directly from the Consequent phrase of the Prin. Theme, begins in measure 14 — in the usual dominant key (*B* major, from *E*).   In the Recapitulation, the I. Subord. Theme is presented completely (including its Codetta) *in A major* — instead of the expected principal key, *E* major.   See measures 8–25 from the change of signature to four sharps.

123. In reference to such *transpositions,* or presentation of Themes in some unexpected key — which is not an uncommon circumstance (par. 167) — the student (both in practice and in analysis) must bear the following conditions in mind: The transposed recurrence of any foregoing material, especially the initial melodic member of the Prin. Theme, must not be accepted hastily as an actual presentation of the Theme itself, in a manner influencing the meaning of the design, but must be examined in all of its bearings upon the latter.   Such a recurrence is *not* the "Theme" itself, but merely an allusion to it, or a structural deduction from it —

(1) If it is not in the legitimate and expected key;

(2) If it is only a portion of the Theme (less than *one entire Part*);

(3) If it does not appear in its expected place in the design.

See Example 49, note *3). This is *not* the Prin. Theme itself, because it is not in the right key (*C*), and, chiefly, because it is no more than a fragment of the Theme. Also Ex. 46, note *2); not the actual Prin. Theme, but merely its thematic motive employed as retransition, for the same reasons. Also

Beethoven, Sonata, op. 10, No. 3, last movement; measures 46–48 are only an *allusion* to the Prin. Theme, because limited to this fragment, and in the wrong key; they represent a section of the retransition. Similar: Rondo, op. 51, No. 1; measures 76–83 allude to the Prin. Theme, but only to utilize its first phrases as material for the retransition (second section). This was a favorite device of **Beethoven,** and is worthy of imitation.

124. On the contrary, such a recurrence may and will actually represent the Theme, *even when transposed* —

(1) If it covers the entire Theme, or a convincingly large proportion (*an entire Part*) of it;

(2) If it ultimately turns back into the legitimate key;

(3) If it appears where expected.

See par. 122*b*. Also, **Beethoven,** Sonata, op. 10, No. 1, first movement, measures 110–127 from the double-bar; the Subord. Theme appears here in *F* major instead of the expected key, *c* minor, — but swings over into the latter key, and begins anew in meas. 128 (compare measures 56–70 from the beginning). In other words, this *is* the Subord. Theme, despite the change of key, — for the given reasons. Also, **Beethoven,** Sonata, op. 10. No. 2, first movement, at the change of signature to two sharps: The following 12 measures *are* the Prin. Theme, although it appears in *D* major, instead of *F* major — compare the first 12 measures of the movement. Four measures later it regains the original key, and is then duplicated there, in ultimate confirmation of its thematic quality. Also, Sonata, op. 7, last movement, measure 28 from the end: The phrase in *E* major is a transposed statement of the Third Part (of the final recurrence of the Prin. Theme) — extended, led back to the original key, and there duplicated, with some alterations. Also, Sonata, op. 22, last movement: The II. Subord. Theme (measures 72–103) is a 3-Part form, with *transposed* Third Part — as every detail proves. Similar: Sonata, op. 14, No. 1, last movement, from first change of signature to the next.

Such transpositions, especially of entire Themes, are frequently encountered in the larger forms of **Schubert,** as will be seen (par. 167).

125. Another misleading device — partly analogous to par. 123 — is the free adoption of any foregoing thematic unit, as basis for quite another factor of the form; or, in other words, the use of the selfsame thematic material for different structural purposes. The student must be on his guard against misinterpretation of these deceptive coincidences, — must not jump at the conclusion that such a member *is* the Theme in question, simply because it looks like it.   See Ex. 55, note *2).

Instances of this kind have already been seen: **Beethoven,** Sonata, op. 26, last movement.   As shown in Ex. 38, No. 1, Ex. 45, and Ex. 47, the transition, I. Subord. Theme, and retransition, are all wrought out of the thematic figure of the Prin. Theme. — Sonata, op. 14, No. 1, first movement (Ex. 37): measures 13–14 are identical with measures 1–2; at first, these figures are a part of the Prin. Theme; their recurrence is, however, a part of the transition. — Same sonata, last movement: The I. Subord. Theme (meas. 14) is similar to the Consequent phrase of the Prin. Theme. — Sonata, op. 14, No. 2, last movement: The transition (meas. 64–72) is based upon the Second Part of the Prin. Theme (meas. 8–16). — Same movement: The first section of the Coda (meas. 160) is so nearly identical with the Second Part of the Prin. Theme, immediately preceding, that it might easily be construed as an intention of repeating the foregoing two Parts; *there,* it was in the Prin. Theme; *here,* it is in the Coda — thus serving a wholly different purpose. — Sonata, op. 22, last movement: The transition-phrase, first stated in measures 18–20, and again (before the II. Subord. Theme) in measures 67–69, is utilized as thematic basis of the entire Second Part of the II. Subord. Theme (measures 80–95). — An unusually misleading example occurs in **Beethoven,** Sonata, op. 2, No. 2, *Largo,* measure 13 from the end: The 8-measure period, from this point, is not the Prin. Theme itself, despite very close resemblance to it, because it is not in the proper place — being unquestionably nothing else than one of the four sections of the Coda, — and because, furthermore, it differs from the Theme (measures 1–8 of the movement) significantly in the (important) fifth measure.

Such instances of the employment of the same thematic factor for widely different aims, are extremely numerous.   And that these coincidences should appear, is precisely as it should be, in good, logically coherent, musical form.   For they contribute to the *unity of the design,* and can easily be so manipulated as to avert monotony or confusion. The student must simply keep his attention bent unwaveringly upon the broad, vital lines of the design as a whole, and not allow these to become obscured.

126. After the presentation of the I. Subord. Theme, in the Recapitulation, attention will be directed to the return of the Prin. Theme; and the same difficulties are involved in this retransition as in the preceding transition, in consequence of the similarity of key.

As before (par. 121*a*), this similarity is sometimes turned to advantage, and an immediate return made to the Prin. Theme, without transition.

Beethoven, Sonata, op. 2, No. 2, last movement, measure 53 from the end; **the** close connection is emphasized by an elision of the cadence.

Generally, however, the final phrase of the I. Subord. Theme (or its Codetta) is dissolved, and led to the prospective dominant in the usual manner.

Beethoven, Sonata, op. 2, No. 3, last movement; at measure 68 from the end, the I. Subord. Theme terminates on its dominant (*G*) instead of its tonic; this is exactly where it closed in the first division (meas. 55 from the beginning), and results from different manipulation of its final phrase — compare carefully. From this dominant, the retransition (*including* the former Codetta) proceeds almost exactly as before. — Sonata, op. 7, last movement, similar (meas. 41–44 from the end). — Sonata, op. 13, last movement, similar; the Codetta (meas. 57 from the end) is reduced to the first of its two phrases, which is duplicated, extended, dissolved, and led to the dominant in the usual way; the "second act" follows, to the re-entrance of the Prin. Theme. — Sonata, op. 22, last movement: The I. Subordinate Theme is re-stated exactly as in the first division, and also its Codetta, *with its duplication and dissolution;* this leads, of course, into the *subdominant* key (meas. 48–50 from the end); it is followed by a pretended announcement of the first phrase of the Prin. Theme, in the subdominant key; this is not, however, the Theme itself, but merely the second section of the retransition (comp. par. 123). The actual Prin. Theme enters a few measures later.

127. The final presentation of the Prin. Theme in the Third Rondo form is its fourth statement, and is therefore (unless unusually significant and attractive) apt to be ineffective, although prescribed in the regular design. For this reason, as intimated in the diagram, it is most common to abbreviate it, or to merge it in the Coda (by way of dissolution), or even to omit it altogether. Compare par. 106.

In **Beethoven,** op. 26, last movement, the final *da capo* (*i.e.*, the Prin. Theme) is entirely omitted. The I. Subord. Theme, with its complete tonic cadence, is followed immediately by the Coda (measure 16 from the end). See also:

Beethoven, Rondo, op. 51, No. 2: The final recurrence of the Prin. Theme is omitted; the I. Subord. Theme (in the Recapitulation) is stated completely, and exactly as before (with slight changes, only); what followed it in the first Division, as retransition, is also added here, but as *first section of the Coda* (measure 48 from the end). The Prin. Theme (Part III) is alluded to, quite strongly, in the second section of the Coda. Compare par. 125 — especially the reference to op. 2, No. 2, *Largo.* — Sonata, op. 2, No. 2, last movement: The final Prin. Theme is abbreviated to its First Part, which is, however, ingeniously extended (meas. 53 from the end). — Sonata, op. 2, No. 3, last movement: The final Prin. Theme (measure 54 from the end) appears fragmentarily, as first section of the Coda. — Sonata, op. 28, last movement: The I. Subord. Theme (in the Recapitulation, measure 145) recurs as before, with its Codetta; the latter, also, is duplicated twice and extended *exactly as before* — therefore terminating a fifth lower (or 4th higher) than at first; the Prin. Theme, as final *da capo*, does not follow, but it is intimated, *in the subdominant key* (*G*), as first section of the Coda. On the other hand, in **Beethoven,** Sonata, op. 7, last movement, the final Prin. Theme appears more elaborate than before, being extended in its III. Part by a characteristic modulation (measures 11–41 from the end).

THE CODA.

128. The consistency of the Coda corresponds here to that of the preceding Rondo forms, and requires no further illustration.

---

129. Beyond this the Rondo form very rarely extends. Further digression from, and return to, the Prin. Theme would divest the form of the necessary compactness and symmetry, so admirably manifested in the First and Third Rondo forms especially; and would produce a discursive, straggling impression, of questionable interest, and inevitably monotonous. Even the Third Rondo form, as has been learned, has no more than two *different* Subord. Themes.

Isolated examples of a more extended form occur in **Mozart,** Sonata, No. 8 (Schirmer edition), last movement; and Sonata, No. 17, last movement. Also:

Beethoven, Violin Sonata, op. 23, last movement.

And the Primitive small "Rondeau" of the 17–18 centuries was often prolonged to include three, and even more, independent digressions or "couplets." (See *Homophonic forms,* par. 108.)

The following Rondos of **Beethoven** have been cited in detail in the above paragraphs. But they should now be thoroughly analyzed as a whole:

Beethoven, Sonata, op. 2, No. 2,

Beethoven, Sonata, op. 2, No. 3,

Beethoven, Sonata, op. 7,

Beethoven, Sonata, op. 13,

Beethoven, Sonata, op. 14, No. 1,   } last movement of each.

Beethoven, Sonata, op. 22,

Beethoven, Sonata, op. 26,

Beethoven, Sonata, op. 28,

Beethoven, Rondo, op. 51, No. 2.   See further:

Beethoven, Violin Sonata, op. 12, No. 1, third movement; (last *da capo* omitted).

Beethoven, Violin Sonata, op. 12, No. 2, third movement; (last *da capo* omitted).

Beethoven, Violin Sonata, op. 12, No. 3, third movement; (Prin. Th. at the beginning of the Recapitulation partly tranposed to the subdominant; final *da capo* merged in the Coda).

Beethoven, Violin Sonata, op. 24, last movement; (I. Subord. Theme, in the Recapitulation, appears in a remote key).

Beethoven, String-Trio, op. 3, last movement; (very broad; II. Subord. Theme long, sectional in form, and imitatory; long Coda, ten brief sections).

Schubert, pfte. Sonata, No. 1, op. 42, last movement (broad).

Mozart, Sonata, No. 13 (Schirmer edition), last movement.

Mozart, Sonata, No. 10 (Schirmer edition), last movement.

Glazounow, pfte. Sonata, No. 2, op. 75, *Scherzo* (no final *da capo*).

Glazounow, pfte. Sonata, No. 1, op. 74, last movement; (regular; final *da capo* merged in the Coda).

Mendelssohn, Violoncello Sonata, op. 45, last movement; (elaborate transitions and retransitions — the latter, in every case, extremely ingenious and effective). — Pfte. Trio, No. I, op. 49, last movement; (very broad, but regular; effective reference to the II. Subord. Theme in the Coda). — Pfte. Trio, No. II, op. 66, last movement (very similar; also contains a climactic reference to the II. Subord. Theme, in the Coda).

Beethoven, Violoncello Sonata, op. 5, No. 1, last movement. — Op. 5, No. 2, last movement.

Beethoven, Symphony, No. 6 (*Pastorale*), last movement — 16 measures of Introduction.

Beethoven, Symphony, No. 4, *Adagio.*

Brahms, String-sextet, No. 1, op. 18, last movement. — Violoncello Sonata, No. 2, op. 99, last movement (Prin. Theme transposed, in the Recapitulation; par. 167a). — Violin Sonata, No. 2, op. 100, last movement (Prin. Theme transposed, in the Recapitulation). — Violin Sonata, No. 3, op. 108, last movement; a superb example; Prin. Theme, 2-Part form, Part II dissolved, as transition; I. Subord. Theme, broad 2-Part form, Part I duplicated, Part II related to Prin. Theme; Codetta (two measures), duplicated and extended, as retransition; first recurrence of Prin. Theme reduced to its First Part — first phrase transposed; II. Subord. Theme (related to Prin. Theme), a group of phrases, imitatory, phrase four extended as retransition; second recurrence of Prin. Theme (Recapitulation), Part I transposed and elaborately extended, Part II as before, but with different methods of dissolution; Coda, last 27 measures.

Beethoven, String-quartet, op. 18, No. 4, last movement: This is the design of the Third Rondo form; but its distinct cadences, and detached periods, assign it to the lower grade of Song-form with Trios. — **Schumann,** pfte. Quintet, op. 44, second movement (*Marcia*) is similar.

EXERCISE 9.

A number of examples of the Third Rondo form, in various styles, but in no *tempo* slower than *Allegretto.*

N.B. — Write for pianoforte, organ, pfte. duo (Violin or 'Cello), or trio.   See par. 197, 1 to 7.

DIVISION THREE.

THE SONATA-ALLEGRO FORMS.

INTRODUCTION.

130. Review par. 70. Of the two distinct classes of the Larger forms, that of the Rondo is based throughout, as has been shown, upon the structural principle of **Alternation.**

The fundamental structural idea of the other class, the Sonata-allegro, is that of **Union,** — the union or association of two contrasting Themes upon quite, or nearly, equal footing. The second Theme should be as significant as the first, and is called "Subordinate" only because it occupies the second place in the thematic order, — the Principal Theme being first in order, naturally.

131. This union of the two Themes (made binding by the necessary transition between them, and further confirmed — as a rule — by the addition of one or more Codettas) constitutes the **Exposition,** which very frequently terminates with a complete tonic cadence, in the key chosen for the Subord. Theme, — and a double-bar.

132. In the larger species of this class, the Sonata-allegro form, the Exposition is followed by a so-called *Development,* and the latter by a *Recapitulation* of the Exposition; therefore the design comprises three Divisions.

In the smaller species, the Sonatina-form, the Exposition is followed at once (or after a few measures of retransition) by the Recapitulation; therefore this design contains two Divisions only.

CHAPTER X.

THE SONATINA-FORM.

133. The term *sonatina*, as diminutive of "*sonata*," is applied without further qualification to the smaller species of this class of forms, and does not imply any special *tempo* or style of music. Comp. par. 142. The diagram of the Sonatina-form is as follows:

Exposition				Recapitulation		
Prin. Theme	*Subord. Th.*	*Re-trans.*		*Prin. Th.*	*Subord. Th.*	*Coda*
Any Part-form.	Related key.			As before.	**Transposed** (to principal key).	
Transition.	(Codetta.)			*Transition* (modified)	(Codetta.)	

134. As pointed out in Ex. 37, note *1), which review, all of the larger forms follow the same schedule up to, and into, the Subordinate Theme. After that they diverge and pursue different courses, according to the purpose of creating either one of the three Rondos, the Sonatina-form, or the Sonata-allegro form. This confirms the principle that the form should be determined by the music, and not the music by the form. The design which the music is to adopt cannot be positively forecast until enough of the latter has appeared to define the choice. The student must, however, make it his aim at first to carry out the *fixed details of each diagram in turn*, and familiarize himself thoroughly with each, until, by comparison, he has fully mastered the distinctive qualities of them all, and can, later on, guide his conception into its proper and most effective channels. Compare par. 118.

THE EXPOSITION.

135. The Principal Theme, in the Sonatina-form, may be in any of the Part-forms (probably not the largest, often only One-Part), and in almost any style and tempo, though usually a slow movement. Review par. 68. As a rule, it will be somewhat less pretentious than that of the larger (Sonata-allegro) species.

136. The transition into the other Theme is in no respect different in purpose from that of any other form, and requires no further explanation; but it is considered an indispensable factor, and is often somewhat assertive.

137. The Subordinate Theme, as intimated, must be regarded as a more significant element, here, than in the Rondo forms, and may therefore be both more elaborate, striking, and of somewhat greater length. It is placed, as usual, in some related key; most commonly in the dominant key from major, or the relative key from minor.

The addition of a Codetta, or even more than one (in the same key), is characteristic, though not imperative in this smaller species — the Sonatina-form.   See Ex. 54, note *1).

138. Whether the Exposition terminates with a complete tonic cadence, or is dissolved and led into the retransition, depends upon the character and current of the music.   No "double-bar" ever appears (as in the Sonata-allegro form — par. 144), as this would interfere with the retransition, and is furthermore needless because the Exposition of a Sonatina-form is never repeated.   But the Exposition should, nevertheless, be conceived as a finished whole, a consummated *union of the two Themes* — free from any symptom of the Rondo, despite the immediate retransition to the Prin. Theme.

THE RETRANSITION.

139. The length and importance of the retransition depends upon circumstances; but it never oversteps the purpose of *mere retransition*, even when fairly lengthy, in the *genuine Sonatina-form*.   Its conduct is determined according to the rules already given.

etc., to

dissolved ("first act" of Transition)

"second act"

etc., 3 meas.
*3)

Prospective dominant

etc., 3 meas.

*1) The original is in Trio-score, of course — which should be carefully consulted. The above example is condensed to a pianoforte version, for convenience.

*2) The Prin. Theme is a regular 8-measure period, duplicated, dissolved, extended, and led to the prospective dominant, where the "second act" of transition begins, — as shown.

*3) The transitional prolongation of the dominant extends through eight measures, in all.

*4) The Subord. Theme is a Group of (four) phrases, quasi Double-period. It begins in the customary dominant key, and continues there for eight measures; then modulates, abruptly, to *G* major, in which (remote) key it terminates, with a complete tonic cadence.

*5) There is no Codetta to the Subord. Theme; but its place is taken by this one-measure extension of the cadence.

*6) The entire retransition is based upon the initial melodic member of the Principal Theme, but employed in such a skilful manner as to prepare for, and yet not *anticipate*, the Theme itself.

See further (the *Exposition* only):

Beethoven, Sonata, op. 10, No. 1, *Adagio:* Prin. Theme (*A*-flat major), Two-Part form, Part II dissolved, as transition (meas. 17–21, 22, 23); Subord. Theme (*E*-flat major) quasi Period, with duplication of each phrase (meas. 24–42); cadence extension, in lieu of a Codetta (meas. 43–44); the Exposition closes with a complete tonic cadence in *E*-flat major (meas. 44); the retransition covers only one measure — *the simple arpeggiated dominant-seventh chord* — meas. 45.

Beethoven, Sonata, op. 31, No. 2, *Adagio:* Prin. Theme (*B*-flat major) is in Two-Part form (Part I, to meas. 17); Part II is dissolved, as transition, and led, rather abruptly, to the prospective dominant (meas. 23); the "second act" extends to meas. 30; the Subord. Theme (*F* major) is a duplicated phrase with tonic cadence (meas. 31–38); the retransition covers four measures, is merely a "second act," upon the prospective dominant, and is patterned after the preceding "transition"; the Recapitulation follows, in meas. 43.

Beethoven, pfte. Trio, op. 9, No. 1, *Adagio:* The final phrase of the Subord. Theme is dissolved, and led directly over into the Recapitulation.

Beethoven, String-Trio, op. 3, *Adagio:* A brief Codetta is added to the Subord. Theme, and extended into a brief (5-measure) retransition.

The Recapitulation, and Coda.

140. As in the Third rondo form, the Recapitulation here is a collective re-statement of the thematic members of the first Division or Exposition; and it involves the inevitable *transposition of the Subordinate Theme*, — as a rule, to the principal key. Review par. 119. This change of key influences the conduct of the transition, as shown in par. 121, which carefully review. Also par. 122.

The illustration given in Ex. 52 (Exposition), is continued, as Recapitulation, in the following manner:

Dominant

Subord. Theme *3)

etc. to   *4)   etc. to

*1) The Prin. Theme is presented as before, but embellished. Compare (in the original) with the first version.

*2) At this point, the final phrase of the Prin. Theme diverges from its original course, and is directed toward the prospective dominant (in this case, *B*). The "second act" is much shorter than before, but runs into the Subordinate Theme in the same manner.

*3) The Subord. Theme is *transposed*, as usual, to the principal key. Compare Ex. 52.

*4) The somewhat unusual (remote) modulation, made in the final phrase of the Subord. Theme, in the Exposition, is made again here — to *C* major — and is followed up, as there, with a little change, so that the Recapitulation closes with a complete tonic cadence *in a minor* (instead of *E* major, as was to be expected).

*5) The Coda begins, with an elision of the cadence, in this remote key. It contains five brief sections, all of which (excepting, perhaps, section 3) are derived from the Prin. Theme. Section 2 is patterned after the retransition. The original key, *E* major, is regained at the end of the second section, and maintained to the end, only excepting one brief modulation in section 4.

See the continuation (as Recapitulation) of the examples given at the end of par. 139:

Beethoven, Sonata, op. 10, No. 1, *Adagio.* — Sonata, op. 31, No. 2, *Adagio.* — Pfte. Trio, op. 9, No. 1, *Adagio.* — String-Trio, op. 3, *Adagio.*
See further (the entire movement of each):
Beethoven, Symphony, No. 8, *Allegretto scherzando.*

Schubert, pfte. Sonata, No. 4, op. 122, *Andante molto;* Prin. Theme (*g* minor), group of four phrases, and Codetta; the Subord. Theme (in an unexpected key — *E*-flat major) is a Two-Part form, and closes with a complete tonic cadence in *b*-flat *minor* (instead of the expected *B*-flat major); the retransition is an apparent extension of the foregoing, and covers 7 measures; the Recapitulation closes in *f* minor, and the first section of the Coda is analogous to the retransition; a later section re-states the Codetta to the Prin. Theme, which was omitted in the Recapitulation. Compare par. 185, "Dislocation of the structural factors."

Schubert, pfte. Sonata, No. 7, op. 164, last movement. The modulatory design is irregular, as follows:
Prin. Theme, *a* minor, Two-Part form, dissolved.
Subord. Theme, *D* major, phrase-group, with elaborate Codetta (in *E* major), duplicated.
No retransition, but an abrupt resumption of the Prin. Theme, *transposed to e minor;* (review par. 124).
Subord. Theme, *G* major, as before, — the Codetta in *A* major.
The first section of the Coda is a partial statement of the Prin. Theme (Part I). Comp. par. 181.

Schubert, pfte. Sonata, No. 2, op. 53, *Andante con moto:* Prin. Theme, large Three-Part form; no transition; Subord. Theme, also broad Three-Part form; retransition, nine measures; in the Recapitulation, the *Third Part* of the Prin. Theme is transposed, in direct preparation for the transposition of the Subord. Theme; the first section of the Coda is a partial statement of the principal member of the Prin. Theme.

Schubert, Unfinished Symphony, *b* minor, *Andante con moto:* The Subord. Theme is greatly extended, and closes in the (remote) key of *C* major; the retransition (12 measures) is a very effective expansion of the *E* of this *C* major chord, as *tonic* of the succeeding Prin. Theme (*E* major).

Mozart, Sonata, No. 7 (Schirmer edition), *Adagio;* Retransition, one measure of "bridging" only; no Coda.

Clementi, "Gradus ad Parnassum" (Schirmer's *compl.* edition), No. 35 (orig. ed. No. 11). — No. 19 (orig. ed. 36); the Prin. Theme transposed to the opposite mode, in the Recapitulation. — No. 24 (44).

Mendelssohn, *Presto agitato in b minor* for the pfte. (preceded by an *Andante cantabile* in Three-Part form). An illustration of the breadth which the Sonatina-form may assume, quite irrespective of its diminutive title: A 4-measure Introduction (par. 178) precedes the Prin. Theme; the latter is in Three-Part form, with complete tonic cadence, followed by an independent Transition-phrase, duplicated and dissolved as usual; Subord. Theme (*A* major and *f*-sharp minor), Two-Part form, broad; Codetta I, 18 measures; Codetta II, 8 measures (duplication dissolved); retransition, 4 measures; Recapitulation, a somewhat extended recurrence of the Exposition; the final phrase of the second Codetta is dissolved into the Coda, the first section of which presents the first (brief) member of the Prin. Theme, greatly spun out; the following two sections are brilliant and effective. Analyze carefully.

Mendelssohn, Symphony, No. 3 (*a* minor), *Adagio:* Introduction, 9 measures; Prin. Theme (*A* major), double-period, with Codetta; no transition; Subord. Theme (*a* minor and *E* major), a Two-Part form, the second Part *very similar to the second Period of the Prin. Theme;* the retransition is rather long — fifteen measures — but unmistakably retransitional in character; Recapitulation fairly exact; very brief Coda.

Mendelssohn, Symphony, No. 4 (*A* major), *Andante con moto:* Introduction, 3 measures; Prin. Theme very broad — Three-Part form with all the repetitions, and a Codetta, duplicated and dissolved, as usual; the retransition covers two measures, derived from the Introduction; in the Recapitulation, the Prin. Theme is *intimated only,* by a fragment of its initial Part, *transposed,* but spun out into a transition; the Coda consists chiefly of a statement — effectively extended — of the foregoing Codetta.

Mendelssohn, 'Cello Sonata, No. 2, op. 58, *Allegretto scherzando;* broad, but regular. — The same Sonata (op. 58), last movement: Another example of extreme breadth which the Sonatina-form may assume; the Prin. Th. is preceded by a lengthy Introduction (see par. 178); the Subord. Theme is large Two-Part form, with two fairly long Codettas (letters "F" and "G"); the retransition (letter "H") is 19 measures in length; the Coda (letter "P") is proportionately long.

Such broad dimensions, though somewhat unusual, are by no means incompatible with the Sonatina design. Since the distinction between the latter and the Sonata-allegro form rests solely with the presence or absence of a genuine Development, it follows that the omission of the latter, *alone,* may not prevent the employment of large and important Themes.

Two unusually concise examples, on the other hand:

Beethoven, Sonata, op. 81a, *Andante* ("l'Absence"): Prin. Theme, *c* minor, a group of four phrases (measures 1–14); Subord. Theme (*G* major), an extended phrase (measures 15–20); no retransition; in the Recapitulation, the Prin. Theme, beginning at its *second* phrase, is transposed to *f* minor and other keys (measures 21–30); Subord. Theme (*F* major — measures 31–36); Codetta, six transitional measures, leading into the next movement.

Mendelssohn, *Andante cantabile* in *B*-flat major, pfte.: Introduction, three measures; Prin. Theme, period, dissolved; Subord. Theme, single phrase, meas. 12–16; Codetta, to meas. 20; retransition, two measures; Recapitulation regular; final Codetta, two measures.

Further: **Schubert,** Mass in *A*-flat, *Kyrie:* The Prin. Theme, in 2-Part form, is built upon the text "Kyrie eleison"; the Sub. Theme, a phrase-group with Codetta, on the text "Christe eleison"; the retransition (orchestra alone) is five measures long. — See also, in the same Mass, the *Benedictus*, — very similar.

Brahms, Symphony, No. 4, op. 98, *Andante* (note the interesting treatment of the Recapitulation). — Violin Sonata, No. 3, op. 108, *Adagio* (very concise, but regular). — Horn-Trio, op. 40, first movement.

Intermediate Grade.

141. As the retransitional material, inserted between the Exposition and its Recapitulation, gradually increases in length, and assumes a more individual and important character, the design approaches the larger Sonata-allegro form; for when this intermediate sentence becomes of sufficient weight to create the impression of an independent Division, the form has advanced from the Two-Division to the Three-Division design. Compare par. 132. As long, however, as the insertion (no matter how lengthy it may be) is *clearly only retransitional in character and purpose,* the form is unquestionably Sonatina; compare par. 139.

About the illustrations referred to above,there can be no doubt. But a number of examples will be encountered, whose precise classification may appear difficult — *not because of concise form, or brevity of Themes* (which has little, if anything, to do with the design), but solely in consequence of the indefinite relative significance of the intermediate "Retransition."

All such questionable examples may be legitimately disposed of as "Intermediate Grades" — between Sonatina-form and Sonata-allegro form.

For illustration:

*1) The presence of Codettas is, in itself, an intimation of the larger design in the composer's purpose. This *third* Codetta, is, to be sure, very brief, and might be regarded as a mere extension of the cadence. But it has some thematic importance, and is duplicated at the beginning of the Coda (meas. 21 from the end).

*2) This double-bar is very significant, and, in connection with the marks that call for a repetition of the entire Exposition, it is almost conclusively indicative of the larger, Sonata-Allegro, form. Comp. par. 144.

*3) The intermediate sentence here is eleven measures long (about one-quarter of the length of the Exposition), and begins, at least, with some evidence of independent purpose. It weakens, however, in the fourth measure, and thereafter is obviously nothing but a genuine retransition. The form is, strictly speaking, "Sonatina", but with a decided advance toward the Sonata-allegro design, as indicated by the double-bar, and the decisive conclusion of the Exposition.

See further:

Beethoven, Sonata, op. 49, No. 2, first movement: The Exposition closes with a double-bar (and repetition-marks) in meas. 52; the intermediate section covers fourteen measures, of which only the last four are obviously retransition. This movement, therefore, represents a still more positive advance toward the larger design.

Beethoven, Sonata, op. 109, *Prestissimo:* The Exposition ends in meas. 70, *without* a double-bar; the intermediate section begins at once, with cadence-elision, and is 35 measures long — just one-half the length of the Exposition; it is a fairly elaborate polyphonic (or, at least, imitatory) development of the *bass-part of the first phrase* (Prin. Th.), and is nowhere — not even at the end — of a distinctly retransitional character. Therefore, this movement should be assigned to the Sonata-allegro forms, with some retrogression toward the smaller design.

Beethoven, Sonata, op. 110, first movement, somewhat similar; no double-bar; intermediate section 17 measures long.

Beethoven, Sonata, op. 106, *Adagio:* Very broad; no double-bar; intermediate section 19 measures, of which the last 9 or 10 are distinctly retransitional, — the form is "Sonatina," with some advance toward the Sonata-allegro design.

Mozart, pfte. Sonata, No. 6 (Schirmer ed.), last movement: The Exposition ends with a double-bar; the intermediate section is 30 measures long, and not at all suggestive of retransition; the form is Sonata-allegro, slightly retrogressive. — Also, pfte. Sonata, No. 8 (Schirmer ed.), *Andante,* — Sonatina-form, approaching the larger design.

EXERCISE 10.

A. A number of examples of the *genuine* Sonatina-form, in *slow* tempo, and with *brief* retransition. See N.B. below.

B. Also one or two examples in *rapid* tempo, and broad design — but with genuine retransition.

C. One example, with double-bar at the end of the Exposition, and a *somewhat* independent, but not lengthy, intermediate section.

N.B. As usual, any instrument, or ensemble, may be chosen for these movements: pianoforte; organ; pfte. and Violin, or 'cello; pfte. Trio, or Quartet; String-quartet, or Quintet. See Exercise 7, *A*, "N.B." See par. 168*b*.

CHAPTER XI.

THE SONATA-ALLEGRO FORM.

142. This term must not be confounded with "Sonata." It refers to a structural *design*, and not to the conventional compound form of composition bearing the titles Sonata, Symphony, Duo, Trio, etc. (par. 199).

It is the design most commonly applied to the first (*allegro*) movement of the Sonata, hence the term: Form of the Sonata-allegro, or "Sonata-allegro form." The term "Sonata-form" is misleading, and should not be used. Further, the title does not imply that it is used *only* for the Sonata-allegro movement: It may be applied to any style of composition in the larger form, and to any *tempo* (or "movement").

The diagram of the Sonata-allegro form is as follows:

:	Exposition			:	Development	Recapitulation				Coda
	Prin. Th.	*Subord. Th.*	*Co-detta.*		Sectional form	*Prin. Th.*	*Sub. Th.*	*Co-detta*		*Coda*
	Any Part-form	Related key	One or more			As before	**Transposed**			
							(to principal key)			
	Transition				*Retransition*	*Transition* (modified)				

(Compare this diagram with that of the Third Rondo form, par. 110, and note both the similarity and the difference.)

143. Note that the Sonata-allegro form, like the Third Rondo form, is another, and the most refined, manifestation of the tripartite structural principle. Compare par. 111. It is the most eminent and artistic grade of the Three-Part form.

144. The double-bar, at the end of the Exposition, is characteristic of the Sonata-allegro form, and is rarely omitted. Its original purpose — to mark the customary repetition of the Exposition — is no longer recognized, inasmuch as this repetition, in the modern Sonata and Symphony, is considered needless, and is not often insisted upon. But the double-bar has a deeper significance: It reinforces the impression of a fully completed union of the two Themes, thus confirming the object of the Exposition; hence the almost invariable addition of one or more Codettas to the Subord. Theme, as these serve to strengthen the impression of finality. And this impression must be assured, even when the repetition, and the double-bar itself, are omitted.

THE EXPOSITION.

145. Review paragraphs 135–137.

The Principal Theme must be sufficiently striking and attractive to challenge attention and excite interest. It may be in any style of melodic and rhythmic conception, and may reflect any emotional mood; may be tragic or gay, rapid or deliberate, lyric or dramatic. But it *must* be significant and worthy of development, no matter how simple in character.

Its form is optional, and will be determined chiefly by its normal proportion to the proposed extent of the movement. The most effective is probably the *Two-Part* form, as this is less complete within itself than the Three-Part.

The first presentation of the Prin. Theme should be as straightforward and unaffected as possible. Its elaboration and development come *later*, as ruling purpose of the whole movement.   See par. 197, 1 to 6.

See **Schubert**, Unfinished Symphony; note the simplicity in the announcement of the Prin. Theme. — **Beethoven**, Ninth Symphony, Prin. Theme of the first movement.   Also other Symphonies of **Beethoven**. — **Brahms**, Second Symphony, Prin. Theme of the first and last movements.   Also Prin. Theme of the First Symphony, last movement.   These are all models of clearness.

146. The transition into the Subordinate Theme may be effected in the usual manner:

1. Through an independent Transition-phrase (which may be decidedly individual; may possess genuine thematic importance; and may be "spun out," through its two "acts," to considerable length). Or,

2. By dissolution of the final phrase of the Prin. Theme.

147. The Subordinate Theme is placed in some other key, usually the closely related dominant or relative of the original key — though other, even remote, keys are possible.   The key to be *avoided* for the Subord. Theme is the *subdominant*.

In rhythmic character, and mood, it should contrast effectively with its companion-Theme.   The form is optional, but is usually smaller (shorter) than that of the Prin. Theme.   (Review par. 84 and Ex. 45.)

148. As implied, the addition of a Codetta is almost imperative, and not infrequently two, three, and even more, Codettas follow the Subord. Theme, generally decreasing successively in length.

The (first) Codetta usually presents a marked contrast, in rhythm and style, to both Themes, and may be *thematically significant;* though it should not create the impression of a *genuine Theme* (wherefore the epithet "closing Theme" is not consistent).   The contents may be wholly new, or may be derived (more or less directly) from the Prin. Theme — or from any foregoing factor.

Each Codetta is, as a rule, duplicated; often with considerable modification and *extension*.   An illustration of Exposition will be found in Ex. 55.

(The student should, and probably will, perceive that every detail in the formation of the Exposition is so consistent, logical, and natural, as to be *self-evident*, and compel unquestioned adoption as the surest and simplest means of securing a truly *effective* presentation of this broad thematic material.   But above all things he must bear in mind that *unlimited freedom is left to the imagination, in the execution of this design.* No two among a million Expositions need be alike, though all follow the fundamental lines of the design with the same strictness.)

149. The end of the Exposition is usually indicated by the double-bar. Review par. 144. The various methods of treating this "ending" may be classified as follows:

a. The Exposition may close with a complete and emphatic tonic cadence, followed by the double-bar, and marks of repetition.

See **Beethoven**, Sonata, op. 2, No. 1, first movement. — Sonata, op. 7, first movement; op. 10, No. 1, first movement; op. 14, No. 2, first movement.

b. The double-bar may be attended by two endings, because of some slight change in the rhythmic condition upon proceeding into the Development.

Beethoven, Sonata, op. 2, No. 3, first movement; op. 10, No. 2, first movement; op. 2, No. 2, first movement.

Or the two endings may indicate a (perhaps slight) harmonic change, involved by the repetition, — as in **Beethoven**, Sonata, op. 13, first movement; and op. 2, No. 1, last movement.

c. Or, of the two endings, the first may be a brief "retransition" back to the beginning (for the repetition), and the second ending a similar "transition" into the first section of the Development.

Beethoven, Sonata, op. 31, No. 2, first movement; Sonata, op. 31, No. 3, *Scherzo* (four measures before the double-bar — see Ex. 55); see also the last movement, four measures before the double-bar. Also op. 27, No. 2, last movement, two measures before the double-bar; op. 28, first movement, four measures before the double-bar.

d. The final phrase of the Exposition may be dissolved, and led — without double ending — first back to the beginning (for the repetition), and then over into the Development. This is practically the same as *c.*

Beethoven, Sonata, op. 10, No. 3, first movement; op. 14, No. 1, first movement; op. 31, No. 2, last movement; op. 31, No. 3, first movement; op. 53, first movement; op. 57, last movement.

e. More rarely, the repetition is omitted, and, in that case, the double-bar may not (usually does not) appear.

Beethoven, Sonata, op. 10, No. 3, *Largo* — light double-bar (measure 29) but no repetition. — Sonata, op. 22, *Adagio;* the Exposition ends in measure 30, without the double-bar, and is followed in meas. 31 by the Development. (The first *light* double-bar, in meas. 12, indicates the end of Part I of the Prin. Theme.) — Sonata, op. 57, first movement; the Exposition ends in measure six before the change of signature (from four flats to the "natural"). — Op. 90, first movement; the Exposition closes, without double-bar, in measure 81. — Symphony, No. II, *Larghetto;* no double-bar.

THE DEVELOPMENT.

150. The middle Division of the Sonata-allegro form is called a "development," because it is devoted to the free manipulation of the various thematic members of the Exposition, with a view to the more complete unfolding (or developing) of their resources. And, since this is the chief aim, all restraint which might hamper the most effective presentation and combination of the foregoing thematic material, is removed; the Development is *free*, in every sense, — not subject to any of the structural conditions which govern the Exposition. Neither the choice of material, the order of presentation, the method of treatment (homophonic or polyphonic), nor the extent of each successive process, — none of these matters are prescribed, but rest solely with the judgment of the composer.

It is in this very respect that the Development constitutes a very necessary and emphatic contrast with the foregoing Exposition and the succeeding Recapitulation. While the Exposition demands some degree of control and regulation, the Development calls forth the untrammeled *imagination and ingenuity* of the writer. The Exposition is the more or less sober and judicious (*not* lifeless or unimpassioned) "presentation" of the various factors; the Development is their illumination and vitalization, their shifting into more interesting positions, in relation to each other and to the whole.

151. *a.* The form of a Development is always *sectional*. (Review par. 55*b*, with reference to the definition of sectional form.)

b. The number of sections is optional.

c. The extent, contents, and style of each section, are also optional. In other words, any section of the Development may derive its material from the Prin. Theme, from the Subord. Theme — from any melodic member of either Theme, — from the transition, or from the Codettas. The only conditions are, that no Theme should appear in its *complete* form; and that *no member should appear in the same key as before* (i.e., as in the Exposition). To this natural rule there are but very few legitimate exceptions. (Comp. par. 162.) It emphasizes the important general principle that the Development, as a whole, *should avoid the original key* — since the latter is the proper domain of the Recapitulation (and of the Coda, to some extent).

d. Further, one or another of the sections may be partly, or even decidedly, new. This, though somewhat less usual, is thoroughly consistent with the purpose of the Development, especially when the new members are analogous, or used in connection and combination with the essential ones.

e. The sections are frequently grouped in pairs — as duplication (especially as *sequence*).

f. A section is not likely to have a complete cadence, because it would arrest the very vital *urgent* quality of the Development. A light semicadence is all that marks the end of a section, as a rule; and even that is not necessary, for a change of style, or exchange of thematic material, sufficiently indicates where a new section begins. In other words, the extent of a section is defined by the retention of the *same style*, or the *same contents*.

152. The ultimate aim of the Development is to regain the original key and prepare for the Recapitulation. Therefore, its final section (possibly more than one) is equivalent to the usual retransition, or to the "second act" of that process.

153. The best, and possibly the only, way to master the unique problem of effective Development is to examine, minutely, the methods adopted by the great masters of composition. Therefore, close scrutiny of the following illustrations (in which every one of the above details will be verified) is extremely important.

Compare the following example, from **Beethoven's** Sonata, op. 31, No. 3, *Scherzo*, with the original:

*1) The Prin. Theme is a regular Three-Part Song-form.

*2) The Transition-phrase is borrowed directly from the Second Part of the Prin. Theme, and suggests the intention of repeating Parts II and III (as is legitimate, and not uncommon. *Homophonic Forms*, par. 105a). See par. 125.

*3) The Subord. Theme *begins* in an unexpected key (the remote *F* major), but passes over into the usual dominant (*E*-flat major) in the 3d Phrase. It, also, is based upon foregoing material: The lower part (left hand) is derived from the Second Part, and the upper from the bass, of the Prin. Theme.

*4) There are two Codettas, respectively two measures, and one measure, in length, closely analogous to the foregoing thematic members, and each duplicated.

*5) The treatment of the ending of the Exposition corroborates the method explained in par. 149c, which see.

*6) The Development embraces five sections of various lengths (fairly brief), the thematic relations of which to the members of the Exposition are clearly demonstrated: Section I, derived from the Prin. Theme, very directly, *but placed in a different key* (see par. 150c); Section II, from the Subord. Theme; Section III, again from the Prin. Theme; Section IV, from the last measure of Part Two (Prin. Theme).

*7) Section IV was conducted to the prospective dominant, and it therefore executed the "first act" of retransition. Section V is the "second act" (all upon this dominant), and represents what is usually called the "retransition" proper.

See the following, also, and note that each of these Developments must be studied *with close reference to its foregoing Exposition,* in order to be of full benefit:

Beethoven, Sonata, op. 2, No. 1, first movement: The Development, after the double-bar, contains six sections; Section I, 7 measures, is derived from the Prin. Theme; Sec. II, 8 measures, from the Subord. Theme; Sec. III, 10 measures, is a sequence of section II, extended; Sec. IV, 8 measures, grows out of section III, and leads to the prospective dominant; Sec. V, 12 measures, is the retransition proper, but is interrupted and followed by a sixth section (7 measures), which is another phase of the "second act," derived from the second measure of the Prin. Theme.

Sonata, op. 2, No. 3, first movement: Sec. I of the Development, 6 measures, is derived from the last Codetta but one; Sec. II, 12 measures, bears close relation to the Second Part of the Prin. Theme, but is a practically new passage, in brilliant broken chords; Sec. III, 4 measures, is a re-statement of the first phrase of the Prin. Theme, in a different key, of course; Sec. IV, 17 measures, is a novel treatment of the first two measures of the Prin. Theme, and is spun out by two *sequences,* the last one extended, and led to the prospective dominant; Sec. V, 9 measures, is the retransition, based upon the initial figures of the Prin. Theme.

Sonata, op. 22, first movement: Sec. I of the Development, 2 measures, corresponds to the last (fourth) Codetta; Sec. II, 4 measures, corresponds to the third Codetta; Sec. III, 7 measures, to the second Codetta. These sections, it will be seen, proceed systematically *backward* from the double-bar. Sec. IV, 10 measures, reverts to the third and fourth Codettas, and is a *sequential* group of phrases. Such sequential formation is a natural and effective device for the Development, for evident reasons. Sec. V, 13 measures, grows out of the preceding one, and is a stirring passage in harmonic figuration; note the progression of the lowermost (bass) part. Sec. VI, 15 measures, is the retransition, all upon the dominant.

Sonata, op. 53, first movement: Sec. I of the Development, 4 measures, grows sequentially out of the last member of the Codetta; Sec. II, 6 measures, re-states the first phrase of the Prin. Theme, in a different key, and extends it; Sec. III, 8 measures, follows up this extension; Sec. IV, 9 measures, is a modified manipulation of the same thematic member; Sec. V, 30 measures, is a long, *sequential,* presentation of the initial phrase of Part Two of the Subord. Theme; note the modulatory design, and the manner in which its last seven measures relax into, and upon, the prospective dominant; Sec. VI, 13 measures, is the retransition, based upon the fourth measure of the Prin. Theme.

Sonata, op. 90, first movement: The conventional double-bar is omitted; the Exposition closes with measure 81; the first section of the Development is an "interlude" of three measures, echoing the foregoing cadence; Sec. II, 7 measures, is derived directly from the first phrase of the Prin. Theme; Sec. III, 9 measures, is based upon the 3rd measure (indirectly upon measures 21–22) of the Prin. Theme — note the bass-progression; Sec. IV, 9 measures, maintains the same rhythm, but is otherwise *new;* it has the "leading" quality of a transition, as dominant, into the next section; Sec. V, 20 measures, is a sequential (or imitatory) presentation of the third phrase of the Prin. Theme, and its final extension leads to the prospective dominant; Sec. VI, 14 measures, is the retransition; it utilizes the dominant in bass, but as *tonic six-four chord*, throughout — thus exemplifying the curious irregularity of leading to the following Theme through its *tonic.* Compare par. 76c. This final section is a singularly ingenious manipulation of the first measure of the Prin. Theme, *into which* the whole unique process finally merges.

Beethoven, Symphony, No. 4, first movement: The Prin. Theme begins, after an independent Introduction, in measure 43. The first section of the Development (immediately after the double-bar) is a two-measure extension of the final Codetta; Sec. II, 16 measures, is derived from the initial measure of the Prin. Theme; Sec. III, 14 measures, continues this figure as bass, against the preliminary notes (16ths) which occur at the very beginning of the Prin. Theme; Sec. IV, 24 measures, combines the first 4-meas. phrase of the Prin. Theme with a new melodic (contrapuntal) member — imitatory; Sec. V, 40 measures, is a long, climactic, presentation of the first measure of the Prin. Theme, in sequential succession; Sec. VI, 8 measures, is the beginning of the retransition; it is patterned after the final measure of the independent Introduction to this movement; note that the *a*-sharp is the enharmonic equivalent of the tonic, *b*-flat; its appearance here is an actual premonition of the coming Theme, which, here again, is entered through its *tonic;* Sec. VII, 16 measures, is derived from the second phrase of the Prin. Theme; Sec. VIII, 32 measures, is patterned after the third section, but with more pointed employment of the "preliminary tones."

Schumann, pfte. Sonata, No. 2, op. 22, first movement: The first section of the Development, 29 measures, is a new melodic member, but closely allied to the foregoing; its presentation is sequential; Sec. II, 16 measures, is also new, though related in character to the Subord. Theme, — also sequential; Sec. III, 11 measures, grows out of the preceding; Sec. IV, 16 measures, reverts to the initial member of the Prin. Theme, — also sequential, and similar in rhythmic treatment to all the preceding sections; Sec. V, 8 measures, is a fairly exact presentation of the first phrase of the Prin. Theme, in a different key; Sec. VI, 18 measures, is also based upon the first phrase (beginning in misleading proximity to the principal key), — also sequential, and led to the prospective dominant, as tonic six-four chord; Sec. VII, 6 measures, is the retransition proper.

Mendelssohn, Symphony, No. 3, *a* minor, first movement (*Allegro un poco agitato*): The first section of the Development, 29 measures, grows out of the final (cadence) member of the Exposition, gradually quickened, and with interspersed fragments of the second measure of the Prin. Theme; Sec. II, 25 measures, is based upon the first phrase of the Subord. Theme, in sequential (or imitatory) presentation; Sec. III, 14 measures, grows out of section II; Sec. IV, 17 measures, is derived from the Second Part of the Prin. Theme; Sec. V, 8 measures, is a nearly exact recurrence of the first phrase of the Codetta; Sec. VI, 13 measures, emerges out of the preceding section; Sec. VII, 19 measures, is the retransition proper.

Brahms, Violoncello Sonata, No. 1, op. 38, first movement: The first section of the Development, 16 measures (beginning one measure after the double-bar), is derived from the first member of the Prin. Theme — compare minutely with the Ex-

position; Sec. II, 7 measures, is a more animated manipulation of the same thematic member; Sec. III, 12 measures, a still more passionate presentation, limited
to the second measure of the Prin. Theme; Sec. IV, 8 measures, a dramatic recurrence
of the first period of the Subord. Theme, in a remote key; Sec. V, 8 measures, is a
duplication of the same period, with complete change of character; Sec. VI, 3 measures, grows out of the last measure of the preceding, with accelerated rhythmic accompaniment, leading to the prospective dominant; Sec. VII, 17 measures, is the
retransition proper, for which the Codetta is utilized.   Nothing could be more
artistic, masterly, and thoroughly effective than this Development, with its admirable
continuity, its thematic unity, and its vivid sequence of "moods," or phases of normal
and vigorous emotional life.   Its careful study will prove extremely instructive to
the observant student.

Glazounow, pfte. Sonata, No. 2, op. 75, first movement: There is no "double-
bar" at the end of the Exposition; at the change of signature from one sharp to five
sharps, the second Codetta is duplicated; the Development follows this, in meas. 7
from the change of signature;   Section I, 17 measures (to next change of signature),
is based upon the first 4-measure phrase of the Prin. Theme, in a sort of diminution,
and canonic, — later spun out melodically; Sec. II, 8 measures, refers to the second
4-meas. phrase of the Prin. Theme; Sec. III, 12 measures (to next change of signature), is derived, ingeniously, from the chief thematic member of the Prin. Theme;
Sec. IV, 24 measures, is a continuation and lengthy extension of the preceding section;
Sec. V, 19 measures (to new signature — 2 sharps), resembles the first section, but
is more elaborate; Sec. VI, 12 measures (to one-sharp signature), is the retransition,
shifting from the basstone *A* to the basstone *C*, which is utilized (as "second act")
as 6th scale-step of the prin. key (*e* minor) — see par. 76*a*.

Schubert, pfte. Sonata, No. 5, op. 143, first movement: Section I of the Development, 10 measures, is derived from the first and second periods of the Prin. Theme;
Sec. II, 13 measures, is a combination of the first and third periods; Sec. III, 14
measures, the same material, with different treatment; Sec. IV, 17 measures, utilizes
the same rhythmic figure, in conjunction with the Subord. Theme; Sec. V, 8 measures,
is the retransition.

Schubert, pfte. Trio, No. 1, op. 99, first movement: Section I of the Development,
8 measures, closely resembles the Prin. Theme (in the opposite mode of the original
key); Sec. II, 19 measures (including a sequential duplication), is similar, but more
elaborate, and extended; Sec. III, 16 measures (sequential duplication), is based
upon the Subord. Theme, with the chief rhythmic motive of the Prin. Theme; Sec.
IV, 14 measures (sequential duplication) is similar, but more elaborate and vigorous;
Sec. V, 6 measures, utilizes the first member of the Subord. Theme, in diminution;
Sec. VI, 12 measures, is derived from the Codetta; Sec. VII, the retransition, is
24 measures long (including sequential duplication), and directly anticipates (*in
other keys*) the first period of the following Prin. Theme. Note the modulatory
design of the whole Development.

THE RECAPITULATION.

154. Review par. 140.

In the Sonata-allegro form, the Recapitulation may be simple and fairly exact, but it is not unlikely to be somewhat more elaborately modified than in the Sonatina-form. In compositions of unusual breadth, and especially where the Exposition is lengthy, it is not uncommon to abbreviate the *Prin. Theme.* As usual, the transition is modified, in view of the transposed location of the Subord. Theme. As a rule, the conduct of the Recapitulation — once the Subord. Theme is reached — follows the lines of the Exposition closely, without much modification or abbreviation, through the Codetta or Codettas, which here become the threshold of the Coda.

Compare the following Recapitulation, from **Beethoven's** Sonata, op. 31, No. 3, *Scherzo,* with the original. See Ex. 55:

*1) Parts I and II of the Prin. Theme are stated *exactly* as in the Exposition; the Third Part, here, is slightly modified — compare the original.

*2) The transition is also exactly as before, entirely without regard to the coming transposition of the Subord. Theme.

*3) The shift of key is made abruptly; Phrase 1 of the Subord. Theme is, at first, one step higher than in the Exposition, but its conduct is so modified as to lead to the proper key at the beginning of the second phrase — which, in other words, is a *fifth lower* (or fourth higher) than before.

*4) The third phrase, and both Codettas, are reproduced precisely as before, but in the *principal key*.

*5) The Coda is very brief — one section only — and consists mainly in the extension of the final Codetta.

The student should continue the analysis of every movement given in par. 153, carefully comparing the Recapitulation, in each case, with the Exposition. Such analysis is of the utmost value, and should be pursued thoroughly, persistently and patiently. No further directions are required. The student must have so trained his faculty of *observation*, by this time, as to recognize and follow without effort every impulse — mental and emotional — of the composer.

THE CODA.

155. The Coda, in a Sonata-allegro form, does not differ from that of the foregoing larger forms, as a rule. But it sometimes assumes greater significance, and may be somewhat more elaborate, than in the Rondos or Sonatina-form. Its purposes are: To round off the form, by taking up any loose thematic ends that may seem to be unfinished; to establish more perfect balance in the proportions of the Divisions; possibly — though rarely — to create an additional climax, or to provide a brilliant finish. Its most natural and general artistic object is, however, to converge the whole design into the *tonic*, and to establish and confirm the latter, as ultimate aim; hence the very common, and usually very marked, inclination into the *subdominant* keys. Review, carefully, par. 93.

In **Beethoven,** Sonata, op. 22, first movement, the Coda is omitted altogether, the Recapitulation closing exactly as the Exposition does. — Sonata, op. 2, No. 2, first movement, the same. — Sonata, op. 2, No. 1, first movement; the Coda (last six measures) is an extension of the final Codetta. — Sonata, op. 10, No. 1, first movement; the "Coda" (last two measures) is nothing more than two vigorous cadence-chords, added to the final Codetta. — Sonata, op. 14, No. 2, first movement; the Coda (last 13 measures), one phrase, duplicated and extended, is a parting glance at the Prin. Theme, with positive subdominant infusion (quasi "plagal" in general effect). — Sonata, op. 27, No. 2, last movement; the Coda (last 43 measures) is typical; it reviews, in a very masterly manner, the contrasting emotional phases of the preceding Divisions, and emphasizes them with additional brief but powerful climaxes. — Sonata, op. 31, No. 1, first movement; the Coda (last 46 measures) is derived wholly from the principal thematic member; it begins like the Development, and in the same key, but is, as a whole, nothing more than an exposition of the dominant and tonic chords — the elements of the perfect cadence. — Sonata, op. 31, No. 2, first movement; the "Coda" (last 10 measures) is merely an expansion of the final tonic chord. — Sonata, op. 7, first movement; the Coda (last 50 measures) contains four sections, which utilize, successively, the Subord. Theme, the last Codetta, and the first member of the Prin. Theme. — Sonata, op. 10, No. 3, first movement; there are six brief sections in the Coda (last 50 measures); Section I is an extension of the last Codetta but one, down into the subdominant key; Sections II and III follow the design of the final Codetta; Section IV grows out of the preceding; Sec. V refers to the thematic motive of the Prin. Theme; Sec. VI is similar, but new in treatment.

156. It is possible for the Coda, with its entire freedom from structural constraint, to assume the proportions and the character of a *"Second Development,"* — following, perhaps, the conduct of the foregoing Development proper, more or less closely. This is particularly likely to happen in very broad Sonata-allegro forms (chamber-music, and symphonies).

See **Beethoven**, Sonata, op. 81*A*, first *Allegro:* The Coda (last 98 measures) embraces five sections; the first one (23 measures), which *begins* similar to the Development, is a frank re-statement of the first period of the Prin. Theme, in related keys, extended; the remaining sections are four different (quasi polyphonic) manipulations of the basic motive which appears in the Introduction (compare par. 166). — Sonata, op. 53, first movement; the Coda covers the last 57 measures, and contains five well-marked sections; it begins like the Development, and maintains the "development" character persistently; Section IV is a distinct statement of the Subord. Theme. — Violin Sonata, op. 30, No. 2, first movement; the Exposition closes in measure 74 (75) — *without* double-bar; the first section of the Development is ostensibly an additional Codetta, which is extended and "developed," in the most genuine fashion; the Coda (last 47 measures) begins in precisely the same manner, and, as a whole, is in close analogy to the Development. — Violin Sonata, op. 23, first movement: The Development and Recapitulation are *repeated together*, after which there is a brief Coda, patterned after the Development. — Violin Sonata, op. 12, No. 2, first movement.

In **Beethoven**, Symphonies II (last movement), V (last movement), VII (last movement), VIII (first movement), — and other of **Beethoven's** larger movements, this relation of the Coda to the Development, either in actual material or in treatment, is still more evident, and intentional.

The following examples of the Sonata-allegro form are to be analyzed very thoroughly. Some of them have been already cited, and partly analyzed. A few trifling irregularities will be found, but they are easily recognized and accounted for; and the infinite diversity of treatment, dictated by the character of the Themes, but strictly within the broad requirements of the form, will prove both instructive and stimulating to the observant student:

Mozart, pfte. Sonata, No. 12 (Schirmer edition), first movement. — Sonata, No. 16, first movement. — Sonata, No. 17, *Andante.* — Symphony in C major ("Jupiter"), first movement (second Codetta new; brief Coda). — Same Symphony, last movement; largely polyphonic; the Coda is a "Second Development"; its second section is a quintuple-fugue exposition, the five subjects of which are derived from the Exposition as follows: I, from the Prin. Theme; II, from the transition; III, from the same, modified; IV, from the "second act" of the transition; V, from the Subord. Theme (*Applied Counterpoint,* Ex. 182).

Schubert, pfte. Sonata, No. 1, first movement. — Sonata, No. 3, op. 120, first movement, (the Development and Recapitulation are *repeated together*, after which a brief Coda follows). — Sonata, No. 5, first movement. — Sonata, No. 10, first movement (ingenious retransition). — Symphony in b minor ("Unfinished"), first movement. — Pfte. Trio, No. 2, op. 100, first movement (very broad; seven Codettas). — Fantasia in G, op. 78, first movement (typical).

Mendelssohn, pfte. Sonata, op. 6, first movement. — Symphony No. 3, *a* minor, second movement. — Violoncello Sonata, No. 1, op. 45, first movement (very broad). — Pfte. Trio, No. 1, op. 49, first movement (very broad; no double-bar; Subord. Theme more prevalent than the Prin. Theme; the Coda contains a new, but related, section — *assai animato*).

Schumann, Toccata, op. 7 (chiefly group-formations, but well-defined Themes; Recapitulation abbreviated; long Coda). — Sonata, op. 14, first movement (no double-bar; the Coda is a genuine "second Development," — practically a re-statement of the Development proper). — Sonata, op. 22, first movement. — Symphony, No. 1, op. 38, first movement, *Allegro molto vivace* (concise Exposition; Development sequential; the Prin. Theme, in the Recapitulation, is introduced through the *tonic*, instead of the dominant, and is presented in augmentation; the Coda contains a wholly new section).

Beethoven, Sonata, op. 2, No. 2, first movement (no Coda). — Sonata, op. 10, No. 1, first movement, (in the Recapitulation, the Subord. Theme is first partly transposed, and then completely re-stated in the original key). — Sonata, op. 10, No. 3, first movement. — Sonata, Op. 22, *Adagio* (small Subord. Theme; no Coda). — Sonata, op. 28, first movement. — Sonata, op. 31, No. 2, first movement. — Same Sonata, last movement (the Coda contains, as second section, the entire Prin. Theme). — Sonata, op. 31, No. 3, first movement (quaint retransition). — Sonata, op. 57, first and last movements. — Sonata, op. 78, first movement (concise). — Sonata, op. 106, first movement (very broad). — Violin Sonata, op. 12, No. 1, first movement. — Violin Sonata, op. 12, No. 3, first movement. — Violin Sonata, op. 24, **first**

movement. — Violin Sonata, op. 47, first movement, *Presto* (broad). — String-quartet, op. 18, No. 1, first movement. — String-quartet, op. 59, No. 1, *Adagio molto* (no double-bar; the Coda re-states the Prin. Theme, and is then dissolved, as transition into the next movement). — Symphony, No. I, op. 21, first movement, *Allegro con brio.* — Symphony, No. III, op. 55, first movement (very broad; the long Development presents, in its later course, a new period, which reappears in the Coda). — Symphony, No. V, first movement. — Symphony, No. VIII, first movement (the Subord. Theme, both times, begins in an unusual key and is then stated in the proper key).

Brahms, pfte. Sonata, op. 1, first movement. — Sonata, op. 2, first movement. — Sonata, op. 5, first movement. — Nothing could be more illuminating and inspiring to the serious student of classic form than the larger works of **Brahms;** therefore the most thorough analysis of the following movements is urged (in each case the *first movement*, unless otherwise noted): Violin Sonatas, op. 78; op. 100; op. 108; first movement of each. — Violoncello Sonatas, op. 38; op. 99. — String-Quartets, op. 51, Nos. 1 and 2; op. 67. — String-Quintet, op. 88. — String-Sextets, op. 18; op. 36. — Pfte. Trio, No. III, op. 87. — Pfte. Quartet, No. 2, op. 26.

Dvořák, Symphony, "The New World," first and last movements.

Rubinstein, "Ocean" Symphony, first movement.

Raff, Symphony, *Im Walde,* first movement (in the Exposition, the Subord. Theme is in the subdominant key; in the Recapitulation, in the dominant key — both singularly irregular).

Glazounow, pfte. Sonata, No. 2, op. 75, first movement. Also the last movement; (at the beginning of the Recapitulation, the Prin. Theme is announced as fugue-subject, and treated accordingly). — Also Sonata, No. 1, op. 74, first movement (regular and very clear).

Maurice Ravel, "Sonatina" in *f*-sharp minor; first and last movements.

Paul Dukas, pfte. Sonata in *e*-flat minor; first and second movements (regular, and clear).

Josef Suk, Suita, op. 21, first movement.

Mac Dowell, "Tragic" Sonata for pfte., op. 45, first movement (with Independent Introduction, — par. 178).

EXERCISE II.

A large number of examples of the ordinary, regular, Sonata-allegro form; chiefly *allegro tempo,* but also occasional experiments with *Andante* or even *Adagio;* any style may be chosen; and, as usual, the movement may be conceived for any instrument, or ensemble of instruments. See par. 197, 1 to 7. *And par. 168b.*

CHAPTER XII.

MINIATURE SONATA-ALLEGRO, AS EXPANDED THREE-PART SONG-FORM.

157. In the foregoing chapters, the course of structural evolution was traced in progressive stages from the Song with Trio, through the three successive Rondos and the Sonatina-form, up to the most perfect design — the Sonata-allegro form.

But this course converges with another, and much more direct, line of evolution — from the *Three-Part Song-Form* itself. For the Three-Part Song-form is the exact prototype of the Sonata-allegro form, and the latter emerges out of the former through the natural and direct process of growth, or general enlargement. For this reason, this derivation of the Sonata-allegro form would appear to be the more normal, although the longer line of development is historically quite as real, and has supplied the composer with the variety of intermediate designs.

158. The correspondence of the smallest and largest genuine tripartite forms is illustrated by the following diagram:

Three-Part Song-form.

Part I	*Part II*	*Part III*
Statement	Departure (Return)	Recurrence
Period-form (Two *phrases*)	Period, or Group-form	Period (Codetta)

Sonata-allegro form.

Exposition	*Development*	*Recapitulation*
Statement	Departure (Return)	Re-statement
Two *Themes*	Sectional form	Two Themes (Coda)

The evidence of growth is exhibited in the disposition to separate and expand the two *phrases* of the First Part into the two entire *Themes* of the Exposition.   Hence, *any sign of a division of the original unbroken First Part into more than one structural factor* indicates the vital budding process which is nature's method of advancing growth.

159. The incipient condition of this advance is seen in those examples of the Three-Part Song-form in which Part I is extended by the addition of a Codetta (which, though never so homogeneous and tiny, does represent a somewhat independent structural factor).

See, first, **Mendelssohn,** Song without Words, No. 7, which is a genuine 3-Part Song-form, without the slightest hint of a separation of the members of the First Part, but which has the typical double-bar, and repetitions.

Then, **Mendelssohn,** Song without Words, No. 39, in which several fairly distinct signs of separation are evident: in measure 7, a symptom of "dissolution"; in measure 9, the advent of a somewhat independent Consequent phrase in a *related key* (the prototype of the Subord. Theme); and, in measure 13, a brief Codetta, duplicated as usual.   This contains, in reality, no more thematic material than a Song-form is entitled to, but it is surely headed in the direction of the Sonata-allegro form.   Note that, in the Third Part, the Consequent phrase is *transposed* to the principal key.

Further: **Beethoven,** Sonata, op. 7, third movement — very similar to the preceding. **Mozart,** Sonata, No. 9 (Schirmer ed.), *Menuetto* (without the Trio).   A decided advance is exhibited in **Beethoven,** Sonata, op. 10, No. 2, last movement: measures 15–23 represent an incipient Subord. Theme; and the following Codetta (to measure 32) is a distinctly marked thematic factor.   In the Third Part, only the Codetta reappears, but *transposed,* and considerably extended (as Coda).   This is still within the domain of the Three-Part Song-form, but is "overgrown."   The line of demarcation is passed in **Beethoven,** Sonata, op. 101, first movement, which is a **Minature Sonata-allegro form :**

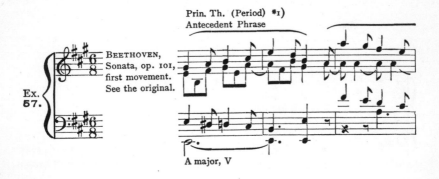

Prin. Th. (Period) *1)
Antecedent Phrase

BEETHOVEN,
Sonata, op. 101,
first movement.
See the original.

Ex. 57.

A major, V

*1) The Principal Theme begins with the *dominant* harmony, and is concise — only a period, including the transition.   The Subordinate Theme (in the dominant key) is longer; probably a Two-Part form, or, at least, a group of three well-defined phrases, the last one (Part II) considerably extended.

*2) There is no double-bar, but the ending of the Exposition is unmistakable. The Development is 20 measures in length, divided into two sections.

*3) In the Recapitulation, the Prin. Theme begins in the opposite mode (*a* minor) and is contracted to a 6-measure period.

*4) From here on, the Subord. Theme and Codetta (*transposed*) are reproduced almost exactly as before, after which a Coda of 18 measures is added. Compare with the original; and compare the whole movement with the diagram in par. 158. This movement might be regarded as a Three-Part Song-form, but its expansion and development into a broader and higher structural purpose cannot fail to be recognized.

See, further:

Beethoven, Sonata, op. 79, first movement; similar, but more obviously Miniature Sonata-allegro form. — Sonata, op. 49, No. 1, first movement (concise Sonata-allegro). — Sonata, op. 2, No. 1, first movement — decidedly Sonata-allegro form, but concise.

Schubert, pfte. Sonata, No. 3, op. 120, *Andante* (Miniature Sonata-allegro form).

Mozart, pfte. Sonata, No. 5 (Schirmer ed.), *Andante;* and No. 6, *Adagio.*

Mendelssohn, Praeludium, op. 104, No. 3. — *Presto agitato* in g minor (concise Sonata-allegro form).

The repetition of the Development and Recapitulation together (as in **Beethoven,** Sonata, op. 10, No. 2, last movement; **Schubert,** Sonata, No. 3, first movement; and a few other of the above movements) is in keeping with the usual repetition of the Second and Third Parts together, in the 3-Part Song-form (see **Beethoven,** the Minuet-movements of the Sonatas).

160. As has been repeatedly shown, it is not dimension, but *individuality of character,* and completeness, even in narrow limits, that define a "Theme." Therefore the sentence may be brief and concise, and still represent a genuine Theme. This is touched upon in par. 85, which review; and is demonstrated in some of the examples for reference at the end of par. 140 (**Beethoven,** Sonata, op. 81*A, Andante;* Sonata, op. 109, first movement).

161. In its "unfolding," the 3-Part Song-form may pursue another course of growth, and become a First Rondo form. This, however, is far less normal and genuine, and must be regarded as an aberration, not to be encouraged, and easy to distinguish from the legitimate process of evolution. See, again, par. 85, and the references there given.

***

NOTEWORTHY VARIETIES OF THE SONATA-ALLEGRO FORM.

162. In some cases, notably in the Sonata-allegro forms of **Brahms,** the Development begins with a marked statement of the Prin. Theme, *in the original key,* and nearly, or exactly, as at the beginning. (Comp.

par. 150 *c.*) This arouses an impression of the Rondo form, or of the Sonatina-form, especially when (as is not uncommon) the double-bar is omitted. But it is always *limited to the first phrase or period* of the Prin. Theme, and soon identifies itself as the *first Section of the Development.* It is wholly justified, as an ingenious substitute for the traditional *repetition of the Exposition* — which is precisely what it represents, until it dissolves into the Development, thus serving a double aim.

This unusual method of beginning the Development is encountered in **Beethoven,** (moderately, and, as it were, tentatively), in Sonata, op. 14, No. 1, first movement; — just one measure, at the beginning of the Development, is exactly like the first measure of the Prin. Theme (in the same key), after which the harmony is deflected. — Also Sonata, op. 31, No. 1, first movement; the first seven measures of the Development correspond exactly to those of the Prin. Theme. — Also Sonata, op. 31, No. 3, first movement. Also **Schumann,** Symphony, No. 1, first *Allegro* (brief). — In all of these examples the double-bar is present, wherefore any misconception of the form is impossible. In **Beethoven,** Sonata, op. 10, No. 1; and op. 14, No. 2 (first movement of each), the Development begins with the first phrase of the Prin. Theme, in the *opposite mode* of the original key.

(It will be remembered, that, as a rule, when the Development utilizes the Prin. Theme at the outset, it is in a *different key:* see **Beethoven,** Sonata, op. 2, No. 2; — op. 7; — op. 28 — first movement of each.)

The method is adopted with fuller consciousness, and to a much greater extent, in **Brahms,** Symphony, No. 2, op. 73, last movement: The Exposition ends in measure 148, — without double-bar; six measures of retransitional bridging follow, and the Development begins, in measure 155, precisely as the whole movement began; practically the entire Development is a manipulation of the members of the Prin. Theme. — Also, Symphony, No. 4, op. 98, first movement: The Exposition closes in measure 137, without double-bar; eight measures of retransitional bridging lead into the Development (meas. 145), whose first Section corresponds exactly to the beginning of the Exposition. Note the impressive augmentation of the principal thematic member, at the beginning of the Recapitulation (measure 247). — Also, Symphony, No. 4, *Allegro giocoso;* The Development begins, as in the above examples, with a direct presentation of the Prin. Theme (partial, of course, but in the original key); in the Recapitulation, the Prin. Theme reappears (13 measures before the *poco meno presto*) a half-step higher than at first (i.e., transposed), and is presented in a wholly different, more serious and lyric, mood from that of the rest of the movement. — Also, Serenade, op. 16, first movement. — I. Pfte.-Quartet, op. 25, first movement. — II. String-Quartet, op. 51, No. 2, last movement. — III. Pfte. Trio, op. 87, first movement.

Beethoven, Symphony, No. 2, last movement; the double-bar is omitted. — Also Symphony, No. 8, last movement; the same.

---

163. To what structural irregularity this particular manner of opening the Development may give rise, will be shown in par. 172.

But there is one noteworthy consequence which is in no sense irregular, and manifests itself in a significant enlargement and enrichment of the Sonatina-form.

164. In this, the **Enlarged Sonatina-form,** there is (as usual) no double-bar; a few measures of retransition lead to the Recapitulation, which begins, of course, with the Principal Theme.   Thus far the form corresponds to that variety of the Sonata-allegro in which, as shown above (par. 162), the Development begins with the first member of the Prin. Theme, in the original key.   But in the Enlarged Sonatina-form a much larger portion (often the whole) of the Prin. Theme is presented, *and spun out as quasi Development* until the Subord. Theme appears, — after which, as usual, the course of the Exposition is closely followed (in the original key), up to the Coda.   Thus:

Exposition			Recapitulation		
Prin. Th.	*Subord. Th.*	Re- trans.	*Prin. Th.*	*Subord. Th.*	Coda
	Related key. Codetta		Extended and " developed "	Transposed. Codetta	

Compare this diagram with that in par. 133, and observe that this manipulation greatly enhances the artistic value of the Sonatina-form, and lends to it a significance almost equal to that of the Sonata-allegro form itself — all of whose structural elements it contains.   Comparison with the diagram in par. 142 shows that it differs from the Sonata-allegro only in the number of its independent Divisions (the Development and Recapitulation being merged by introducing the *process* of Development during the statement of the Prin. Theme).

See **Brahms,** Symphony, No. 1, op. 68, last movement (*Allegro non troppo*).   The Prin. Th. is a 3-Part Song-form, with a duplication of Parts II and III (measures 1–9–17–25–33);   Part III (as Part V) is dissolved, and becomes transitional in meas. 45;   the Subordinate Theme is a 2-Part Song-form (see measures 57–71), the Second Part leading *without cadence* into the First Codetta (measure 87, duplicated in meas. 95);   the Second Codetta begins in meas. 107, duplicated in measure 111.   The Exposition closes in meas. 122 — without double-bar (as usual in the Sonatina-form); measures 123–4 are the retransition.   The Recapitulation begins in meas. 125; section I is Part I of the Prin. Theme;   section II, Part II of the Prin. Theme (meas. 133), deflected into *E*-flat major, and extended; section III is based upon Part III of the Prin. Theme, in *E*-flat major (meas. 143), spun out, and infused with new material; section IV corresponds exactly to Part V of the Prin. Theme, in the original key — meas. 159 to 171; section V is a "development" in character, utilizing the former transitional material; sec. VI (meas. 183) continues the process, duplicated in meas. 188; section VII (meas. 196) resumes the style of section V; section VIII (meas. 207) alludes strongly to the Prin. Theme; section IX (meas. 218) is new; section X (meas. 224) is the transition, quite different from the former one, into the Subord. Theme (meas. 240). From this point, the course agrees exactly with that of the Exposition, leading into the Coda in the same manner as before into the Recapitulation.

Beethoven, String-quartet, op. 18, No. 3, *Andante con moto;* very similar, but more concise.

The structural plan of the Enlarged Sonatina-form is carried out with singular definiteness of purpose, and in so original and logical a manner that it seems to establish a new and legitimate form, in

Brahms, Symphony, No. 3, op. 90, last *Allegro.* (First number the measures up to 200.)

The EXPOSITION:

> *A.* First Antecedent phrase (measures 1–4);
> *B.* First Consequent phrase (meas. 5–8);
> *C.* Second Antecedent phrase (meas. 9–13);
> *D.* Second Consequent phrase (meas. 14–18); ⎱ Part I of Prin. Theme (*f* minor).
> *E.* Part II (meas. 19–29);
> *F.* Part III (meas. 30–35); Dissolution —
> *G.* Sequence, and transition (meas. 36–45);
> *H.* Prospective dominant, "second act," new transition-motive (meas. 46–51);
> *J.* Subord. Theme, *C* major, Part I (meas. 52–61);
> *K.* Subord. Theme, Part II (meas. 62–74);
> *L.* Codetta I, with duplication (meas. 75–95);
> *M.* Codetta II, extended, dissolved as retransition (meas. 96–107).

The RECAPITULATION (the lettered groups corresponding to the above):

> *A.* Extended (meas. 108–113);
> *B.* In augmentation (meas. 114–119);
> *C.* Extended (meas. 120–129);
> *D.* In augmentation (meas. 130–133), and spun out as "development" (meas. 134–148);
> *E.* "Developed" (meas. 149–171);
> *F.* Extended (meas. 172–181);
> *G.* Partial (meas. 182–187);
> *H.* As before, *transposed* (meas. 188–193);
> *J.* As before, transposed to *F* major (meas. 194–203);
> *K. L.* As before;
> *M.* As before; dissolved, again, but this time into the Coda.

See also:

Brahms, Serenade, op. 11, last movement.

Brahms, 2nd Pfte. quartet, op. 26, last movement.

Brahms, 1st String-quartet, op. 51, No. 1, last movement.

---

165. The Basic Motive. Another noteworthy method of enriching the resources and widening the structural scope of the Sonata-allegro form, consists in adopting a sort of *double thematic basis* for the Prin. Theme, — somewhat after the manner of the first species of the Double-fugue, in which the Subject is a *dual* quantity, instead of a single thematic thread. This appears to be distinctive of the Symphony; but its application to any Larger form seems feasible.

Of these two thematic factors, the first assumes the importance of a *Basic Motive*, which underlies the whole movement, or, at least, all of its more essential parts. It is announced *first*, and alone, and may be a melodic, or a full harmonic, motive. That it is in no sense merely introductory, is proven at once by the fact that the initial member of the Prin. Theme, which follows immediately, *is built contrapuntally upon the basic motive.*

For illustration:

(Part III) (Prin. phrase, expanded)

etc.

Basic Motive (contrary motion)

Subord. Theme
(Basic Motive)

etc.

(derived from Prin. phrase)

etc. *1)

Basic Motive (contrary motion)

No. 2.

*1) It is left to the student to trace the masterly manipulation of both these thematic threads through the entire movement, — especially to note the prevalence of the chromatic Basic Motive, which, through all its manifold metamorphoses, is always recognizable and keenly assertive.

*2) In this movement, the Basic Motive, brief as it is, is fully equal to, if not superior to, the Prin. Theme itself in importance, and permeates the structure in a singularly ingenious and vitalizing manner. The student will find inspiration in the thorough exploration of the movement, and the (enthusiastic — not cold-blooded) analysis of its fabric.

*3) For the details of the inner accompaniment, see the original.

*4) Here, again, the Basic Motive and the actual Principal Theme are so intimately interwoven, that they appear coördinate in thematic significance and in the degree of attention which each compels. But the student will recognize that the former is properly called the **basic** motive, for the entire melody of the Prin. Theme is adjusted contrapuntally to it (or derived contrapuntally from it). Both are wholly absent, however, from the Subord. Theme, which presents a very striking contrast in key, measure and character, and provides the chief sections of the Development. Again, the student is urged to make an exhaustive study of this masterly movement, and to note, constantly and earnestly, the *manner and spirit in which the structural plan is executed.* If these thematic devices were employed with complacent calculation, and the lines drawn merely with clever technical ease — as lifeless arabesques — the music would be to some extent interesting and even artistic, but not inspiring. These symphonic movements, however, are vitalized by an emotional energy and warmth of passion that is at times almost overpowering in its intensity; and the structural devices are applied *in the control of this surging passion, and as the last and most eminent means of preserving the unity and concentration of the whole.*

166. A remote suggestion of such a double thematic basis, though in a totally different and less significant sense, may be detected in those larger forms with an *Independent Introduction* (par. 178*d*), for which, in a few cases, a specific motive is chosen, and later alluded to (in the movement proper).

For example: **Beethoven,** Sonata, op. 81*A*, first movement. The first three chords of the Introduction are, to a considerable extent, "thematic":

BEETHOVEN, op. 81*A.*

But though this motive of the Introduction does appear in, and almost pervades, the succeeding Sonata-allegro, it is in no sense as a *Basic* motive, but more as an auxiliary thematic member, or *companion* of the Principal Theme (not its contrapuntal *source*, as in the examples of **Brahms**).

In **Beethoven,** Sonata, op. 13, first movement, there is also an independent Introduction, one of the members of which reappears, very briefly, in measures 4–6, 10–12 of the Development; and also as "Interlude," before the Development (properly speaking, as first section of the Development), and again in the Coda. This, also, is merely an incidental — not a "basic" — motive. In **Beethoven,** Sonata, op. 78, first movement, the brief introductory phrase might be expected to assume a thematic purpose, but it has no further bearing upon the *Allegro.*

---

167. Transposed Themes. The important principle of Contrast is sometimes effectively emphasized by the (as a rule misleading, and therefore somewhat hazardous) practice of *transposition.*

a. This is applied strikingly to the Principal Theme, which, *in the Recapitulation,* occasionally appears — at least partially — in some other than the original key.

In order to comprehend fully how this may be done without impairing the structural purpose, the student should thoroughly review par. 123, and especially par. 124.

See, again, **Beethoven,** Sonata, op. 10, No. 2, first movement: The Prin. Theme, at the beginning of the Recapitulation (two-sharp signature) is, for a while, in *D* major instead of *F* major.

Beethoven, Sonata, op. 78, second movement (Sonatina-form, with additional statement of the Prin. Theme at the end — par. 181): In the Recapitulation, the Prin. Theme is presented in *B* major, instead of *F*-sharp major.

Brahms, Symphony, No. 4, *Allegro giocoso* (already cited, in par. 162).

Schubert, Sonata, No. 3, last movement (Pr. Th. transposed to the sub-dominant key).

Schubert, Sonata, No. 6, first movement (the same).

Schubert, Sonata, No. 7, first movement (the same). Last movement of the same Sonata (Prin. Th. transposed to the dominant key).

b. This modulatory shifting process is so frequently applied to the Subordinate Theme (which has often been seen to choose its key with complete freedom, and even with disregard of the principle of relation to the principal key — both in the Exposition and in the Recapitulation), that no further discussion or illustration is necessary.

For a particularly interesting example, see **Beethoven,** Symphony, No. 8, first movement, and last movement: The Subord. Theme begins, in every case, in an unexpected key, but (also in every case) swings over into the proper key after one Period. See also **Beethoven,** Sonata, op. 53, first movement. — Sonata, op. 31, No. 1, first movement. — Sonata, op. 31, No. 3, last movement. No other master employs the device of transposition quite so freely, or so effectively, as does **Schubert.**

---

168. *a.* **Polyphony, in the Larger Forms.** The use of polyphonic as well as homophonic texture, in the execution of the Larger designs of composition, as pointed out in par. 2, has been witnessed in many of the foregoing examples. But there are cases where the adoption of the polyphonic or imitatory style, and contrapuntal treatment generally, is not merely incidental (or peculiar to the Development), but pervades the Themes themselves, and thus enters vitally into the purpose and character of the movement; and such examples may be classed among the noteworthy varieties of the Larger Forms. For illustration:

Brahms, 'Cello Sonata, op. 38, last movement: As a whole, this is a Double-fugue, in Sonata-allegro form (with a Dislocation — par. 185); the Prin. Theme is a fugal exposition, chiefly of Subject *A*; the Subordinate Theme begins with Subject *B*. — String-quintet, op. 88, last movement; an admirable example of an elaborate Fugue in strict Sonata-allegro form (no double-bar).

Also, **Beethoven,** String-quartet, op. 59, No. 3, last movement; practically a Fugue, in Sonata-allegro form (no double-bar). — Sonata, op. 101, last movement: the Development is an elaborate *fugato*, upon the first phrase of the Prin. Theme, and a general imitatory atmosphere pervades the movement; it is not, however, a Fugue as a whole. — Sonata, op. 110, last movement: This is, roughly speaking, a Sonatina-form; the Prin. Theme is a lyric *Adagio* (with Introduction — par. 178), the "Subord. Theme" is a Fugue; in the Recapitulation, the Fugue, besides being transposed, is manipulated in *contrary motion*. — **Mendelssohn,** Sonata, op. 6, third movement, is similar, excepting that here the Prin. Theme is *fugato*, and the Subord. Theme lyric.

Other interesting examples of more or less essentially polyphonic character:

Mozart, *C* major Symphony, last movement (Quintuple fugue). — **Mozart,** Overture to *Die Zauberflöte.* — **Beethoven,** Symphony, No. 9, *Scherzo.* — Sonata, op. 10, No. 2, last movement. — **César Franck,** Violin Sonata in *A*, last movement (canonic Prin. Theme).

b. In this connection, attention may be directed to the employment of the extremely vital device of **Melody Expansion** in the Larger Forms. See, first, *Homophonic Forms*, par. 32.

It is analogous to the thematic modification known as Augmentation, but differs from this in that it is not applied to the whole member, bodily, but consists in expanding (rhythmically enlarging or lengthening) single tones, or tone-groups, or repeating tone-groups, so as to "stretch" the melodic phrase, so to speak, over a larger number of measures.

As "Augmentation," it appears frequently in the music of Bach and other contrapuntists; also in that of Haydn and Mozart. As "Melody Expansion" it is suggested, only, in Beethoven; and is applied with more definite purpose in Mendelssohn (*Homophonic Forms*, Example 44). But it was reserved for Brahms to make thoroughly conscious, vital and truly significant use of Melody Expansion, as a practically new and powerful factor of legitimate structural development, and consistent thematic derivation.

For illustration:

Ex.
60.

No. 1.   *Allegro non troppo*
BRAHMS, Violin-
Concerto, op. 77,
first movement.

Original melodic sentence

Later form:

5.   expanded   6.

7.   modified and expanded

7½.   8.   expanded   *tr*   etc.

Allegro vivace

No. 3.

BRAHMS, 'Cello Sonata, op. 99, first movement.   Meas. 1.   2.   3.   4.

Original melodic sentence (8 measures)

5.   6.   7.   8.   Immediate duplication, in

expanded form:

Meas. 1.   2.   (repetition of 1 and 2)   3.

extension   4.   expanded   5.

6.   7.   8.   extension   *3)   etc.

*1) In this example, the expansion of the melodic sentence assumes the unusual form of "imitation," — expansion in which different voices participate. The principle is the same, of course. See the original.

*2) The measures are numbered, for convenient comparison. Here the process of expansion is clearly exhibited. *See the original*, in order to appreciate the full significance of the harmonic associations, in the accompaniment.

*3) Here, both repetition and expansion are active. *See the original*.

Another illustration may be seen in Ex. 58, No. 1; Part III of the Principal Theme is an expanded version of Part I (involving repetitions, also).

EXERCISE 12.

A. Two or more examples of the Miniature Sonata-allegro form.

B. An example of the Concise Sonata-allegro form (with brief, but thoroughly characteristic, Themes).

C. Two or more examples of the Enlarged Sonatina-form.

D. An example of the Sonata-allegro form, with Basic Motive and Prin. Theme.

E. An example of the Sonata-allegro form, with transposition of the Principal Theme, in the Recapitulation.

F. An example of the Sonata-allegro form, with polyphonic treatment.

CHAPTER XIII.

IRREGULAR FORMS.

INTRODUCTION.

169. *a.* It is but natural that an occasional deviation from the regular or conventional arrangement and treatment of the essential factors of the form should occur. These irregularities do not, however, contradict the fundamental principles of musical structure, but are the decidedly rare exceptions which prove the rules. They contain nothing which violates or obscures any of the vital lines of the designs, since their object, dictated always by the particular character of the music itself, is merely to lay more emphasis upon one or another of the thematic members, or to provide more effective contrasts and better balance of parts; in a word, to obtain a more telling presentation of the thematic material.

b. The student has observed that the various members and divisions of the form are of two distinctly opposed kinds:

1. The *thematic* components (Prin. Theme, Subordinate Theme, and the Codettas), whose treatment is regulated by fairly strict conditions; and

2. What might be termed the *episodic* components (the Transition, Retransition, the Development, and the Coda), which are treated with almost absolute freedom, and conform to no other law than that imposed by the imagination and good judgment.

170. A very common general cause of irregularity is traceable to the manner of treating these "episodic," or free, factors of the form. There is no telling, for example, when a retransition, impelled by the impetus of the musical material, may expand into a developing section; or when the extension or dissolution of one of the basic phrases, ingenuously begun, may be spun out, similarly, into a "development," or into an episodic division, or be transformed into a *new* thematic member; or when a Coda may assume both unexpected contents and length.

This is quite as it should be, for it prevents the necessary controlling influence of the fundamental thematic conditions from hampering the equally necessary freedom of conception and expression; and it enables the musical ideas themselves to define the most appropriate form of each part and of the whole.

171. The Irregularities may be roughly divided into four classes:

1. Exchanges or Mixtures of the Thematic factors
2. Augmentations
3. Abbreviations (omissions)
4. Alterations in the order of the thematic factors ("dislocations")

} of the regular designs.

EXCHANGES, OR MIXTURES.

1. THE RONDO WITH DEVELOPMENT.

172. The two classes of Larger forms — Rondo, and Sonata-allegro — are radically differentiated, as has been seen; and it is for this very reason that an occasional fusion, or exchange, may take place between the two, in a perfectly recognizable (and therefore permissible) manner. Such a fusion occurs, now and then, *in the Third Rondo form* (more rarely in the Second Rondo), *when a Development takes the place of the Second Subordinate Theme.*

The roving, generally urgent, often polyphonic, character of a "Development" is so well-defined (par. 150) that it cannot be confounded with any other factor of the design, and, therefore, its presence (as irregularity) in the Rondo cannot be mistaken.

See **Beethoven**, Sonata, op. 27, No. 1, last movement. It is a "Third Rondo, with Development," and has the following design:

First Division			Middle Div.	Recapitulation		*1)
Prin. Th.	*I. Sub. Th.*	*Prin. Th.*	*Development, instead of II. Sub. Th.*	*Prin. Th.*	*I. Sub. Th. transposed, as usual*	*Coda*

*1) Compare this with the diagram in par. 110. The details are as follows:

Principal Theme, E-flat major, Part I (meas. 1–8); Part II (meas. 9–16), repeated (17–24); Part III (meas. 25– – –), dissolved (meas. 28), transition (29–35);

I. Subordinate Theme, B-flat major (meas. 36–56);

Codetta (meas. 56– – –), extended (to meas. 72);

Retransition (meas. 72–81);

Principal Theme, Parts I and II (meas. 82–97); Part II duplicated, as before, but dissolved and led to a cadence in G-flat major (meas. 98–106);

Development, section I, polyphonic (meas. 106–131); section II, extension (meas. 132–139) to the prospective dominant; section III, retransition, an ingenious digression from the dominant, and back to it (meas. 140–166);

Recapitulation (meas. 167– – –), as usual. The Recapitulation ends with the Codetta, which is extended and led to a dominant semicadence; the Coda follows at once, the final *da capo* being omitted (but alluded to in the final section).

173. It is obvious that this thematic arrangement elevates the Rondo form, and leads it toward the Sonata-allegro form, of which the distinctive feature is the *Development*. It interrupts, for a time, the characteristic structural process of the Rondo, namely: the constant alternation of a Prin. Theme with various *new* Themes, — and substitutes the leading principle of the Sonata-allegro: the elaboration or development of the *original* thematic material. See further:

Beethoven, Sonata, op. 31, No. 1, last movement (Third Rondo, with Development in place of the II. Subord. Theme. The final *da capo* is omitted, as such; but the principal motive is represented in the Coda). — Sonata, op. 90, last movement (Third Rondo, with Development — at the change of signature; Recapitulation complete). — String-quartet, op. 18, No. 1, last movement (Third Rondo form, with elaborate Development; the I. Subord. Theme begins each time a 5th too high, and then drops into the proper key; the last *da capo* is merged in the Coda). — Pfte. Trio, op. 9, No. 2, last movement (Third Rondo, with Development; both retrans-

itions lead to a heavy dominant chord, followed, singularly, by a light double-bar —
to mark the form; — the final *da capo* is omitted, but alluded to in the Coda). —
Violin Sonata, op. 30, No. 2, last movement (Third Rondo, with Development).
— Violin Sonata, op. 30, No. 3, last movement (a very unusual design for a modern
sonata-movement, suggestive of the *old-fashioned Rondeau*, in which a brief Principal
phrase alternates with quite a number of similarly brief "Subordinate" phrases. This
alternating process continues for 90 measures, and is then followed by a genuine
Development, to meas. 141, where the Principal phrases again appear, followed by a
fairly lengthy Coda).

Mozart, Sonata, No. 12 (Schirmer edition), last movement (Second Rondo, with
additional Development, as extension of the second retransition, similar to par. 174,
which see; the II. Subord. Theme is genuine).

Mendelssohn, "Midsummer Night's Dream," *Scherzo* (Third Rondo, with Development). — Étude, op. 104, No. 5, *F* major, (Second Rondo form, with Development).

Schubert, Sonata, No. 9, *A* major, last movement (Third Rondo, with Development. The design is legitimate and clear, but is rendered *extremely broad* by
persistent duplications — especially in the I. Subord. Theme — after Schubert's
favorite manner. In the Recapitulation, the Prin. Theme is first stated, tentatively, in *F*-sharp major). — Sonata, No. 10, *B*-flat major, last movement (Third
Rondo, with Development; also very broad design, but perfectly clear; the Prin.
Theme has a unique modulatory beginning, which influences all the retransitions;
three large Codettas follow the I. Subord. Theme).

Brahms, 2nd pfte. Concerto, op. 83, last movement (Third Rondo, with Development). — 3rd pfte. Trio, op. 87, last movement (the same; Part I of the Prin. Th.
omitted in the Recapitulation). — Serenade, op. 16, last movement (the same).

Beethoven, Symphony, No. 3, *Marcia funebre* (Second Rondo, with Develop-
ment; the I. Subord. Theme is in the same key, but opposite mode; Part III of the
Prin. Theme is transposed, in every instance, to the subdominant key). — Symphony,
No. 7, *Allegretto* (Second Rondo, with Development; at the beginning, there are
three complete repetitions of the Prin. Theme; in the Coda, a portion of the Subord.
Th. appears as Section I, and the first Period of the Prin. Th. as Section III).

174. The insertion of a Development has been seen to occur chiefly
in the Third Rondo form, and occasionally in the Second Rondo. There
is no apparent place for it in the *First Rondo form*, because none of the
thematic members could maintain its integrity, if replaced by a Development. But it is nevertheless practicable to create the impression
of a "developing" section, even in the First Rondo form, by *spinning
out the retransition* (as intimated in par. 170), after the specific manner
of a Development.

See **Brahms,** Symphony, No. 2, op. 73, *Adagio:*
Prin. Theme (*B* major), 3-Part period (meas. 1–17);
Transition-phrase (meas. 17–27); "second act" (meas. 28–32);

Subordinate Theme (F-sharp major), 3-Part form (measures 33–44);

Codetta (meas. 45–49);

Retransition, as fairly elaborate "Development" (meas. 49–67; there is a curious "false start" of the Prin. member in meas. 65);

Prin. Theme, as before, but modified (meas. 68–80);

The *Coda* begins in meas. 81, precisely as the Transition-phrase did, and reverts, briefly, to the "development" style.

Also **Brahms,** Ballade, op. 10, No. 1 (similar; the Subord. Theme is in the same key, but opposite mode; it is extended in the manner of a Development; the Prin. Theme, as *da capo,* is abbreviated to its First Part, which is then extended in lieu of a Coda).

175. The *Third* Rondo form with a Development bears a misleading resemblance to that variety of the regular Sonata-allegro form in which the Development begins with a partial statement of the Prin. Theme exactly as at the beginning of the Exposition (par. 162).

This is best illustrated by a comparative diagram:

*1)	First Division			Middle Div.	Recapitulation		
	Prin. Th.	*I. Sub. Th.*	*Pr. Th.*	*Development,* instead of *II. Sub. Th.*	*Pr. Th.*	*I. Sub. Th.*	*Prin. Th.* and *Coda*
		Retransition					

*2)	: Exposition :		Development		Recapitulation		
	Prin. Th.	*Sub. Th.*	*Pr. Th.* as 1st Section	*— following Sections*	*Prin. Th.*	*Subord. Th.*	*Coda*

*1) Third Rondo form, with Development (par. 172).

*2) Regular Sonata-allegro form, with first member of the Prin. Th. as Section I of the Development.

The distinction lies, of course, in the purpose of the composer, according to which it must be clearly shown whether the form is to be "Rondo" (exhibiting the principle of *Alternating* Themes), or "Sonata-allegro" (Exposition of *Associated* Themes). It will manifest itself in the location of the double-bar, or of the heavy bar which separates the Divisions — as shown in the diagram. In the *presence* of a double-

bar, there can be no misconstruction. In the *absence* of a double-bar,
the distinction depends upon the extent and quality of the first retransition (which may support the Rondo-impression); but also, and
chiefly, upon the *quantity of the Prin. Theme* that is presented at this
point: If it is only a fragment, it will clearly prove to be no more than
the first section of a genuine Development; but if it is a genuine and
fairly complete presentation of the Prin. Theme, it will establish the
Rondo form.

The difference is clearly exhibited in **Beethoven**, Sonata, op. 31, No. 1: The *first
movement* is a Sonata-allegro of the above type; the *last movement* is a Third Rondo
with Development.

II. The Sonata-allegro with a Middle Theme in, or instead of, the Development.

176. This comparatively unimportant irregularity is the result
of a slight concession of the Sonata-allegro design to the Rondo-prin-
ciple. It consists in introducing into the Development, or partly
substituting for the latter, a more or less *new thematic episode*, which
may, in extreme cases, assume precisely the rank and effect of a "Second
Subordinate Theme," and which, in any case, interrupts, or greatly
limits, the process of genuine "Development." Compare par. 173,
which is here reversed; the Sonata-allegro exhibits *new* traits, after its
Exposition is completed, instead of confining itself to its own original
thematic members. The justification of this treatment is pointed out
in par. 151*d*, which review.

A characteristic example is found in **Beethoven**, Sonata, op. 2, No. 1, last movement: After the usual double-bar, a wholly new thematic factor appears — instead
of the expected Development. This new episode, or Middle Theme, is a complete
3-Part Song-form, with all the repetitions, and assumes the nature and significance
of an additional "Subord. Theme." After it has reached its full tonic cadence, the
process of "development" is begun, in the usual way, and carried on, through the
retransition, to the return of the Prin. Theme (Recapitulation). See further:

    Beethoven, Sonata, op. 10, No. 3, *Largo:* A light double-bar (without repetition)
marks the end of the Exposition; instead of a "Development," an entirely new
melodic sentence is announced, which, with its extension, leads to the Recapitulation. — Sonata, op. 10, No. 1, first movement: The Development begins, legitimately, with a member of the Prin. Theme (in the opposite mode — 12 measures); the
following section is a new Middle Theme, extending to the Recapitulation. — Sonata,
op. 14, No. 1, first movement: The first section of the Development is derived from

the Prin. Theme; the second section is a Middle Theme; the third section is the usual retransition.

Mozart, Sonata, No. 16 (Schirmer edition), *Andante:* With the exception of the first beat, the entire second Division is a new Middle Theme.   In **Mozart,** Sonatas, Nos. 4, 6, 7, 15, the first movement of each, the Development contains more or less new material.

Schubert, Sonata, No. 4, op. 122, last movement (also first movement). — Sonata, No. 6, op. 147, last movement. — In Sonatas No. 7 and 8 (first movement of each), a large section of the Development is new.

Schumann, Symphony, No. 2, op. 61, *Adagio* (third movement): The form is concise, but legitimate and clear; the Exposition ends in meas. 62 (without double-bar); the 12 measures which follow constitute a new thematic member, and lead to the Recapitulation (in measure 74).

Brahms, 2nd pfte. Concerto, op. 83, second movement (*Allegro appassionato*): An extremely interesting and powerful, but unique, movement; a regular Exposition leads to the usual double-bar; a genuine Development follows, the third (or fourth) section of which leads to an unexpected complete tonic cadence in the original key; hereupon the signature changes (to two sharps) and a characteristic Middle Theme, strongly suggestive of a "Trio," follows (par. 183); it also has a complete tonic cadence, but (at the change of signature, back to one flat) is carried over into a re-transition, which leads into the genuine Recapitulation (with the customary transposition of the Subord. Theme); the Coda is brief. — See also, **Brahms'** *Rhapsodie* in g minor (op. 79, No. 2): Prin. Theme, Two-Part form, with an important Codetta; Sec. I of the Development (8 measures) is derived from the Prin. Theme; Section II is its sequence; Sec. III, from the Codetta; *Sec. IV is new,* and assumes the rank of a "Middle Theme"; it is in Two-Part form, dissolving into the retransition.

AUGMENTATIONS.

177. An augmentation of any one of the regular designs results from the insertion, or addition, of one or more complete, but extraneous, structural factors — not included, or expected, in the original plan. Such extra members may appear at the beginning, or during the Exposition; possibly, though more rarely, in the later course of the movement.

178. Independent Introduction or Coda. Probably the most common augmentation consists in an independent *Introduction*, placed before the Exposition.

a. This may be brief and unessential:

Beethoven, Sonata, op. 78, first four measures. — **Mendelssohn,** Caprice, op. 33, No. 2.

b. Or it may be longer; may be in Group-form, or in complete Two- or Three-Part Song-form; and may possess, both in character and contents, independent significance.

c. In this case, the Introduction differs, as a rule, completely from the movement proper, in style and in tempo (being almost always much slower — *andante,* or *adagio*). And it may be either a general means of establishing the key, without any *thematic* reference to the following *Allegro:*

Beethoven, Symphony No. 1, first movement; Symphony No. 2, first movement. In the Symphonies, No. 4 and No. 7, there is first a lengthy independent Introduction (in slower tempo), and then an additional, brief, direct introductory phrase of a few measures, in the *Allegro* tempo. — Sonata, op. 111, first movement. — **Mendelssohn,** Caprice, op. 33, No. 1.

d. Or it may be thematically related to, or even constructed systematically upon, thematic members of the movement proper:

Beethoven, Sonata, op. 57, last movement, first 19 measures. — **Brahms,** Symphony, No. 4, op. 98, *Andante,* first four measures. — Symphony, No. 1, op. 68, first movement. — Pfte. Sonata, op. 2, last movement.

In **Beethoven,** Sonata, op. 13, and especially in Sonata op. 81*A,* (first movement of each), fragments of the Introduction recur during the following Development, and Coda.

The final phrase of an independent Introduction is usually dissolved and led to a heavy *dominant* ending, often considerably expanded. The key is, naturally, the same as that of the movement proper.

In **Brahms,** Symphony, No. 1, last movement, it is in the opposite mode (*c* minor); this introduction is constructed wholly upon thematic members of the following *Allegro;* it is therefore "independent" *only in tempo,* but wholly related *in contents.* Its thorough analysis will prove most instructive.

e. To some extent analogous, is the insertion of an independent section in the Coda — usually the final section — in contrasting (usually quicker) *tempo.* This, however, can scarcely be regarded as an irregular augmentation, since the Coda (like the Development) has a right to any number of Sections, with any contents.

See **Beethoven,** Sonata, op. 53, end of the last movement (*Prestissimo*). — Symphony, No. 5, end of the last movement (*Presto*). — **Brahms,** Symphony, No. 3, end of the last movement (*slower* tempo). — **Mendelssohn,** Symphony, No. 3 (*a* minor), end of the last movement (slower tempo). — This factor is strikingly significant in **Brahms,** Sonata, op. 5, *Andante;* the form is First Rondo, but the independent Coda has the appearance and importance of a II. Subord. Theme, in the subdominant key.

179. Double Subordinate Theme. In Sonata-allegro (possibly also in Rondo) designs of unusual breadth, or conceived with a certain exuberance of conceptive imagination, it is sometimes possible to identify *two Subordinate Themes in succession* (in the Exposition, of course). This is a very rare augmentation, and its presence can be verified only in those cases where that thematic member which corresponds to the *first Codetta* is so elaborate and extensive as to claim attention as a genuine *Theme.* Such analysis seems reasonable, and convenient, in the following:

Beethoven, Sonata, op. 2, No. 3, first movement: Prin. Theme, *C* major, Part I (measures 1–13); Part II, dissolved (meas. 14–23); transition (meas. 24–26); *Subordinate Theme "A"* (in *g* minor, dissolved, meas. 27–43); transition (meas. 44–46); *Subordinate Theme "B"* (in *G* major), Part I (meas. 47–61); Part II (corresponding to Part II of the Prin. Theme, meas. 62–77); Codetta I (meas. 78–84); Codetta II (meas. 85–90); Double-bar.

Also in **Beethoven,** Sonata, op. 7, first movement: *Subordinate Theme "A"*, measure 41; *Subordinate Theme "B"*, meas. 60. The latter (Sub. Th. *"B"*) might be regarded as the First Codetta, but it has full "thematic" value. The real first Codetta appears in meas. 93.

Still more convincing is **Mozart,** Sonata, No. 17 (Schirmer edition), first movement:

Prin. Theme, *F* major, measures 1–31; Transition-phrase, duplicated, and dissolved into the prospective dominant (meas. 32–41); *Subordinate Theme "A"*, *C* major (meas. 42–57); Transition-phrase, duplicated, and dissolved, again, into the dominant (meas. 58–66); *Subordinate Theme "B"*, *C* major (meas. 67–89); I. Codetta (meas. 89 etc.). It is evident that no other interpretation of this design is so consistent as that of an Augmentation, consisting in the addition of another Subordinate Theme. And the same condition is unmistakably present in **Chopin,** *e* minor pfte. Concerto, op. 11, last movement: A very broad *Third Rondo form,* in which, besides the usual *tutti*-insertions, — par. 180*b,* — there is a I. Subordinate Theme which appears in two wholly distinct thematic divisions: I. Subordinate Theme *"A"*, in meas. 120, and I. Subordinate Theme *"B"*, in meas. 171–173, etc. These might, it is true, be regarded as the First and Second *Parts,* respectively, of one Subordinate Theme; but their radical difference in character is much more suggestive of individual Themes.

A somewhat similar thematic insertion, though of a less common type, occurs in **Beethoven,** Sonata, op. 49, No. 1, last movement:

After the Prin. Theme, in complete (though Incipient) Three-Part Song-form, the transition leads to a distinctly independent thematic period, in the opposite mode (meas. 20) — followed by two measures of bridging, which lead to the Subordinate Theme proper; and the same insertion occurs again, slightly altered, at the end of the Subord. Theme, before the retransition. This insertion might be called an "Intermediate motive."

180. The Concerto-allegro.   Additions, or insertions, of a very significant and conspicuous nature appear in the various movements of the *Concerto*, which, as a natural consequence of the association of an individual Solo-part with an equally vital orchestral accompaniment, are almost invariably a positive augmentation of the usual, regular, designs.

a. The most noteworthy of these (more common in the earlier, than in the modern, Concerto), is a preliminary presentation of the chief thematic material of the Exposition; not as an Introduction, but as a sort of **pseudo-Exposition,** sometimes all in the principal key, preceding the actual Exposition.

It is generally assigned to the orchestra alone, as in the first movement of **Beethoven,** pfte. Concertos, Nos. 1, and 2 and 3; and in his Violin Concerto. — **Brahms,** 1st pfte. Concerto, op. 15; and Violin Concerto. — **Mendelssohn,** Violin Concerto.

But the Solo-instrument sometimes participates, especially at the very beginning, as in the first movement of **Beethoven,** pfte. Concertos, Nos. 4 and 5. **Brahms,** 2nd pfte. Concerto, op. 83.

This introductory Exposition, and the following genuine Exposition, represent, in a sense, the customary *repetition of the Exposition.*   This repetition never occurs in the Concerto, and therefore the usual (heavy) double-bar, with repetition-marks, is invariably omitted.

Examine, thoroughly, the beginning of **Beethoven's** 3rd pfte. Concerto, op. 37, and note the relation of the introductory Exposition to the subsequent genuine one.

b. Besides this extra member, at the outset, the Concerto-movements are further augmented by fairly frequent **"tutti"** passages, for the orchestra alone; inserted — for necessary contrast — as Interludes, chiefly at the end of the thematic statements in the Solo-part (between the Exposition and the Development; sometimes between the Themes; and at the end of the Recapitulation, leading into the *Cadenza*).

See **Beethoven,** pfte. Concerto, No. 3, first movement (analyze the whole movement, thoroughly): Orchestral Exposition; regular Exposition; "tutti"-insertion at the end of the Exposition; Recapitulation; "tutti"-insertion and *Cadenza;* Coda.

Also the last movement of **Chopin's** *e* minor Concerto (cited in par. 179).

c. The conventional **Cadenza** is also a distinctly extraneous insertion.   It occurs at (or within) the cadence-harmony of the Recapitulation (that is, before the Coda), whence its name.   The *Cadenza* has, as a rule, no structural significance, and is therefore never essential. Its chiefly superficial purpose is to provide for the Solo-performer a specific opportunity to display his technical dexterity. But its mere presence does, nevertheless, exert an influence upon the impression of the whole, which cannot be ignored; therefore, it is considered necessary to mould it in some degree of consistency with the rest of the movement; to derive its contents from foregoing thematic members; and to exercise fine artistic discrimination. In many (older) concertos, the place for the *Cadenza* is designated, and its achievement is then left to the Solo-performer, who might even improvise its contents. The wisest course is, no doubt, for the composer, if he wants it, to incorporate his own *Cadenza*, or its equivalent, into his work; as in

Schumann, pfte. Concerto in *a* minor, first movement; **Grieg,** pfte. Concerto in *a* minor, first movement; **Mendelssohn,** Violin concerto, first movement, — and others.

181. Sonatina-form with final da capo. The Sonatina-form is not infrequently augmented by an additional presentation of the Prin. Theme at the end of the Recapitulation. In the examples given in Chap. X, an apparent extra *da capo* of this kind was sometimes observed; but in the genuine Sonatina-form this would be no more than a fragmentary allusion, as *first section* (or perhaps some later section) *of the Coda.*

(See again, for example, **Beethoven,** Sonata, op. 10, No. 1, *Adagio*, in which the Coda, measure 22 from the end, begins with the first phrase — only — of the Prin. Theme. This is not enough to constitute an augmentation of the formal design.)

As real augmentation, this final *da capo* must represent the whole, or at least one whole Part, of the Prin. Theme, in the original key of course. When it is, thus, an *obvious* recurrence of the Prin. Theme, it establishes a significant relation to the Second Rondo form — from which the Sonatina-form differs (externally) only in that the *same* Subord. Theme appears twice, instead of two different ones. Compare the following diagram with that in par. 133, and with that in par. 97:

Exposition			Recapitulation		Extra Member	
Prin. Th.	*Sub. Th.* related key.	*Re-trans.*	*Prin. Th.*	*Sub. Th.* transposed. Retransition	*Prin. Th.*	Coda

See **Beethoven,** Sonata, op. 78, last movement: The Prin. Theme, at the beginning of the Recapitulation, is transposed to the subdominant key, and is abbreviated; after the Recapitulation, it is stated, with evident purpose, in the proper key (34 measures from the end), but somewhat abbreviated, and finally merged in a brief Coda.

Similar: **Chopin,** Sonata, op. 58, *b* minor, last movement: Introduction, 8 measures; in the Recapitulation, the Prin. Th. is transposed to the subdominant key; it reappears, in the original key, complete, before the Coda.

Schubert, Sonata, No. 8, *c* minor, *Adagio.*

Mozart, Sonata, No. 13 (Schirmer edition),*Andante;* concise, but clear.

Brahms, 2nd Pfte.-quartet, op. 26, *poco adagio.*

Beethoven, String-quartet, op. 18, No. 6, last movement: Independent Introduction; the reappearance of the Prin. Theme after the Recapitulation, both before and in the Coda, is persistent.

Schumann, Symphony, No. 3, op. 97, third movement: The design is unusual, approaching the Group-form; Prin. Theme, period (measures 1–5); Subord. Theme, (Part I, meas. 6–10; Part II, meas. 11–15, complete *tonic* cadence); Prin. Theme ("Codetta" in effect), with new Consequent phrase (meas. 16–21); Subord. Theme (meas. 22, extended to meas. 34); Retransition, one measure; Prin. Theme, again (meas. 36–40); Coda to the end.

182. The enlargement of the Rondo by the addition of another (third) Subordinate Theme, must be accounted for as an augmentation of the Third Rondo form.

See par. 129.   And glance, again, at **Mozart,** Sonata, No. 8, last movement; and No. 17, last movement. — **Beethoven,** Violin Sonata, op. 23, last movement.

See also, **Beethoven,** *Rondo a capriccio,* op. 129, which contains three different Subordinate Themes and two complete Developments.

183. Larger Forms with "Trio."   The "Trio" is a structural division peculiar to the Dance-forms, and is usually confined to the Menuet, March, Scherzo, and related compositions of that domain. Its presence in one of the Larger forms may result partly from a refinement of the dance-form, as shown in paragraphs 95 and 96, whereby the "Trio" emulates a real Subordinate Theme.   Or it may occupy an independent place in a Larger form, *in consequence of the enlargement of the principal division* (the first, or principal, Song-form).

This is illustrated clearly in the *Scherzo* of **Beethoven's** 9th symphony: the principal division is magnified into a complete Sonata-allegro form (as indicated in paragraphs 157, 158); wherefore, the form of the entire *Scherzo* must be defined as a "Sonata-allegro with Trio."

See also **Mozart,** Sonata, No. 9 (Schirmer ed.), *Menuetto* — already cited in par. 159; the "Menuetto" is a Miniature Sonata-allegro, and to this is added the usual "Trio" (and *da capo*). — The 1st Rhapsodie of **Brahms** (op. 79, No. 1) is similar, though less pronounced; the principal division is a broad Three-Part Song-form; Part I has two Codettas, and is repeated; Part II is sectional; Part III is extended, but *without* the two Codettas; and to this Principal Song-form a "Trio" is added.

Brahms, 2nd 'Cello Sonata, op. 99, *Allegro passionato,* is a First Rondo form, with "Trio."

Beethoven, 3rd 'Cello Sonata, op. 69, *Scherzo,* — a First Rondo form, with "Trio"; the "Trio" and *da capo* repeated.

Mendelssohn, Trio, op. 66, *Scherzo,* — a Sonatina-form, with "Trio"; the *da capo* is so abbreviated as to represent the Coda only.

To the examples cited in par. 96 (section 4) may be added the following, somewhat more significant, movements:

Brahms, Symphony, No. 2, third movement: This would probably be called a Song-form with Trio; but the "Trio" is derived from the principal Song, and the Trio and *da capo* are duplicated, with important changes. The design approaches the First Rondo in character and spirit (with duplication). — Violin Sonata, No. 2, op. 100, *Andante and Vivace;* very similar. — String-quintet, op. 88, *Grave;* also similar. — Also, **Beethoven,** Sonata, op. 54, first movement.

ABBREVIATIONS, OR OMISSIONS.

184. The omission of an important thematic member is not likely to occur anywhere but in the Recapitulation, though possible at other points, especially in the Rondo.

The most common of these abbreviations, is the *omission of the Prin. Theme after the Development,* in the Sonata-allegro form. The retransition, at the end of the Development, leads directly into the Subord. Theme, instead of into the Prin. Theme. Thus:

Exposition		Developm.	Recapitulation	
Prin. Th.	*Subord. Th.*		*Subord. Theme* only (trans-	Coda
	Codetta	Retrans.	posed). Codetta	

Compare this diagram with the one in par. 164 (the Enlarged Sonatina-form), which it resembles. The difference lies in the character of the Development: In the Enlarged Sonatina, it is actually the Prin. Theme, in a "developed" form of extension; here it is a *genuine Development,* which the Prin. Theme would follow, were it not omitted.

The omission is owing, usually, to the fact that the Development deals very largely with members of the Prin. Theme, and therefore renders another announcement of the latter unnecessary.

See **Chopin,** pfte. Sonata in *b*-flat minor, op. 35, first movement: The Development sets in, normally, after the double-bar, and covers 57 measures, to the "dominant" at the beginning of the retransition; seven measures of the latter lead into the *Subord.* (instead of the Prin.) Theme.

Chopin, Sonata in *b* minor, op. 58, first movement, very similar: The first phrases (about 16 measures) of the Prin. Theme are omitted, at the beginning of the Recapitulation; then follows one characteristic (later) phrase of the Prin. Theme, and the transition, — leading to the Subord. Theme.

Brahms, *Capriccio,* op. 116, No. 1: clearly an omission of the Prin. Theme, at the beginning of the Recapitulation.

Mendelssohn, Song without Words, No. 5. — *Praeludium,* op. 35, No. 3.

Mendelssohn, *g* minor pfte. Concerto, last movement: The Subord. Th. is in the same key as the Prin. Theme; in the Recapitulation *the Subord. Theme is omitted,* but is alluded to in the Coda. — In the first movement of the same Concerto, the Recapitulation is greatly abbreviated. — *D* minor Concerto, last movement: The Subord. Theme, here also, is omitted in the Recapitulation. — Symphony, No. IV, *Saltarello;* the same. *Rondo brillante,* op. 29: The Prin. Theme is omitted in the Recapitulation, but intimated in the Coda.

The example of **Brahms** (Sonata, op. 5, *Andante*), cited in par. 178*e*, might also be analyzed as a *Second* Rondo form, with a conspicuous omission of the Prin. Theme as final *da capo.* And, similarly, the fairly numerous examples of Second and Third Rondo forms, in which the final *da capo* is merged in the Coda, or even wholly omitted (review par. 106, and par. 127), may be regarded as Abbreviated designs. A similar omission of the final Prin. Theme *in the First Rondo form* would appear to be contradictory; but this analysis is suggested in **Beethoven,** Violin Sonata, op. 24, *Adagio:* The Prin. Theme is a Three-Part Song-form (meas. 1–37); what follows (in the opposite mode) appears to be a duplication, but very soon diverges into a fairly convincing Subord. Theme (17 measures long); the remaining sections are plainly Coda *only* — the Prin. Theme, as such, is omitted.

"DISLOCATIONS" OF THE DESIGN.

185. The alterations in the legitimate order of thematic members, to which the name "Dislocations" may be given, appear only in the Recapitulation; and are more common in the Sonata-group than in the Rondo-group. They do not admit of specific classification, but appear to be quite arbitrary and sometimes whimsical, although, in some cases, the reason is clear and well-grounded. They can best be understood by analysis of the following examples:

Brahms, 'Cello Sonata, op. 38, last movement — a Concert fugue (double) in Sonata-allegro form. In the Recapitulation, the Prin. Theme appears *after* (instead of before) the Subord. Theme.

Chopin, Concerto in *e* minor, *Romance:* Third Rondo form; in the Recapitulation, the I. Subord. Theme (at the 4-flat signature) *precedes* the Prin. Theme, instead of following it.

Mozart, Sonata, No. 15 (Schirmer ed.), second movement: Same as the preceding example; it is a Third Rondo form, and the I. Subord. theme *precedes* the Prin. Theme, in the Recapitulation. — Sonata, No. 14, last movement: The form is vague, owing to the similarity of the Prin. Theme and I. Subord. Theme; but it is probably a Third Rondo form, with a Development instead of the II. Subord. Theme; the latter is followed by the *I. Subord. Theme* (instead of the Prin. Theme, which, however, reappears completely in the Coda). — Sonata, No. 14, first movement: In the Recapitulation, the 1st Codetta appears *before* (instead of after) the Subord. Theme.

Mendelssohn, "Midsummer Night's Dream," *Scherzo:* In the Recapitulation of this Rondo with Development (already cited), the two *phrases* of the I. Subordinate Theme are presented in reversed order — the Consequent phrase *preceding*, instead of following, the Antecedent phrase.

Beethoven, String-quartet, op. 59, No. 2, last movement: Third Rondo with Development; in the Recapitulation, the I. Subord. Theme *precedes* the Prin. Theme.

186. Upon arriving at the conclusion of the Irregular designs, the student may be inclined to assume that *any* arrangement of the thematic factors is possible, and may doubt the justice or necessity of insisting upon any "regular" design. There is some apparent reason for such doubt; and it is probable that many a fantastic form has been composed, emanating from the untrammeled imagination, that is quite as effective and convincing as those that accept the guidance of the conventional lines. (Witness the "Group-forms," "Sectional forms," the "Fantasia," and some of the soul-compelling products of the "Tone-poem" style.) But, in the first place, the student's extensive analysis and observation will convince him that the legitimate or "regular" designs *far outnumber* the irregular ones; and, in the second place, he will recognize that the irregularity is always incidental, rather than essential; that it is due to emotional and imaginative impulses *within* the confines of the normal design, and does not overthrow any *vital* condition of the structural scheme as a whole.

EXERCISE 13.

A. An example of the Rondo with Development. Any instrument or ensemble may be chosen. Review notes to Exercise 10 ("N.B.").

B. An example of the Sonata-allegro with a Middle Theme.

C. A Sonata-allegro, with Independent Introduction (and, perhaps, Independent Coda).

D. A Concert-allegro, with "orchestral" Augmentations, and Cadenza.

E. A Sonatina-form with additional (final) *da capo.*

F. A *Scherzo*, in Sonata-allegro form, with "Trio."

G. A Sonata-allegro, with omission of the Prin. Theme in the Recapitulation.

H. An example of the Third Rondo form, with reversed presentation of Themes in the Recapitulation (*i.e.*, the Subord. Theme *before* the Prin. Theme).

CHAPTER XIV.

ISOLATED UNIQUE DESIGNS.

187. The examples of Larger Forms whose analysis follows, are not classed among the Irregular designs, because they are not in any sense typical, but merely isolated specimens of unusual thematic arrangement which do not admit of ordinary classification. Their justice and effectiveness is not called in question, inasmuch as, in common with all structural designs, regular or fantastic, they evidently appealed to the composers as the most appropriate method of presentation for the specific quality of the music itself.

a. **Beethoven,** Symphony, No. 5, *Andante.* This is ostensibly a First Rondo form, and is an illustration, as unique as it is effective, of the "Expansion" of an otherwise regular design by the process of *duplication* (free repetition — see par. 12*d*). The Prin. Theme is a Three-Part Song-form; Part I contains four phrases (measures 1, 5, 11, 16), the fourth phrase practically a duplication of the third; Part II is a Double-period (measures 23, 27, 32, 39); Part III is a nearly literal recurrence of Part I (measures 50–71); this is followed by a modified duplication of Parts II and III. (Part II, meas. 72–98; Part III represented by two repetitions of its first two phrases, finally dissolved, meas. 99–123); what follows is a sort of Interlude, which, however, represents the Subord. Theme, although it contains no new members (meas. 124–157); the retransition follows, and contains three sections (measures 158, 167, 176), the second of which resembles the Prin. Theme, but is in the opposite mode and obviously belongs to the act of retransition; the Prin. Theme recurs in meas. 185, and is reduced to its First Part only; the Coda begins in meas. 206, and contains four sections. (The *Allegretto* of **Beethoven's** 7th Symphony, cited at the end of par. 173, is similarly "expanded" by duplications of the Prin. Theme.)

b. **Beethoven,** Symphony, No. 9, *Adagio*, is ostensibly a First Rondo form, enlarged by duplication, and the insertion of a Development (as retransition). Its design is thus:

Prin. Theme, B-flat major (with two measures of unessential *Introduction*), a Period, the Consequent phrase of which is repeated, extended, and dissolved;

Subord. Theme, D major, a Period, duplicated, extended and dissolved;
Prin. Theme, B-flat major, complete, but modified; } Duplication of the first
Subord. Theme, G major, complete, but modified; } presentation.
Development, as *retransition;*
Prin. Theme, 22 measures, as before, cadence evaded and led into the *Coda,*
which embraces six sections.

c. Somewhat similar is **Schubert,** Sonata, No. 5, op. 143, last movement. The
form is Sonatina, enlarged by a duplication of the Exposition:
Prin. Theme, a minor, Two-Part form, and transition;
Subord. Theme, F major, Three-Part Period (three *phrases,* with all the repetitions).
Retransition of three measures;
Prin. Theme, a minor, partly transposed; } Duplication of the
Subord. Theme, C major (proper key); } foregoing.
Retransition, 42 measures;
Prin. Theme, abbreviated; } Recapitulation.
Subord. Theme, A major (proper key); }
Brief *Coda.*

d. **Beethoven,** String-quartet, op. 59, No. 1, second movement. This might
best be defined as a Group of Themes — a Prin. Theme, and two Subordinates — in
the following order: Prin. Theme (*B*-flat major); I. Subord. Theme (*d* minor);
Prin. Theme, reconstructed; II. Subord. Theme (*f* minor, Three-Part form, with
repetitions); Development, as long retransition; Prin. Theme (transposed to *G*-flat
major, and with a new contrapuntal melody); I. Subord. Theme (*g* minor); Retransition; Reconstructed Prin. Theme (*F* major, *E* major, *d* minor, *B*-flat major);
II. Subord. Theme (*b*-flat minor); Coda, beginning in *b*-flat minor.

e. **Brahms,** 1st Pfte. quartet, op. 25, last movement, *Alla Zingarese:* A very broad
Third Rondo form, with several irregularities; the II. Subord. Theme is a complete
"Song with Trio"; the final *da capo* (Prin. Theme) is abbreviated by the omission of
Part I, and merged in the Coda.

f. **Mendelssohn,** *Scherzo capriccioso,* in *f*-sharp minor: Fantastic and irregular,
but approximating the Third Rondo form. It has the following design:
Prin. Th. — I. Sub. Th. — Prin. Th. (brief). — II. Sub. Th. — I. Sub. Th. —
Prin. Th. — II. Sub. Th. — Prin. Th. (brief). — Coda.

g. **Mendelssohn,** Overture to "Melusine." This might admit of several ap-
proximate definitions, the most tempting of which is, to declare the first 46 measures
an Introduction (par. 178d). But these measures are so significant, so genuinely
thematic, and are interwoven so essentially with the texture of the whole, that it
seems more reasonable to define them as *an additional Principal Theme.* The
presence of two Subordinate Themes has been demonstrated (par. 179), and this
suggests the possibility of a similar two-fold Principal Theme, contradictory as it
may appear. Further, an analogous structural idea is conveyed, in embryo, in the
Basic motive which may accompany, and even transcend in importance, the Principal
Theme (par. 165). In the above Overture, the graceful opening measures, in *F* major,
would be called "Prin. Theme, *A*," and the following dramatic member, in *f* minor,
"Prin. Theme, *B*."

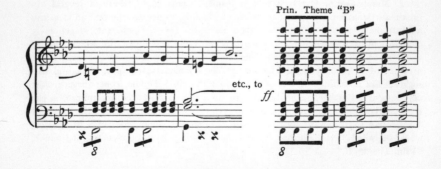

MENDELSSOHN, "Melusine"

Both of these appear in the Development, in the Recapitulation (briefly), and in the Coda. As to the rest, the movement is plainly Sonata-allegro form, with the usual contrasting (lyric) Subord. Theme.

h. **Brahms,** 1st pfte. Concerto, op. 15, first movement. This is similar, but less pronounced. It is plausible, perhaps inevitable, to accept Prin. Theme *"A"* and *"B,"* although *"B"* (which appears at the beginning of the *actual* Exposition — in the Solo-part), is decidedly less vital than *"A,"* which opens the introductory Exposition, and pervades the movement.

BRAHMS, op. 15.

etc.

Other examples of unique structural arrangement might be cited, but these are sufficient to direct the student's attention to what he may expect to encounter, in his general analysis, especially of the more modern Larger Forms.

CHAPTER XV.

THE OVERTURE.

188. As the name indicates, the Overture (always orchestral) is an opening number — primarily of the Oratorio or Opera.   It is, however, usually an independent movement, complete in itself, and therefore may be detached from its original dramatic associations, and be employed as a separate number upon any concert program.   This circumstance has given rise, in two conspicuous instances (the Concert-overture and the Tone-poem), to a modified application of the term "Overture," whereby, similar to the occasional use of the term "Prelude," it may signify an entirely independent composition, with *general* reference, only, to some dramatic subject.

189. The Overture admits of a five-fold classification, as follows:
1. The Oratorio Overture;
2. The Dramatic or Classic Overture;
3. The Potpourri Overture;
4. The Concert-Overture; and
5. The Tone-poem.

190. The Overture to an **Oratorio** is most commonly an orchestral fugue, or other polyphonic form, in keeping with the dignity of the sacred subject; usually with an independent Introduction in slower tempo.

See **Handel,** the "Messiah." — **Mendelssohn,** "Elijah."

191. The **Dramatic** or **Classic Overture** refers directly to a drama, play, melodrama, opera, or theatrical presentation of any kind. Its title is therefore usually *personal* — for example, "Hamlet," "Romeo and Juliet," "Prometheus," "Faust"; or is borrowed directly from the title of the drama which it precedes: *e.g.*, "The Tempest."

Its design is almost invariably the Sonata-allegro form, often with an independent Introduction.

See **Mozart's** operas "Don Giovanni," "Figaro." — **Cherubini,** "Medea." — **Beethoven,** the four Overtures ("Leonore" and "Fidelio") to his opera "Fidelio." — **Wagner,** "The Flying Dutchman." — **Weber,** "Der Freischütz." — **Boiëldieu,** "La Dame blanche." — And the Overtures to the dramatic plays: **Beethoven,** "Coriolan," "Egmont." — **Mendelssohn,** "Midsummer Night's Dream." — **Goldmark,** "Sakuntala."

See also, the other Overtures of **Beethoven;** the Overtures of **Cherubini, Mozart, Schumann, Weber.**

Similar in purpose, but of inferior *structural* significance, are the brief (and not detachable) "Introductions" or "Preludes" to such Operas as **Verdi's** "Aida"; **Wagner's** "Lohengrin," "Tristan und Isolde."

192. The **Potpourri-Overture** is always connected with the lighter or comic type of Opera, or Operetta. Its design is the group-form, or sectional form, sometimes approaching the regular arrangement of a Larger form, but most commonly a mere series of melodic episodes, selected from the music of the opera itself, with a view to individual and collective attractiveness.

See **Flotow,** "Martha." — **Rossini,** "William Tell." — Also **Wagner,** "Die Meistersinger," the Overture to which, though a work of commanding contrapuntal character, great breadth, and eminent artistic significance, belongs properly to the "Potpourri" class.

193. The **Concert-Overture** is designed for "concert" performance, and is therefore, in a sense, transferred from the theatre to the concert hall. Thus it is, also, to some extent sundered from the drama, and divested of immediate connection with any dramatic theme. (This, of course, refers to the *specific* Concert-overture, and not to those Dramatic Overtures which actually precede an opera, and are merely inserted in a concert-program because of their intrinsic musical value.) For this reason, the title of a concert-overture may be personal or impersonal; may refer to some character in sacred or secular history ("Joan of Arc," "Samson"); or in mythology ("Hercules' Youth"); to some abstract idea ("Spring"); or even to some concrete subject, if susceptible of poetic or emotional environment, or suggestive of shifting moods (**Mendelssohn,** "Calm Sea and Prosperous Voyage"; "Fingal's Cave"). Or it may refer to the drama in a more general or indirect way, without the necessity or the intention of actual connection with any Play which bears the same name; for example, the "Faust"-overture of **Wagner;** "1812" of **Tschaikowsky;** "Melusine"; "Sakuntala"; — which may, or may not, serve as actual introduction to the corresponding theatrical presentation.

The form of the Concert-overture is also usually Sonata-allegro; but is often very broad, and may be treated with much freedom (or irregularity), in order to provide for the brilliancy and independent effectiveness imperatively necessary in case of isolated performance.

In what manner this classic design (the Sonata-allegro form) may be applied to, or may be modified and adjusted to, the successive dramatic details of the chosen subject, must be left to the student's ingenuity. Almost every drama, and even wholly abstract subjects, provide natural contrasting episodes, which may be represented by the successive members of the design. (By way of very broad suggestion: "Hamlet" and "Ophelia," or "Romeo" and "Juliet," would naturally serve as types for the Prin. Theme and Subordinate Theme, res₁ectively; and other episodes would lend themselves plausibly enough to the Codettas, Development, and so forth.) This may shock the enthusiastic young composer's sensitive poetic conception; but he should know that a musical composition *with definite structural outlines* is invariably more powerful and convincing than one whose form is vague, and whose intent is uncertain. And, further, if the student is wise enough to confine himself to one strong general impression, as *central dramatic idea* (instead of dissipating this impression by wandering through numerous accidental phases of the dramatic *narrative*), he may be sure that the sequence of members represented by the Sonata-allegro form is far more consistent, natural, and effective than any arbitrary design could be, which he might devise. See par. 194, 197.

See further: **Brahms,** "Academic Festival-Overture," op. 80; "Tragic Overture," op. 81. **Weber,** "Jubel-Ouverture." **Mendelssohn,** Overtures, op. 24, op. 101.

194. The **Tone-poem** or **Tone-picture** is not an Overture, in the accepted sense of that term. But it is more closely related to that class of composition than to any other, and, in fact, may best be defined as a development of the idea embodied in the Concert-overture. As the title indicates, the Tone-poem refers to some poetic idea, or narrative; most frequently it adopts some motto, or some brief literary product, either poetry or prose, as basis for musical illustration; and since it therefore follows the order of incidents or thoughts presented in the motto or text, and successively gives them musical expression, the style is properly called "program music." A typical example is "Die Ideale" of **Liszt** (a "description" of a complete poem by Schiller).

The sectional form, or Group-form, must of necessity be adopted, because the free presentation of an arbitrary series of dramatic or emotional episodes could scarcely be made to conform to the firmly set diagram of any regular Larger form. In this, as in every other respect, the Tone-poem stands for the last degree of freedom, and is farthest removed from the absolute musical conception which falls so readily into the pulse of the *regular* designs — because these designs are such true and simple exponents of the universal laws of structure. To what extent, and in what manner, this freedom is to be used, rests solely with the musical conscience of the composer.

195. Music has always been regarded and defined as a vehicle for the expression of emotion (feeling, sentiment, passion), and the reflection of "moods." This is doubtless true, inasmuch as the specific *sound* of the varied intervals, chords and other tone-combinations (coupled with rhythm and dynamics) does appear to possess a close and universally recognizable analogy to various emotional phases; some chords "sound" joyous, and others sombre; some seem to represent hateful, others amiable, attributes (compare the "yearning" harmonies in the first scene of "Die Walküre," with the deadly hatred suggested by *Hagen's* chords in "Die Götterdämmerung"). But music can, with its multitude of varying rhythms, its infinite shades of dynamics, and the direction and speed of its lines, closely imitate actual physical movements and conditions; and may, therefore, to some extent, "illustrate" the shifting motions of an active narrative: For example, the slow or swift ascent or descent of material objects, and a multitude of natural sounds (the flight of an arrow, the rocking of a boat, the gentle movement of a zephyr, the roll of thunder, the downpour of rain — as in the thunderstorm in **Beethoven's** 6th Symphony; the hollow clicking of bones, as in the "Dance of the Dead" of **Saint-Saëns** ; the gallop of horse, as in **Raff's** "Lenore"-Symphony, and **Liszt's** "Mazeppa"; the murmur of a spinning wheel; the tread of giants, the clumsy winding of a dragon, as in **Wagner's** "Rheingold"; — see also the numerous "descriptive" episodes in the first Part of **Haydn's** "Creation,"and in the plague-choruses in **Handel's** "Israel in Egypt"; also, as an interesting example of musical suggestion, **Bach,** Organ compositions, Vol. V, Peters edition, No. 13 — the *pedal-bass* of the chorale elaboration, *Durch Adam's Fall* — constant descending diminished-seventh progressions).

But they who would defend the integrity of music declare that these are all purely *external* adjuncts, not inherent qualities, of musical material, and that they should serve no other purpose than *to emphasize the inherent meaning* of the tone-relations and tone-associations; that music can be, and should be, an *absolute* art, and is not to be *applied* to the superficial and childish illustration or description of anything outside of the specific province of pure musical expression — that its noblest use is exemplified in the classic symphonies and Chamber-works, which are absolute music-creations, pure Music, *per se*.   They also voice the suspicion that the composer who utilizes these exterior traits of music for the illustration of physical episodes and movements, does so from insufficient knowledge of the true meaning of the musical "parts of speech," and therefore caricatures, instead of *discoursing* in a language that is vastly more subtle, more searching and powerful in its appeal than mere words can ever be.

Extreme views are always wrong.   Everything that is, is right, in its proper place, and **in proper proportion.**   All error lies in exaggeration.

The student is urged to weigh these conflicting opinions seriously and thoroughly; to form his own conviction, and to follow, unfalteringly, his artistic impulses and beliefs.   (See *Homophonic Forms*, par. 97e.)

The application of what might be called the physical qualities of music, for suggestion and imitation, may be considered almost imperative in the Opera; in the accompaniment to Songs; and in that melodramatic species of the Tone-poem called musical Recitation (recitation with "descriptive" musical accompaniment — as "Enoch Arden" of **Richard Strauss**).

196. Examples of the Tone-poem are sufficiently numerous.   The student will find ample material for examination and analysis in the twelve *Sinfonische Dichtungen* of **Liszt ;** but may add to these "Till Eulenspiegel," "Ein Heldenleben" and "Sinfonia Domestica" of **Richard Strauss ;** and any other modern examples that he may encounter.

---

197. In the conception and composition of the Overture, or, for that matter, of any of the Larger Forms, the student must bear the following General Principles in mind:

1. The Themes should be presented in a simple, clear manner. Cadences should be fairly frequent, and sufficiently forcible to give the hearer a clear impression of the architecture of the movement.   At least from time to time the hearer must get his bearings, since nothing is truly enjoyed that is not comprehended.

2. The thematic members should, nevertheless, be distinctly characterized.   A good Theme is always easily recognizable.

3. There must be sufficient symmetry of construction, and corroboration of members; this is obtained by very frequent (almost constant) application of the process of duplication.

4. On the other hand, there must be sufficient *contrast*. This refers to smaller as well as to larger factors, and should be fairly frequent and striking, though not too abrupt or too extreme.

The arch-enemy of all art-creation is Monotony, and this must be carefully avoided. Hence, the process of extension and expansion must be freely employed, in order to vary the phrase-lengths (distance between cadences); and no end of imagination and ingenuity must be applied in *modifying* the necessary repetitions and duplications.

5. Exaggeration, in every respect, should be guarded against.

6. Clearness of design (for the hearer) and a perfectly sure consciousness of the successive steps in the execution of the structural design (for the composer), can best be secured by reasonable regard for the conditions of the simple, smaller, forms. For example, *the natural association of an Antecedent and Consequent phrase;* the relation of the Parts (in the Song-form) to each other; the ever-present operation of the principles of repetition or duplication, of parallel construction, of extension and expansion — in the progressive structure, or in the spinning-out, of the fundamental phrases and periods.

7. Perhaps most important of all, there must be a constant maintenance — and increase — of interest; and a constant forward striving, a steady impulse and "push," that keeps the musical spirit thoroughly alive. This very element must, however, be emphasized by the contrasting *relaxations*, from time to time, which provide variety, and prepare for the next climax — but without wholly checking the undercurrent of energy.

8. For the Dramatic Overture, and Concert-Overture, some "dramatic" design is necessary. But this should be followed in its broadest lines, only, and not so closely as to hamper the purely musical expression, and the adherence to an effective structural design (than which, as hinted, none is more reliable than one of the *regular forms*, as a rule).

EXERCISE 14.

One example each, at least, of the Dramatic Overture, the Concert-overture, and the Tone-poem.

DIVISION FOUR.

CHAPTER XVI.

THE COMPOUND FORMS.

198. Compound forms are those larger collective compositions which contain a number of different and independent movements.

The oldest of these is the **Suite,** which, however, being originally a collection of Dances only, did not utilize any of the Larger Forms. Later, some degree of artistic refinement was imparted to the Suite by introducing one or more numbers of a scholastic type, as the Prelude, Gigue (contrapuntal) and Fugue; but these, also, required none of the Larger Forms. The numbers of the Suite (and of the Serenade, Divertimento, etc.) were usually all in the same key, and the number of the Dances, or "Movements," was optional.

The more modern Suite is no longer solely a collection of Dances, and often contains some elaborate movements, and Larger Forms; but dance-forms and allied types are usually present, and complete freedom governs the choice of styles, and the number of movements, which are thrown together more loosely, and not inter-related, and definite, as are the movements of the Sonata or Symphony (par. 199; 206).

See the Suite for pianoforte by **d'Albert,** op. 1 (conventional Dance-forms); the Suites for orchestra by **Franz Lachner ;** the Serenades for String-orchestra by **Robert Volkmann ;** Serenades for full orchestra by **Brahms,** op. 11, and op. 16.

In some cases the distinction between the Suite and the Sonata approaches the vanishing-point, and the titles are then apt to be exchanged. **Beethoven** calls his op. 26 a "Sonata "; but the term "Suite" would be more appropriate, since the four movements are a set of Variations, a Scherzo, a Funeral March, and a "Toccata" in Rondo form. And op. 21 of **Josef Suk** is called a Suite, for no obvious reason; for the first movement is a genuine Sonata-allegro (though of a somewhat fantastic character); the second movement is a Menuetto (which claims a rightful place in the Sonata); the third is an *Adagio* ("Dumka," or Folk-song); and the fourth, a genuine Rondo. **Mozart,** Sonata, No. 15 (Schirmer ed.) might be designated Suite: its three movements are "Allegro," "*Rondeau en Polonaise*," "Theme and Variations."

199. The most artistic and significant compound form is the Sonata, — not the "Sonata-form," but the **complete Sonata** (par. 142). The early Sonata consisted of three "Movements," so contrasted that the slow movement (in a different key) appeared between two rapid movements (in the same key). The order was, therefore:

1. An *Allegro*, of a somewhat serious, stately, or spirited character;

2. An *Adagio, Largo*, or *Andante*, usually lyric, sometimes dramatic, or even elegiac, and always dignified;

3. An *Allegro, Allegretto*, or *Presto*, of a more lively, gay, or brilliant character (often a Rondo).

For typical examples, see **Mozart,** Sonata, No. 17 (Schirmer ed.); also No. 16.
Beethoven, Sonata, op. 10, No. 1; op. 13; op. 31, No. 1 and No. 2.

200. To these three movements there was later added (in the early String-quartet, and Symphony) a fourth movement, and for this a Dance-form was borrowed from the Suite, to provide a good contrast with the original three styles. At first the Minuet was chosen, and usually inserted as third movement:

Haydn, any one of the twelve well-known Symphonies. **Beethoven,** Sonata, op. 2, No. 1; op. 22; op. 31, No. 3.

In many instances a more sturdy, or rapid, type of Minuet was employed:

Mozart, Symphony in *E*-flat. **Beethoven,** Symphonies, Nos. 1 and 4.

And when the "Minuet" was still more accelerated, and assumed a playful or humorous character, it was called *Scherzo.*

Beethoven, Sonata, op. 2, No. 2; op. 2, No. 3; op. 28. Symphonies, Nos. 2 and 3.

Sometimes this third movement, while retaining the usual 3–4 measure and the general character of a Dance-form, had no specific title, but took the tempo-designation (*Allegretto, Allegro*):

Beethoven, Sonata, op. 7, *Allegro;* Symphony, No. 3. **Brahms,** Symphony, No. 1, *Poco Allegretto e grazioso;* Symphony, No. 4, *Allegro giocoso* ("Scherzo").

201. This association of four movements:

1. Serious *Allegro.*
2. *Adagio* or *Andante.*
3. *Minuet* or *Scherzo.*
4. Brilliant *Allegro.*

became the established, conventional, form of the complete Sonata, and any digression from this scheme of movements is regarded as an irregularity.

For example, the Scherzo *precedes* the slow movement in the second and third Symphonies of **Schumann.**

In **Beethoven,** Sonata op. 27, No. 1, the first movement is *omitted* — the Sonata beginning with the slow movement; also in the next Sonata, op. 27, No. 2. This probably accounts for **Beethoven's** cautious title for both: *Sonata quasi una Fantasia.* In **Beethoven,** Sonata, op. 10, No. 2, the slow movement is omitted.   In the Sonata, op. 78 (*Allegro ma non troppo; Allegro vivace*) there is neither a slow movement nor a Minuet.   Op. 90 is similar.   In op. 54 (*Menuetto; Allegretto*) the opening *Allegro* and the slow movement are omitted.   See also op. 111.

In op. 27, No. 1 — as stated — the opening *Allegro* is omitted; but another slow movement is inserted before the final *Allegro.*   In **Schumann,** Symphony, No. 3, there are five movements — an additional slow movement preceding the final *Allegro.*

202. *a.* As a rule, only the slow movement is placed in some other (usually related) key.

Thus, in **Beethoven,** Sonata, op. 2, No. 2: *Allegro vivace, A* major; *Largo, D* major; *Scherzo, A* major and *a* minor; *Rondo, A* major.

But other key-conditions occasionally prevail:

Beethoven, Sonata, op. 2, No. 1 — all four movements in the *same* key. — Op. 10, No. 3; op. 14, No. 1; op. 28 — similar (though the opposite mode appears).

Brahms, Symphony, No. 1: first movement, *c* minor; second movement, *E* major; third movement, *A*-flat major; fourth movement, *C* major (Introduction, *c* minor). Symphony, No. 2: the four movements are in *D* major, *B* major, *G* major and *D* major, respectively.

b. The structural design of the several movements is, to some extent, optional.   But the following choice is most common:

For the first *Allegro*, the Sonata-allegro form; for the slow movement, the First Rondo form (in the Symphony, sometimes Sonatina or Sonata-allegro form); for the Minuet or Scherzo, the 3-Part Song-form, with one or two Trios; for the Finale, the Second or Third Rondo form, or, occasionally (especially in the Symphony), the Sonata-allegro form.

203. *a.* The legitimate complete Sonata is not a haphazard collection of movements, as is the Suite, but is an artistic *unit*.   Therefore a more or less palpable organic relation, a certain unity of "mood," might be expected to prevail throughout the movements.   (This is analogous to par. 66, which review.)   This was evidently not demanded of the early Sonata and Symphony, which seem to aim, rather, to secure marked contrasts; but the higher artistic idea of establishing "spiritual" relation between the movements, so that they shall successively represent progressive phases of the *collective* artistic purpose of the composer, is being cultivated in the modern Sonata and Symphony with increasing consciousness. It can scarcely be claimed for the earlier works of even **Beethoven,** but becomes increasingly noticeable in his later periods; and is positively present in some of the Symphonies and Chamber works of **Brahms.**

b. The determination to thus *unify* the Sonata is manifested, technically, by instituting *actual thematic relations* between the movements.

See **Brahms,** 1st Violin Sonata, op. 78. In the first place, the rhythmic figure ♪ ♪ ♩ is conspicuous in all three movements. And, second, the Prin. Th. of the Adagio becomes the II. Subord. Th. of the last movement.

Glazounow, Sonata, op. 75: Movements one and three are based upon the self-same thematic figure 𝄞 ♩ ♩ ; and the thematic melody of the II. Subord. Th. of the second movement reappears in the Coda of the last movement.

Vincent d'Indy, String-quartet, op. 45: The thematic figure of four tones

Ex. 63.

is adhered to, as basic motive, throughout all four movements. It occurs at the outset of each movement, but is soon followed by other melodic members; and also forms a sort of thematic impulse to the other structural members of the movements.

Brahms, Symphony, No. 1: The Basic Motive of the first movement (given in Ex. 58, No. 1) is reëchoed in measures 4–6 of the *Andante.*

Brahms, pfte. Sonata, op. 1: The principal thematic figure of the first movement constitutes, in altered rhythmic form, the initial figure of the last movement; and the first phrase of the *Scherzo* is derived from the plagal ending of the preceding (slow) movement.

Beethoven, Symphony, No. V: The principal melodic phrase of the Third movement reappears in the last movement, in the last section of the Development (as retransition). Also, the rhythmic figure ♩ ♩ ♩ | ♩. ‖ is common to the first and third movements, and reappears, quickened, in the Subord. Theme of the last movement.

Beethoven, Sonata, op. 101: The initial phrase of the first movement recurs, as quasi Introduction, before the last movement.

Brahms, Symphony, No. III: The melodic motive of the Prin. Th. in the first movement, is reverted to, in the independent Coda of the Finale, so that the Symphony ends, so to speak, as it began.

Tschaikowsky, Symphony, No. V, in *e* minor: The introductory motive of the first movement enters vitally into the structure of the Finale.

Schumann: Symphony, No. III: The fourth (slow) movement refers thematically to the Finale.

Florent Schmitt, pfte. quintet, op. 51: The last movement contains Themes from the first movement.

Brahms, String-quartet in *c* minor, op. 51, No. 1: The initial motives of the first and last movements are identical.

Brahms, String-quartet, op. 67: The last Variation, in the Finale, reverts to the Prin. Th. of the first movement, — similar to Symphony, No. III, cited above.

See further: **César Franck,** Violin Sonata in *A*. — **Liszt,** *E*-flat major pfte. Concerto. — **Saint-Saëns,** *c* minor pfte. Concerto.

204. When written for pianoforte or organ, the term "Sonata" is employed; and even when two solo-instruments are chosen (as "Duo"), the work is more commonly called a "Sonata" (Violin Sonata, 'Cello Sonata, etc.).

When three solo-instruments are used, the work is called a "Trio" (pfte. Trio, String Trio, Horn Trio, Clarionet Trio, etc. — the latter two always implying the presence of the pianoforte). A Sonata for four instruments is designated a "Quartet," and so on, up to Septet, Octet, or even Nonet. When more than this number of instruments are employed, the term "Sinfonietta" or "Symphony" is used.

205. A **Concerto** is a Sonata for some solo-instrument, invariably with *orchestral* accompaniment (pfte. Concerto, Violin Concerto, etc.). In a Double-Concerto, two solo-instruments are engaged: **Brahms,** op. 102; **Beethoven,** op. 56.

206. The **Symphony** is a Sonata for full orchestra. Being the most serious and dignified form of musical composition, it is not customary to introduce into the Symphony any movements of a less distinguished or regular type than the Sonata-allegro or Rondo forms, — excepting, of course, the conventional Minuet, Scherzo, or allied Song-form with Trio. The adoption of the Variation form, by **Beethoven,** as Finale of his III. Symphony, and of the Chaconne, by **Brahms,** as last movement of his IV. Symphony, is therefore regarded as exceptional.

207. The term Symphony, or Symphonic poem, is, nevertheless, not infrequently applied to an expanded form of the Tone-poem (par. 194). The title seems to be wholly defensible in the case of those genuinely "symphonic" works which reflect in a very general way, and without pronounced detailed musical "description," some universal idea or impression.

For example: The Forest Symphony, and Lenore Symphony, of **Raff**; the Ocean Symphony of **Rubinstein**; the New World Symphony of **Dvořák**; the Columbus Symphony of **Abert**; "Joan of Arc" of **Moszkowski**. Perhaps, also, the Pastorale Symphony of **Beethoven,** and the "Rustic Wedding" of **Goldmark,** — to which category belongs the "Characteristic Sonata" of **Beethoven,** op. 81*A*, for pianoforte.

The descriptive, or programmatic, quality is more pronounced, and the symphonic rank (as such) proportionately lowered in the "Dante" Symphony of **Liszt**; "Scheherazade" of **Rimsky-Korsakoff**; *"Tod und Verklärung"* of **Richard Strauss**; and many other modern orchestral works, to which the title "Symphonic poem" is usually frankly given.

Date Due

NOV 6 1936		
Elizabeth House		
My 8 37 NOV 28 60		
Ju 6 7/15/72		
9:00 am		
N 1945		
9:00 am		
FE 5 48		
NO 48		
DE 4 '50		
APR 19 55		
MAY 9 58		
OCT 16 58		
NOV 25 02		
⊕		